ALSO BY BRITTAINY CHERRY

THE ELEMENTS SERIES

The Air He Breathes

The Fire Between High & Lo

The Silent Waters

The Gravity of Us

THE *Fire* BETWEEN *High & Lo*

THE ELEMENTS SERIES

THE *Fire* BETWEEN *High & Lo*

BRITTAINY CHERRY

sourcebooks
casablanca

Published by Sourcebooks Casablanca, an imprint of Sourcebooks
P.O. Box 4410, Naperville, Illinois 60567-4410
(630) 961-3900
sourcebooks.com

Originally self-published in 2016 by Brittainy Cherry.

Cataloging-in-Publication Data is on file with the Library of Congress.

Printed and bound in Canada.
MBP 10 9 8 7 6 5 4 3

For those with a fire inside them, thriving for better tomorrows.

For those who need to know

that their past mistakes do not define them.

This one's for you.

Dear Reader,
May you feel the
love that I have
for both Logan +
Alyssa within
the pages.

PROLOGUE
Alyssa

The boy in the red hoodie kept staring at me in the checkout line.

I'd seen him before, many times, including earlier that Monday morning. Every day, he and his friends hung out in the alleyway behind the grocery store where I worked. I'd see them when my boss made me break down boxes and toss them outside.

The boy in the red hoodie always showed up with his friends each day. They'd make a ton of noise, smoking cigarettes and cursing up a storm. He stood out, because the other guys laughed and smiled. He seemed mute, almost as if his mind lived far away from his surroundings. His lips hardly ever turned up; I wondered if he knew what smiling was. Maybe he was a person who simply existed instead of lived.

Sometimes we'd lock eyes, and I'd always look away.

I found it hard to look into his caramel eyes, because they looked sadder than any eyes his age should've ever looked. Deep, purplish bags sat under them, along with wrinkle lines, but still, he was handsome. A handsomely tired boy. No boy should've looked that exhausted or that gorgeous all at once. I was almost certain he'd lived one hundred years of struggle all within his youth. I could tell he'd been through worse private wars than most of the people walking the earth just by the way he stood: shoulders rounded forward, back never straight.

But not all of him looked so broken.

His medium-length dark hair was always perfect. Always. Sometimes he'd pull out a small comb and run it through his locks, as if he was a greaser from the 1950s. He always wore the same kind of outfits too: either a plain white T-shirt or a plain black T-shirt, and sometimes the red hoodie. His jeans were always black, along with his black shoes, which were tied with white shoestrings. I didn't know why, but even though the outfits were simple, they gave me goose bumps.

I noticed his hands too. His hands were constantly wrapped around a lighter he flicked on and off, nonstop. I wondered if he was even aware that he did it. It seemed almost as if the flame shooting from the lighter was a part of his existence.

A mundane expression, tired eyes, perfect hair, and a lighter in hand.

What kind of name would fit a guy like that?

Hunter, maybe. It sounded kind of bad boyish—which he was, I assumed. Or Gus. Gus the greaser. Greasy Gus. Or Mikey—because it sounded sweet, which would be the complete opposite of what he seemed to be, and I enjoyed things like that.

But his name didn't currently matter.

What mattered was that he was standing across from me. He showed more expression than I'd ever seen from him as he stood in the alleyway. His face was beet red and his fingers were fidgety as he stood in my checkout line at the grocery store. There was such a strong, poignant embarrassment in his eyes as he swiped his food stamps card over and over again. Each time, it was declined. *Insufficient funds.* Each time, he grew gloomier. *Insufficient funds.* He bit his bottom lip. "That doesn't make sense," he murmured to himself.

"I can try it up here on my register if you want. Sometimes those machines are wonky." I offered him a smile, but he didn't smile back. His face was filled with stern lines of coldness. His brows were knit and aggressive, yet he handed me his card. I slid it through my machine and frowned. *Insufficient funds.* "It's saying there isn't enough money on the card."

"Thank you, Captain Obvious," he mumbled.

Rude.

"This is bullshit." He huffed, his chest rising and falling. "We just got money on it yesterday."

Who was "we"? *None of your business, Alyssa.* "Do you have another card we could try?"

"If I had another card, don't you think I would've tried it?" he barked, making me jump a little. Hunter. He had to be a Hunter. Mean, bad boy Hunter. Or maybe Travis. I'd read a book once with a Travis in it, and he was a very bad boy. Travis was so bad that I had to close the book to keep myself from blushing and screaming all at once.

He took a breath, studied the line of people forming behind him, and then locked his stare with mine. "I'm sorry. I didn't mean to yell."

"It's okay," I replied.

"No. It's not. I'm sorry. Can I just leave the shit here for a second? I have to call my mom."

"Yeah, sure. I'll just suspend the order for now; then we can ring up your items once we get the issues worked out. No worries."

He almost smiled, and I almost lost it. I didn't know he knew how to *almost* do that. Maybe it was just a twitch in his lips, but when they slightly curved, he looked so handsome. I could tell he didn't partake in the act of smiling very often.

As he stepped to the side and dialed his mom's number, I tried my best not to eavesdrop on his call. I took the next customers' orders, but still, my nosy ears and eyes kept finding their way back to him.

"Ma, I'm just saying, I feel like a fucking idiot. I swiped the card, and it keeps getting declined... I know the PIN. I entered the PIN... Did you use the card yesterday?" he asked. "For what? What did you get?"

He moved the phone from his face as his mom spoke to him and rolled his eyes before putting the receiver back to his ear.

"What do you mean, you bought thirty-two cases of Coca-Cola?!" he shouted. "What the hell are we going to do with thirty-two cases of Coca-Cola?"

Everyone in the grocery store turned toward him. His gaze met mine, and the embarrassment returned to him. I smiled. He frowned. Heartbreakingly handsome.

Slowly he turned his back to me and returned to his call. "How are we supposed to eat for the next month? Yeah, I get paid tomorrow, but that's not gonna be enough to... No. I don't want to ask Kellan for money again... Ma, don't cut me off. Listen. I have to pay rent. There's no way I'll be able to—" Pause. "Ma, shut the hell up, okay?! You spent our food money on Coca-Cola!"

Short pause. Crazy arm movements of anger.

"No! No, I don't care if it was Diet Coke or Coke Zero!" He sighed, running his fingers through his hair. He set the phone down on the ground for a few moments, shut his eyes, and took a few deep breaths. He picked it back up. "It's fine. I'll figure it out. Don't worry about it, all right? I'll figure it out. I'm hanging up. No, I'm not mad, Ma. Yeah, I'm sure. I'm just hanging up. Yeah, I know. It's okay. I'm not mad, okay?

I'm sorry I yelled. I'm sorry. I'm not mad." His voice became as low as it could, but I couldn't stop listening. "I'm sorry."

When he turned back to me, I'd finished helping the last customer in my line.

He shrugged his left shoulder and stepped closer, rubbing the back of his neck. "I don't think I'm gonna be able to get those things today. Sorry. I can put the stuff back on the shelves. Sorry. Sorry." He kept apologizing.

My gut tightened. "It's okay. Really. I'll handle it. I'm getting off work now anyway. I'll put it all back."

He frowned again. I wished he would stop doing that. "Okay. Sorry." I wished he'd stop apologizing too.

When he left, I glanced inside his grocery bags. Studying the items in the bags was heartbreaking. The stuff added up to a total of eleven dollars, and he couldn't even afford that. Ramen noodles, cereal, milk, peanut butter, and a loaf of bread—items I'd never had to think twice about buying.

You never knew how good you had it until you saw how bad someone else did.

"Hey!" I shouted, chasing after him in the parking lot. "Hey! You forgot these!"

He turned around slowly and narrowed his eyes in confusion.

"Your bags," I explained, handing them to him. "You forgot your bags."

"You could get fired."

"What?"

"For stealing groceries," he said.

I hesitated for a moment, a bit confused as to why his first thought would be that I stole the food. "I didn't steal them. I paid for them."

Bewilderment filled his stare. "Why would you do that? You don't even know me."

"I know you're trying to take care of your mom."

He pinched the bridge of his nose, shaking his head back and forth. "I'll pay you back."

"No, don't worry about it." I shook my head. "It's no big deal."

He bit his bottom lip and brushed his hand over his eyes. "I'll pay you back. But…thank you. Thank you…uh…" His eyes fell to my chest, and for a second, I felt a level of discomfort, until I realized he was retrieving my name from my name tag. "Thank you, Alyssa."

"You're welcome."

He turned and went on his way again.

"What about you?!" I shouted his way, hiccupping once or twice—or maybe fifty times.

"What about me?" he asked, not turning to face me, still walking.

"What's your name?"

Hunter?

Gus?

Travis?

Mikey?

He could've definitely been a Mikey.

"Logan," he said. He kept walking, not looking back once.

I placed my shirt collar in my mouth and chewed on it; it was a bad habit my mom always yelled at me about, but my mom wasn't there, and small tiny butterflies were taking over my stomach.

Logan.

He looked like a Logan, now that I thought about it.

He came back a few days later to pay me back. Then he began show-ing up weekly to buy a loaf of bread or some more ramen noodles or a pack of gum. He always came to my checkout lane. At some point, Logan and I began to talk during transactions. We learned that his half brother was dating my sister, and they had been together for what felt like forever. At some point, he almost smiled. Then once, I swore he even laughed. We kind of became friends, starting with small exchanges of words and building up to bigger conversations.

When I'd leave work, he'd be sitting on the parking lot curb, wait-ing for me, and we'd talk even more.

Our skin tanned together under the burning sun. We left each night beneath the flaming stars.

I met my best friend in the checkout lane of a grocery store.

And my life was never the same again.

PART 1

His soul was set in flames,
and he scorched anyone who stood too close.

She stepped closer,
unafraid of the ashes they were destined to become.

CHAPTER 1
Logan

TWO YEARS, SEVEN GIRLFRIENDS, TWO BOYFRIENDS, NINE BREAKUPS, AND A STRONGER FRIENDSHIP LATER

I'd watched a documentary on pie.

Two hours of my life were spent sitting in front of a tiny television, watching a library DVD on the history of pie. It turned out pie had been around since the ancient Egyptians. The first documented pie was created by the Romans; they made a rye-crusted goat cheese and honey pie. It sounded completely disgusting, but somehow, at the end of the documentary, all I wanted was that freaking pie.

I wasn't much of a pie eater, more into cake, but at that moment, all that flew through my mind was the thought of a flaky crust.

I had all the things needed to go upstairs to our apartment to make the pie too. All that stood in my way was Shay, my now ex-girlfriend, who I'd spent the past few hours sending mixed signals to.

I was crappy at breaking up with girls. Most of the time, I'd text them a simple "Not working, sorry" or have a five-second phone call to cut it off, but I couldn't with this one, because Alyssa told me breaking up with someone over the phone was the worst thing a person could ever do.

So I'd met up with Shay in person. Terrible idea.

Shay, Shay, Shay. I wished I hadn't found the need to have sex with her that night—which we had. Three times. *After* I broke up with her. But now it was past one in the morning, and…

She. Wouldn't. Leave.

She wouldn't stop talking either.

The cold rain whistled as we stood in front of my apartment building. All I wanted to do was go to my bedroom and relax for a bit. Was that too much to ask? Smoke a bit of pot, start a new documentary, and make a pie or five.

I wanted to be alone. No one liked being alone more than I did.

My cell phone dinged, and I saw Alyssa's name appear on the screen with a text message.

Alyssa: Is the good deed done?

I smirked to myself, knowing she meant me breaking up with Shay.

Me: Yeah.

I watched the three dots appear on my phone, waiting to see Alyssa's reply.

Alyssa: You didn't sleep with her though, did you?

More dots.

Alyssa: Oh God, you slept with her, didn't you?

Even more dots.

Alyssa: MIXED SIGNALS!

I couldn't help but chuckle, because she knew me better than anyone else. Alyssa and I had been best friends for the past two years, and we were the complete opposite of each other. Her older sister was dating my brother, Kellan, and at first, Alyssa and I were convinced we had nothing in common. She happily sat in church while I smoked pot around the corner. She believed in God while I danced with demons. She had a future while I somehow seemed trapped in the past.

But we had certain things in common that somehow made us make sense. Her mom barely tolerated her; my mom hated me. Her dad was a jerk; my dad was Satan.

When we realized the small things we did have in common, we spent more time together, growing closer each day.

She was my best friend, the highlight to my shitty days.

Me: I slept with her once.
Alyssa: Twice.
Me: Yeah, twice.
Alyssa: THREE TIMES, LOGAN?! OH MY GOSH!

"Who are you talking to?" Shay whined, breaking my stare from my phone. "Who could possibly be more important than having this conversation right now?"

"Alyssa," I said flatly.

"Oh my gosh. Seriously? She just can't get enough of you, can she?" Shay complained. It wasn't new though; every girl I'd dated in the past two years had a way of being extremely jealous of Alyssa's and my relationship. "I bet you're screwing her."

"Yeah, I am," I said. That was the first lie. Alyssa wasn't easy, and if she was, she wouldn't be easy with me. She had standards—standards I didn't meet. Also, I had standards for Alyssa's relationships—standards no guy could ever meet. She deserved the world, and most people in True Falls, Wisconsin, only had crumbs to offer.

"I bet she's the reason you're breaking up with me."

"Yeah, she is." That was the second lie. I made my own choices, but Alyssa always backed me, no matter what. She always gave me her input, though, and let me know when I was in the wrong in all my relationships. She was painfully blunt sometimes.

"She wouldn't ever really get with you, though. She's a good girl, and you—you're a piece of shit!" Shay cried.

"You're right." That was the first truth.

Alyssa was a good girl, and I was the boy who never had a chance of calling her mine. Even though sometimes I'd look at her crazy blond curly hair and my mind would think about what it'd be like to maybe hold her close and slowly taste her lips. Maybe in a different world, I would've been enough for her. Maybe I wouldn't have been screwed up since I was a kid and would've had my life together. I would've gotten into college and had a career, something to show for myself. Then I could've asked her out and taken her to some fancy restaurant and told her to order anything on the menu because money wasn't an issue.

I could've told her how her blue eyes always smiled, even when she frowned, and that I loved how she chewed on the collar of all her T-shirts when she was bored or anxious.

I could've been someone worthy of loving, and she would've allowed me to love her too.

In a different world, maybe. But I only had the here and now, where Alyssa was my best friend.

I was lucky enough to have her in that form.

"You said you loved me!" Shay wept, allowing the tears to fall down her cheeks.

How long had she been crying? She was a professional crier, that one.

I studied her face as I slid my hands into my jean pockets. Goddamn. She looked a mess. She was still high from earlier, and her makeup was smeared all over her face.

"I didn't say that, Shay."

"Yes, you did! You said it more than once!" She swore.

"You're making shit up." I would've traced my memory to see if those three words slipped out of my mouth at some point, but I knew they didn't. I didn't love. I barely liked. My fingers brushed against my temple. Shay really needed to get in her car and drive far, far away.

"I'm not stupid, Logan! I know what you said!" Her words were confident in the belief that I loved her. Which, as a whole, was pretty sad. "You said it earlier tonight! Remember? You said you fucking loved me?"

Earlier tonight?

Oh crap.

"Shay, I said I love *fucking* you. Not that I fucking *love* you."

"Same thing."

"Trust me, it's not."

She swung her purse in my direction, and I allowed it to hit me. Truth was I deserved it. She swung again, and I allowed it once more.

She swung a third time, and I grabbed the bag, yanked it—and her—toward me. My hand landed on her lower back, which she arched at my touch. I pressed her body close to mine. Her breaths were heavy and tears were still rolling down her cheeks.

"Don't cry," I whispered, turning on my charm to try to get her to leave. "You're too beautiful to cry."

"You're such an asshole, Logan."

"Which is exactly why you shouldn't be with me."

"We've been broken up for three hours, and you've become a completely different person."

"That's funny," I muttered. "Because last I checked, it was you who became different, when you hooked up with Nick."

"Oh, get over it. That was a mistake. We didn't even have sex. You're the only boy I've slept with in the past six months."

"Uh, we've been dating for eight months."

"What are you, a math guru? That doesn't matter."

Shay was my longest relationship in the past two years. Most of the time, it was a month tops, but with Shay, we made it a total of eight months and two days. I didn't know why exactly, other than her life was almost a carbon copy of mine. Her mom was far from stable, and her father was in prison. She didn't have anyone to look up to, and her sister was kicked out of their house by their mom because she got knocked up by some jerk.

Maybe the darkness in me saw and honored the darkness in her for a little while. We made sense. But as time went by, I realized that it was because of the similarities that we truly didn't belong together. We were both too messed up. Being with Shay was like looking at a mirror and seeing all your scars staring back at you.

"Shay, let's not do this. I'm tired."

"Okay. I forgot. You are Mr. Perfect. People make bad calls in life," Shay explained.

"You made out with my friend, Shay."

"It's just that: making out! And I only did it because you cheated on me."

"I'm not even sure how to reply to that, seeing as how I never cheated on you."

"Maybe not with sex, but emotionally, Logan. You were never fully there and committed. This is all Alyssa's fault. She's the reason you never really committed to me. She's such a stupid bit—"

I held my hand up to her mouth, halting her words. "Before you say what you're about to say, don't." I lowered my hand, and she remained quiet. "I told you from day one who I was. It's your own fault for thinking you could change me."

"You're never going to be happy with anyone, are you? Because you are so hung up on a girl that you'll never have. You're going to end up sad, alone, and bitter. Then you'll figure out what you had when you were with me!"

"Can you just leave?" I sighed, brushing my hand against my face. I blamed Alyssa for this.

"Break up with her in person, Lo. That's the only way a real man would do it. You can't break up with someone over the phone."

She had some awful ideas sometimes.

Shay kept crying.

God, those tears.

I couldn't handle the tears.

After a few snotty sniffles, she glanced at the ground before holding her head high, a spark of confidence finding her. "I think we should break up."

I appeared shocked. "Break up?" *We already did!*

"I just feel like we're two people going in two opposite directions."

"Okay," I said.

Her fingers flew over my lips and she shushed me, even though I wasn't talking. "Don't be so emotional about it. I'm so sorry, Logan. But it's just not going to work out."

I snickered internally at her, making it seem like the breakup was her idea. I stepped back and placed my hands on my neck. "You're right. You're too good for me."

Why are you still here?

She moved over to me. "You'll find someone good. I know it. I mean, granted, she might look like an ape, but still." She jogged toward her car, opened the door, and climbed inside.

As the car pulled off, my gut tightened, and regret overtook me. I started sprinting toward her car in the pouring rain, shouting her name. "Shay! Shay!" I waved my hands into the darkness, running for at least five blocks before she came up to a red light. I banged on her driver's window and she screamed, out of fright.

"Logan! What the heck are you doing?!" she cried, rolling down her window. Her confusion turned into a proud smirk and she narrowed her eyes. "You want to get back together, don't you? I knew it."

"I…" I huffed. I wasn't an athlete at all; that was more of my brother's field of expertise. I tried to catch my breath, holding my hands against the edge of her window. "I—I…n-need…"

"You need what? What, baby? What do you need?" she asked, running her hand gently against my cheek.

"Pie."

She sat back, confused. "What?"

"Pie. My pie supplies that we bought earlier. They're in the back of your car."

"Are you freaking kidding me?!" she screeched. "You chased me down for blocks and blocks for pie ingredients?!"

I arched an eyebrow. "Um, yeah?"

She reached into the back of her car, snatched the bag up, and slammed it against my chest. "You are so unbelievable! Here's your stupid crap!"

I smirked. "Thanks."

Her car pulled off, and I couldn't help but laugh when I heard her shout, "You owe me twenty bucks for that goat cheese!"

The second I stepped foot into my apartment, I pulled out my cell phone and sent a text.

Me: Next time I break up with a girl, I'm doing it via text
    message.

Alyssa: That bad?

Me: Dreadful.

Alyssa: I feel bad for her. She really liked you.

Me: She cheated on me!

Alyssa: And yet you still found a way to sleep with her
    three times.

Me: Whose side are you on?

Dots.

Alyssa: She's such a monster!
I'm so happy she's out of your life.
No one deserves to date such a psychotic person.

She's disgusting.

I hope she accidentally steps on Lego pieces for the
    remainder of her life.

There was the response I needed.

Alyssa: Love you, best friend.

I read her words and tried to ignore the pull in my chest. *Love you.* I never said those kinds of things to people, not even to Ma or Kellan. But sometimes, when Alyssa Marie Walters said she loved me, I kind of wished I could say it back.

But I didn't love.

I hardly liked.

At least that was the lie I told myself daily to keep from getting hurt. Most people thought love was a reward, but I knew better than that. I'd seen my mom love my father for years now, and nothing good ever came from it. Love wasn't a blessing, it was a curse, and once you invited it into your heart, it only left scorch marks.

CHAPTER 2
Alyssa

Me: Hey, Dad. Just checking in to see about you coming
to the piano recital.

Me: Hey! Did you see my last text?

Me: Hey, me again. Just texting to see if you're okay. Erika
and I are worried.

Me: Dad?

Me: ??

Me: Are you still awake, Lo?

I stared at my cell phone, my heart pounding in my chest as I sent the text message to Logan. I checked the time, sighing heavily.

2:33 a.m.

I should've been sleeping, but I was thinking about Dad again. I'd sent him a total of fifteen text messages and left ten voicemails in the past two days, yet I still hadn't heard back from him.

I laid my phone against my chest, taking deep inhales and exhales.

When it started vibrating, I was quick to answer. "You should be sleeping," I whispered through the phone receiver, secretly happy that he answered. "Why aren't you sleeping?"

"What's wrong?" Logan asked, ignoring my question.

A light giggle escaped my lips. "What makes you think something's wrong?"

"Alyssa," he said, stern.

"Ass-Crack didn't call me back. I called him twenty times this week, and he didn't call me back." Ass-Crack was the name we'd graced my dad with after he walked out on our family. He and I had been extremely close, the two musicians of the family, and when he left, a part of me floated away with him. I didn't talk about him a lot, but even though I never said the words, Logan always knew that it bothered me.

"Forget about him. He's a piece of trash."

"I have the biggest summer piano recital of my career coming up, and I don't know if I can do it without him there." I tried my best to keep my emotions in check. I tried my best not to cry, but I was losing the fight that night. I worried about him more than Mom and Erika did. Maybe because they never really understood who he was, as an artist, as a performer. The two of them had very reality-based minds that came with a lot of stability. Dad and I were kind of floating spirits, dancing in the wildfires.

But lately, he hadn't called. And I was so, so worried.

"Alyssa," Logan started.

"Lo," I whispered, a light tremble in my voice. "When I was little, thunderstorms used to freak me out really bad. And I'd run into my parents' bedroom and beg them to let me sleep with them. Mom never let me because she said I had to learn that storms wouldn't hurt me. Ass-Crack would always agree with her too. So I'd go back to my bedroom, huddle under my blankets, listen to the thunder, and try my hardest not to see the lightning. Within a minute, my bedroom door would open, he'd have his keyboard in his hands, and he'd play music beside my bed until I fell asleep. Most days, I'm strong. I'm okay. But tonight with the storm and all the ignored calls…he's breaking me tonight."

"Don't let him, Alyssa. Don't let him win."

"I just…" I began to cry over the line, and I started to break down. "I'm just having a sad moment, that's all."

"I'm coming over."

"What? No. It's late."

"I'm coming."

"The buses stopped running at two, Logan. Plus, my mom closed the gate to the property and locked up. You couldn't get in anyway. It's fine." Mom was a hotshot lawyer and had money—a lot of money. We lived at the top of a hill, with a huge gate around our property. It was pretty impossible to get into after Mom locked up at night. "I'm fine," I promised. "I just needed to hear your voice and for you to remind me that I'm better off without him."

"Because you are," he explained.

"Yeah."

"No, Alyssa. Really. You are better than Ass-Crack."

My sobbing grew heavier, and I had to cover my mouth with one hand just so he wouldn't hear how hard I was crying. My body shook in bed, and I fell apart, tears falling against my pillowcase, my thoughts making me even more anxious.

What if something had happened to him? What if he was drinking again? What if…?

"I'm coming over."

"No."

"Alyssa. Please." He almost sounded like he was begging.

"Are you high?" I asked.

He hesitated, which was enough of an answer for me. I could always tell when he was high, mainly because he was almost always stoned. He knew it bothered me, but he always said he was a hamster on the wheel, unable to change his ways.

We were so different in so many ways. There wasn't much that I'd ever done. I pretty much went to work, played the piano, and hung out with Logan. He had a lot more experience in things than I could've ever imagined. He used drugs that I couldn't even name. He lost himself almost weekly, usually after crossing paths with his father or dealing with his mom, but somehow he always found his way home to me.

I tried my best to pretend that it didn't bother me, but sometimes it did.

"Good night, best friend," I said softly.

"Good night, best friend," he replied, sighing.

His hands were tucked behind his back, and he was soaked from head to toe. His normally wavy brown hair was lying flat against his head, strands covering his eyes. He was wearing his favorite red hoodie and his black jeans that had more rips than any pair of pants should've ever had. And he had a goofy grin on his face.

"Logan, it's three thirty in the morning," I whispered, hoping not to wake my mom.

"You were crying," he said, standing in my front doorway. "And the storm wasn't stopping."

"You walked here?" I asked.

He sneezed. "It wasn't that far."

"You climbed the gate?"

He twisted a little, showing me the rip in his jeans. "I climbed the gate, plus"—he pulled his hands from behind his back, showcasing a pie pan, wrapped in aluminum foil—"I made you a pie."

"You made a pie?"

"I watched a documentary on pie earlier today. Did you know that pie has been around since the ancient Egyptians? The first documented pie was created by the Romans, and it was a rye-crusted—"

"Goat cheese and honey pie?" I cut in.

His face dropped with shock. "How did you know?!"

"You told me yesterday."

He grew a bit bashful. "Oh. Right."

I laughed. "You're high."

He snickered, nodding. "I'm high."

I smiled. "It's a forty-five-minute walk from your place to mine, Logan. You shouldn't have come that far. And you're shivering. Get inside." I grabbed his dripping wet hoodie by the sleeve and yanked him down the hall to the bathroom connected to my bedroom. Closing the door behind me, I sat him down on the closed toilet seat. "Take off your hoodie and shirt," I ordered.

He smirked mischievously. "Aren't you going to offer me a drink first?"

"Logan Francis Silverstone," I groaned. "Don't be weird."

"Alyssa Marie Walters. I'm always weird. That's why you like me."

He wasn't wrong.

He took off his hoodie and shirt, tossing them into the bathtub. My eyes danced across his chest for a second, and I tried my best to ignore the butterflies in my stomach as I wrapped three towels around his body. "What the heck were you thinking?"

His caramel eyes were gentle, and he leaned in closer to me, locking his stare with mine. "Are you okay?"

"I'm fine." I ran my fingers through his hair, which was so cold and soft. He studied my every move. I grabbed a small towel, kneeled in front of him, and shook my head as I started drying his hair. "You should've stayed home."

"Your eyes are red."

I snickered slightly. "So are yours." Thunder rumbled outside, and I jumped out of my skin. Logan placed a comforting hand against my arm, and a small hiccup escaped my lips. I stared at his fingers lying against me, and his stare fell to the same place. Clearing my throat, I stepped away from him. "Do we eat pie now?"

"We eat pie now."

We headed to the kitchen quietly, hoping to not wake my mom, but I was almost certain she wouldn't wake up due to the number of sleeping pills she took each night. Logan jumped on the countertop, shirtless with soaked jeans, holding his pie.

"Plates?" I offered.

"Just a fork," he replied.

Grabbing a fork, I jumped on the countertop beside him. He took the fork, scooped up a large piece of pie, and held it out toward me. I willingly took a bite, closed my eyes, and fell in love.

Gosh.

He was the best cook. I wasn't certain of it, but I doubted many people could pull off a goat cheese and honey pie. Logan not only pulled it off, he gave life to it. It was creamy, fresh, totally delish.

I closed my eyes and opened my mouth, waiting for another bite, which he gave me. "Mmm," I lightly sighed.

"Are you moaning over my pie?"

"I'm definitely moaning over your pie."

"Open your mouth. I want to hear you do it again."

I cocked an eyebrow at him. "You're being weird again." He smiled. I loved that smile. So much of his life involved frowns that whenever he smiled, I learned to cherish that moment. He scooped up a piece of the pie and hovered it by my lips. He started making plane noises, moving the spoon as if it were flying through the air. I tried my best not to laugh, but I did. Then I opened my mouth, and the plane landed. "Mmm," I moaned.

"You are such a good moaner."

"If I had a dollar for every time I heard that," I mocked him.

He narrowed his eyes. "You'd have zero dollars and zero cents," he mocked back.

"You're a jerk."

"Just to be clear, if there are any guys calling you a good moaner other than me, *jokingly*, I'll kill them."

He always said he'd kill any boy who looked my way, and a big part of why my relationships never worked out probably had something to do with that fact—they were all deathly afraid of Logan Francis Silverstone. I didn't get the fear, though. To me, he was just a big teddy bear.

"This is the best thing I've eaten all day. It's so good that I want to frame the fork."

"That good?" he smirked.

"*That good*," I said. "You should really think about going to culinary school like we talked about before. You would be amazing."

He huffed, a slight frown finding him. "College isn't for me."

"It could be, though."

"Next subject," he said, scrunching his nose.

I wouldn't push it. I knew the subject was a touchy one for him. He didn't think he was smart enough to ever get into any kind of school, but that wasn't the truth. Logan was one of the smartest people I knew. If only he saw himself the way I saw him, his life would change forever.

Stealing the fork from his grip, I scooped more into my mouth, moaning loudly, to make the conversation much lighter. He smiled again. *Good.* "I'm seriously so happy you brought this, Lo. I've actually hardly eaten all day. My mom said I need to lose twenty pounds before I start college in the fall, because I'm in danger of the freshman thirty."

"I thought it was the freshman fifteen?"

"Mom said since I was already overweight that it would turn out to be even more than the average student. You know, she loves me like that."

He dramatically rolled his eyes. "What a sweetheart."

"I'm not supposed to eat after eight at night."

"Luckily, it's past four in the morning, so it's a new day! *We must eat all the pie before eight!*"

I giggled, quickly covering his mouth with my hands to keep him from shouting anymore. I felt his lips lightly kiss the palms of my hands, and my heart skipped once. I pulled my hands away slowly, feeling the butterflies forming, and cleared my throat. "It's a tough job, but someone has to do it."

We did it too; we ate the whole thing. As I went to clean the fork in the sink, he grabbed my hand. "No, we can't clean it. We have to frame it, remember?"

As his hands held mine, my heart skipped twice.

Our eyes met, and he stepped closer. "And just so you know, you're beautiful the way you are, Aly. Screw your mom's opinion. I think you're beautiful. Not just in the superficial ways that fade over time, but I mean in every way possible. You're just a beautiful fucking person, so screw other people's thoughts. You know how I feel about people."

I nodded, knowing his motto by heart. "'Fuck people. Get a pet.'"

"That's right," he smirked, releasing his hold on my hand. I missed his touch before it even left. He began yawning, which distracted me from my erratic heartbeat.

"Tired?" I asked.

"I could sleep."

"You'll have to be gone before my mom wakes up."

"Aren't I always?"

We went into my bedroom. I gave him a pair of sweatpants and a shirt that I had stolen from him a few weeks ago. After he changed, we climbed into my bed and lay side by side. I'd never slept in the same bed with a boy before, other than Logan. Sometimes, I'd awaken with my head on his chest, and before I pulled away, I'd listen to his heartbeats. He was a heavy breather who inhaled and exhaled through his mouth. The first time he stayed over, I didn't sleep a wink. Yet as time went by, his sounds began to remind me of home. As it turned out, home wasn't a certain place; home was a feeling from the ones for whom you cared most, a feeling of peace that calmed the wildfires of your soul.

"Still tired?" I asked as we lay in the darkness, my mind still wide awake.

"Yeah, but we can talk."

"I've just been wondering. You've never explained to me why you love documentaries so much."

He brushed his hands through his hair before placing his hands behind his head and staring at the ceiling. "One summer, I stayed with my grandpa before he died. He had this documentary on the galaxy that got me hooked on wanting to know more about…everything. I wish I remembered the name of the documentary, because I'd buy it in a heartbeat. It was like *Black Hole*…or *Black Star*…" He frowned. "I don't know. Anyway. He and I started watching more and more documentaries together; it became our thing. It was the best summer of my life." A wave of sadness seemed to hit him as he glanced down. "After he died, I just kept up the tradition. It's probably one of the only traditions that I'd ever had."

"You know a lot about the stars?"

"*A lot* about the stars. If there was a good enough place in this town, I'd show you the stars without all the light pollution and show you a few of the constellations. But sadly, there isn't."

"That's too bad. I would love that. I've been thinking, though. You should make a documentary about your life."

He laughed. "No one would want to watch that."

I tilted my head in his direction. "I would."

He gave me half a smile before he wrapped his arm around me, pulling me into the curve of his body. His warmth always sent sparks flying through me.

"Lo?" I whispered, half awake, half asleep, and secretly falling for my best friend.

"Yeah?"

I opened my mouth to speak, but instead of words, a quiet sigh left me. My head fell against his chest, and I listened to the sound of his heartbeats, counting each one. *One… Two… Forty-five…*

Within minutes, my mind slowed down. Within minutes, I forgot why I was so sad. Within minutes, I was asleep.

CHAPTER 3
Logan

Ma and I didn't have cable in our apartment, which was fine. I didn't mind much. When I was a kid, we had cable, but it didn't seem worth it because of my dad. He was the one who paid the cable bill, and he always complained about me sitting in front of the television watching cartoons. It was as if he hated that I was somewhat happy for a few moments during the day. Then one day he came into our home, took the television, and canceled the services.

That was the day he moved out of the apartment.

That was also one of the best days of my life.

After some time, I found a television in a dumpster. It was a small nineteen-inch television with a DVD player, so I'd check out a bunch of documentaries from the library and watch them at home. I was the person who knew too much about everything, baseball, tropical birds, and Area 51, all due to the documentaries. Yet at the same time, I knew absolutely nothing.

Sometimes Ma watched them with me, but most of the time, it was a solo gig.

Ma loved me, but she didn't like me much.

Well, that wasn't true.

Sober Ma loved me as if I was her best friend.

Drugged Ma was a monster, and she was the only one who lived in our house lately.

I missed Sober Ma some days. Sometimes when I shut my eyes, I'd remember the sound of her laugh and the curve of her lips when she was happy.

Stop, Logan.

I hated my mind, how it remembered. Memories were daggers to my soul, and I hardly had any positive ones to hold on to.

I didn't care, though, because I kept my mind high enough to almost forget about the crappy life I lived. If I stayed locked in my room, stocked up on documentaries, with some good shit to smoke, I could almost forget that my mom stood on a corner a few weeks ago, trying to sell her body for a few lines of blow.

That was a call I never wanted to get from my friend Jacob.

"Dude. I just saw your mom on the corner of Jefferson and Wells Street. I think she's…um…" Jacob paused. "I think you should get down here."

Tuesday morning, I was sitting in my bed, staring at my ceiling, while a documentary on Chinese artifacts played as my background music, when she shouted my name.

"Logan! Logan! Logan, get in here!"

I lay as still as I could, hoping she'd stop calling me, but she didn't. Pushing myself up from my mattress, I headed out of my bedroom to find Ma sitting at the dining room table. Our apartment was tiny, but we didn't have much to put inside it anyway. A broken-down sofa, a dirty coffee table with stains, and a dining room table with three different chairs.

"What do you need?" I asked.

"I need you to clean the windows from the outside, Logan," Ma said, pouring herself a bowl of milk and placing five Cheerios inside the cracked bowl. She said she was on a new diet and didn't want to get fat. There was no way that she weighed more than a hundred and twenty pounds, and being five feet nine inches tall, I thought she was almost skeletal.

She looked exhausted. Did she even sleep last night?

Her hair was a mess that morning, but no more a mess than her entire existence. Ma always looked broken down, and I couldn't think of a time when she didn't. She always painted her fingernails on Sunday morning and always chipped it off by Sunday night, leaving little spots of color remaining on her nails throughout the week until the next Sunday morning when she repeated the task. Her clothes were always dirty, but she would spray Febreze on them at four in the morning before ironing them. She believed that Febreze was a decent replacement for washing our clothes at the local laundromat.

I disagreed with her technique and snuck her clothes out whenever I could to wash them. Most people probably walked past spare change on the ground, but for me, it could've meant clean pants that week.

"It's supposed to rain all day. I'll clean them tomorrow," I replied. I wouldn't, though. She'd forget soon enough. Plus, cleaning our third-floor apartment windows without a balcony seemed a bit ridiculous. Especially during a rainstorm.

I opened the fridge door to stare at the bare shelves. It had been empty for days now.

My fingers stayed wrapped around the handle of the refrigerator. I opened and closed it, almost as if food would magically appear to fill my noisy stomach. Right then, like the wizard he was, the front door opened, and my brother, Kellan, came in behind me, holding grocery bags in his hand and shaking the rainwater from his jacket.

"Hungry?" he asked, nudging me in the arm. Maybe Ma was only eating Cheerios because that was all we had.

Kellan was the only person I'd ever trusted—other than Alyssa. We looked almost like twins, except he was stronger, more handsome, and more stable. He had a classic buzz cut, designer clothes, and no bags under his eyes. The only bruises that ever showed up on his skin were from a tackle during a college football game—which didn't happen that often.

He lucked out with a better life, simply because he had a better dad. His father was a surgeon. My dad was more of a street pharmacist who dealt drugs to the neighborhood kids and to my mother.

DNA: sometimes you win, sometimes you lose.

"Geez," he said, looking into the refrigerator. "You'll need more stuff than what I bought."

"How did you even know we needed food?" I questioned, helping him unload the bags.

"I called him," Ma said, eating one of her Cheerios, slurping on the milk. "It's not like you were gonna feed us."

My hands formed fists, and I pounded them against my sides. My nostrils flared, but I tried to contain my anger from her comment. I hated that Kellan had to step in and save us so often from ourselves. He deserved to be far, far away from this lifestyle.

"I'll pick up some more things and drop them off after my night class."

"You live an hour away. You don't have to drive back out here."

He ignored me. "Any requests?" he asked.

"Food would be good," I grumbled, along with my stomach.

He reached into his backpack and pulled out two brown paper bags. "Food."

"You cooked for us too?"

"Well, kind of." He took the bags and dumped them on the countertops. Random food items, uncooked. "I know when you came to stay with me for a bit, we watched a lot of that cooking show where they just give you random supplies and you have to make a meal. Alyssa told me you thought about becoming a chef."

"Alyssa talks too much."

"She's crazy about you."

I didn't argue that.

"So," he smirked, tossing a potato my way, "I have a bit of time before I go to work. Make something happen, chef!"

I did too. He and I sat eating my fancy grilled cheese with ham, three kinds of cheese, and a garlic aioli sauce. On the side, I made homemade hash browns with a spicy bacon-flavored ketchup.

"How is it?" I asked, my eyes glued to Kellan. "Do you like it?" Without thought, I placed half my sandwich in front of Ma. She shook her head.

"Diet," she murmured, eating her last Cheerio.

"Dang, Logan," Kellan sighed, somehow tuning out Ma's comment. I wished I could do that. "This is amazing."

I smirked, a spark of pride. "Really?"

"I bit into the sandwich and literally almost died from how good it was. If I believed in heaven, it would've been solely due to that sandwich."

My smile widened. "Right?! I kind of outdid myself."

"Fucking brilliant."

I shrugged my shoulders with that smug look on my face. "I'm kind of amazing." I couldn't thank Kellan enough—that was the most fun I'd had in a long time. Maybe someday I could go to college… Maybe Alyssa was right.

"I gotta get going, though. You sure you don't want a ride anywhere?" Kellan asked.

I wanted out of the apartment, that was for sure. But I wasn't certain if my dad would be stopping by, and I didn't want him alone with Ma. Whenever he was alone with her, her skin was always more purple than when I left her.

It took a certain kind of demon to ever lay his hands on a woman.

"No. I'm good. I work at the gas station later today anyway."

"Isn't that, like, an hour-long walk away from here?"

"No. Forty-five minutes. It's fine."

"You want bus fare?"

"I can walk."

He dug into his wallet and put money on the table. "Listen." He leaned in closer to me and whispered, "If you ever want to stay at my dad's place… It's closer to your job."

"Your dad hates me," I interrupted.

"He doesn't."

I gave him an are-you-fucking-kidding look.

"Okay. You might not be his favorite person, but to be fair, you did steal three hundred dollars from his wallet."

"I had to make rent."

"Yeah, but, Logan, your first thought shouldn't have been to steal it."

"Then what should it have been?" I asked, growing upset, mostly because I knew he was right.

"I don't know. Maybe asking for help?"

"I don't need anyone's help. Never have, never will." That pride I had was always so harsh. I understood why some called it the deadliest sin.

Kellan frowned, knowing I was in need of an escape. Being in that apartment so long had a way of driving one crazy. "All right then." He walked around to Ma and placed his lips against her forehead. "Love you, Ma."

She kind of smiled. "Bye, Kellan."

He moved behind me, placing his hands on my shoulders, and softly spoke. "She's even thinner than the last time I saw her."

"Yeah."

"That scares me."

"Yeah, me too." I saw the worry weighing heavy on his mind. "Don't worry, though. I'll get her to eat something."

His concern didn't vanish. "You look kind of smaller too."

"That's just because of my high metabolism," I joked. He didn't laugh. I patted him on the back. "Seriously, Kel. I'm okay. And I'll try to get her to eat. I promise to try, okay?"

He released a weighted sigh. "Okay. I'll see you later. If you're not back from work when I stop by tonight, I'll see you next week." Kellan waved goodbye, and before he stepped out of the apartment, I called his name. "Yeah?" he asked.

I shrugged my left shoulder. He shrugged his right.

That was how we always said *I love you* to each other. He meant so much to me. The person I someday dreamed of becoming. Yet still, we were men. And men didn't say, "I love you." Truth was I didn't say those words to anyone.

Clearing my throat, I nodded once. "Thanks again. For..." I shrugged my left shoulder. "Everything."

He gave me a soft smile and shrugged his right. "Always." With that, he left.

Shrugging our shoulders was how we always said…to anyone.

My stare fell to Ma, who was talking to her bowl of milk. Figures.

"Kellan's the perfect son," she muttered to the milk before tilting her head my way. "He's so much better than you."

Where's Sober Ma?

"Yeah," I said, standing up to take my food into my bedroom. "Okay, Ma."

"It's true. He's handsome and smart and takes care of me. You don't do shit."

"You're right. I don't do shit for you," I mumbled, walking away, not wanting to deal with her crazed mind that morning.

As I walked, I became startled when a flying bowl glanced off my left ear and shattered against the wall in front of me. Milk and shattered glass splashed all over me. My head tilted back toward Ma, and she had a sly smile on her lips.

"I need those windows cleaned today, Logan. Right now. I have a date coming to pick me up tonight, and this place is *disgusting*!" she shouted. "And clean up that mess."

My blood began to boil, because she was such a mess. How'd someone get so far gone in life? Once they were so far gone, was there any chance of them ever coming back? *I miss you so much, Ma…* "I'm not cleaning that up."

"Yes, you are."

"Who are you going out on a date with, Ma?"

She sat up straight as if she was some kind of royalty. "None of your business."

"Really? Because I'm pretty sure the last person you went out on a date with was some scumbag who picked you up on a corner. The time before that, it was my deadbeat father, and you came back with two broken ribs."

"Don't you dare talk about him like that. He's good to us. Who do you think pays most of our rent? Because it definitely isn't you."

A just-graduated-high-school, almost eighteen-year-old who couldn't make rent—I was such a loser.

"I pay half, which is more than you can say, and he's nothing but a piece of shit."

She slammed her hands on the table, irritated by my words. Her body had a slight tremble to it, and she was becoming more fidgety. "He's more of a man than you could ever be!"

"Oh?" I asked, charging toward her, starting to search her pockets, knowing exactly what I would find. "He's more a man? And why is that?" I questioned, finding the small baggie of cocaine in her back pocket. I dangled it in her face and watched the panic spill over her face.

"Stop it!" she shouted, trying to grab it from me.

"No, I get it. He gives you this, and that makes him a better man than I could ever be. He beats you, because he's a better man. He spits in your face and calls you shit, because he's a better man than me. Right?"

She started tearing up, not at my words, because I was certain she rarely ever heard me, but from fear that her white powdered friend was in danger. "Just give it to me, Lo! Stop!"

Her eyes were hollow, and it was almost as if I was fighting with a ghost. With a heavy sigh, I tossed the baggie on the table and watched her wipe at her nose before opening it up, finding her razor blade, and setting up two lines of coke on the dining room table.

"You're a mess. You're a goddamn mess, and you're never going to get better," I said as she sniffed up the powder.

"Says the boy who's probably going to walk into his bedroom, shut the door, and snort up your own treat that your daddy gave you. He's the big bad wolf, but little red riding hoodie boy keeps calling him back to get his fix. You think you're any better than me or him?"

"I am," I said. I used, but not too much. I had control. I wasn't wild.

I was better than my parents.

I had to be.

"You're not. You have the worst of both of us in your soul. Kellan is good. He'll be okay forever. But you?" She set up two more lines of coke. "I'll be surprised if you ain't dead by twenty-five."

My heart.

It stopped beating.

Shock rocketed through me as the words fell from her lips. She didn't even flinch when she said them, and I felt a part of me die. I wanted to do the complete opposite of what she thought I'd do. I wanted to be strong, be stable, be worthy of existence.

But still, I was that hamster on the wheel.

Going round and round and getting absolutely nowhere.

I walked into my bedroom, slammed my door, and lost myself in the world of my own demons. I wondered what would've happened if I never said hello to my father all those years ago. I wondered what would've happened if we never crossed paths.

LOGAN, SEVEN YEARS OLD

I met my father on a stranger's front porch. Ma took me to some house that night and told me to wait outside. She said she'd run in fast, and then we would go home, but I guessed she and her friends were having a lot more fun than they thought they would.

The porch was trashed, and my red hoodie wasn't the best for the winter cold, but I didn't complain. Ma always hated when I complained; she said it made me look weak.

There was a broken-down metal bench on the porch that I sat against, my legs bent into my chest as time passed by. The railing of the porch had peeling gray paint and cracked wooden slats along with frozen snow that was never shoveled away.

Come on, Ma.

It was so cold that night, I could see my breath, so to entertain myself, I kept blowing hot air out of my mouth.

People went in and out of the house throughout the night and hardly even noticed me sitting on the bench. I reached into my back pocket and pulled out a small pad of paper and the pen that I always had with me and started to doodle. Whenever Ma wasn't around, I kept myself busy by drawing.

I drew a lot that night, until I started to yawn. Eventually I fell asleep, tucking my legs inside my red hoodie and lying down against the bench. When I was sleeping, I didn't feel as cold, which was kind of nice.

"Hey!" a harsh voice said, waking me from my sleep. The moment my eyes slightly opened, I was reminded of the coldness. My body began to shiver, but I didn't sit up. "Hey, kid! What the fuck are you doing here?" the voice questioned. "Get up."

I sat up and rubbed my eyes, yawning. "My ma is inside. I'm just waiting." My eyes focused in on the guy speaking my way, and my eyes widened with nerves. He looked mean and had a big scar running down the left side of his face. His hair was wild, peppered with black and white, and his eyes kind of looked like mine. Brown and boring.

"Yeah? How long have you been waiting?" he hissed with some kind of cigarette hanging between his lips.

My eyes moved up to the darkened sky. It was light when Ma and I arrived. I didn't answer the man. He groaned and sat down next to me. I scooted closer to the edge of the bench, as far away from him as I could get.

"Chill the fuck out, kid. Ain't no one gonna hurt you. Your mom's a junkie?" he asked. I didn't know what that meant, so I shrugged. He snickered. "If she's in that house, she's a junkie. What's her name?"

"Julie," I whispered.

"Julie what?"

"Julie Silverstone."

His lips slightly parted and he tilted his head, looking my way. "Your mom's Julie Silverstone?"

I nodded.

"And she left you out here?"

I nodded again.

"That bitch," he muttered, standing up from the bench with his hands in fists. He started for the front door, and as he opened the screen door, he paused. He took the cigarette from between his lips and held it out to me. "You smoke pot?" he questioned.

It wasn't a cigarette at all. I should've known by the smell. "No."

His brows furrowed. "You said Julie Silverstone, right?" I nodded for the third time. He placed the joint in my hands. "Then you smoke pot. It will keep you warm. I'll be back with your bitch of a mother."

"She's not a"—the door slammed before he could hear me complete my sentence—"bitch."

I held the joint between my fingers and shivered in the cold.

It will keep you warm.

I was freezing.

So I took a puff and choked on my own coughing.

I coughed hard for a long time, stomping out the joint into the ground. I didn't understand why anyone would do that—why anyone would ever smoke. That was the moment I vowed to never smoke again.

When the man came out, he was dragging Ma along with him. She was hardly awake and sweaty.

"Stop yanking me, Ricky!" she yelled at the man.

"Shut the hell up, Julie. You left your damn kid out here all night, you fucking crackhead."

My fists formed and I puffed out my chest. How dare he talk to Ma like that! He didn't know her. She was my best friend, other than my brother, Kellan. And that guy had no right to talk to Ma like that. Kellan would've been so mad if he heard that guy. Good thing he wasn't here and was with his father on some kind of ice fishing trip.

I didn't know people could fish when there was ice out, but Kellan told me all about it last week. Ma said ice fishing was for weirdos and losers.

"I told you, Ricky! I ain't using anymore. I—I promise," she stuttered. "I just stopped here to see Becky."

"Bullshit," he replied, pulling her down the steps. "Come on, kid."

"Where are we going, Ma?" I asked, following behind my mom, wondering what was going to happen next.

"I'm driving you two home," the man replied. He put Ma in his passenger seat, where she closed her eyes and slumped over. Then he opened the back door for me, slamming it shut after I climbed inside. "Where do you stay?" he asked, climbing into the driver's seat and driving off, away from the curb.

His car was shiny and nice, nicer than any car I'd ever seen. Ma and I took the bus everywhere, so being in his car kind of made me feel like royalty.

Ma started hacking and coughing and tried her best to clear her throat. "See, that's why I had to see Becky. My landlord is being a dick and told me that I didn't pay the last two months! But I did, Ricky! I paid that asshole, and he's acting like I didn't. So I came to see Becky to get some money."

"Since when does Becky ever have money?" he asked.

"She didn't. She didn't have money, I guess. But I had to see. Because the landlord said I can't come back if I didn't have the money. So I'm not sure where we should go. You should let me go check with Becky really quick," she muttered, opening her passenger door as the car drove.

"Ma!"

"Julie!"

Ricky and I shouted at the same time. I reached for her shirt from the back seat, and he pulled her shirtsleeve, jerking her in his direction, shutting the door with her.

"Are you crazy?!" he hollered, his nostrils flaring. "Dammit. I'll pay your bill tomorrow, but tonight you'll stay at my place."

"You'll do that, Ricky? God, we'd appreciate that a lot. Wouldn't we, Lo? I'll pay you back. I'll pay you back every cent of it."

I nodded, feeling the heat finally kick in from the car.

Warmth.

"I'll grab the kid some food too. I doubt you fed him." He reached into his pocket and pulled out a pack of cigarettes and a lighter shaped like a hula dancer. As he flicked the lighter on, the hula dancer moved side to side. I became hypnotized with the movement, unable to take my eyes off it. Even when he finished lighting the cigarette, he flicked it on and off nonstop.

When we arrived at Ricky's apartment, I was blown away by how much stuff he had. Two sofas and a huge armchair, paintings, a huge television with cable, and a refrigerator filled with enough food to feed the world. After eating, he set me up on one of the sofas, and I began to drift to sleep, listening to Ma and him whisper in the hallway nearby.

"He has your eyes," she mumbled.

"Yeah, I know." His voice was filled with spite, but I wasn't sure why. I listened to his footsteps grow closer to me and opened my eyes to see him bending down next to me. His hands clasped together, and he narrowed his eyes. "You're my kid, huh?"

I didn't reply.

Because what was I supposed to say?

A sly smirk fell from the side of his mouth, and he lit a cigarette, blowing smoke into my face. "Don't worry, Logan. I'll take care of you and your mom. Promise."

NOW

At four in the morning when I finally came down from my high, I lay in my bed, staring at the ceiling.

Me: Are you up?

I stared at my phone, waiting for the dots to appear, but they didn't. When my phone rang, I took a breath.

"I woke you up," I whispered into the receiver.

"Only a little," Alyssa replied. "What happened?"

"Nothing," I lied. "I'm fine."

You'll be dead by twenty-five.

"Was it your mom or your dad?" She always knew.

"Mom."

"Was she high or sober?"

"High."

"Did you believe whatever she said or not?"

I hesitated and started flicking my lighter on and off.

"Oh, Lo."

"Sorry for waking you. I can hang up. Go back to sleep."

"I'm not tired," she yawned. "Stay on the phone with me until you're able to fall asleep, all right?"

"All right."

"You're okay, Logan Francis Silverstone."

"I'm okay, Alyssa Marie Walters."

Even though it felt like a lie, it was one that her voice almost always made me believe.

CHAPTER 4
Logan

I never truly celebrated my birthday before two years ago when I met Alyssa. Kellan always took me out to dinner, and I loved that. He was pretty great at reminding me that I wasn't alone in the world, but Alyssa went bigger than ever each year for my birthday. Two years ago, we went to Chicago to watch a documentary special on Charlie Chaplin at an old theater; then she took me out to a fancy restaurant that I was way too underdressed for. She came from a lifestyle where fancy dinners were normal; I came from a world where dinner wasn't always available. When she noticed my discomfort, we ending up walking down the streets of Chicago, eating hot dogs and standing under the giant bean.

That was the first best day of my life.

One year ago, there was a film festival going on in upper Wisconsin, and she rented out a cabin for us to stay in. We watched each and every film together for the whole weekend. We stayed up late discussing which movies inspired us and which were made by people who probably dropped a lot of acid.

That was the second best day of my life.

But today was different. Today was my eighteenth birthday, it was past eleven at night, and Alyssa hadn't called me once.

I sat in my bedroom watching the DVD on Jackie Robinson while I listened to Ma stumble around the apartment. A pile of bills sat beside my bed, and I felt a tight knot in my stomach from fear of not making rent. If we weren't able to make rent, Dad would never let us live it down. And if I asked him for help, I was certain Ma would pay the price.

I reached under my bed and pulled out an envelope, checking the money I had saved up on my own. The words on the envelope made me sick.

College funds.

What a joke.

I counted the money. *Five hundred and fifty-two dollars.* I'd been saving for two years now, ever since Alyssa made it seem like a thing I could do someday. I spent a lot of time thinking that one day I'd save enough to go to school, get a solid career, and buy a house for Ma and me to live in.

We'd never have to rely on Dad for anything. The home would be ours and only ours. We'd get clean too. No more drugs, only happiness. Ma would cry because she was happy, not because he beat her.

Sober Ma would come back, the one who used to tuck me in when I was young. The one who used to sing and dance. The one who used to smile.

It'd been such a long time since I'd seen that version of her, but a part of me held on to the hope that one day, she'd come back. *She has to come back to me.*

I sighed, taking out some cash from my college funds to pay the electric bill.

Three hundred and twenty-three dollars left.

And just like that, the dream seemed a bit further away.

Taking out a pencil, I began to doodle on the electric bill. Drawing and zoning out on documentaries were my main ways to escape reality. Plus, a weird curly-haired girl who smiled and talked too much had been appearing in my mind. Alyssa took up a lot more of my thoughts than she should have. Which was weird, because I didn't really give a shit about people or what they thought of me.

Caring about people made it too easy for them to mess with my mind, and my mind was already pretty much destroyed due to my love for my twisted mother.

"No!" I heard shouting from the living room. "No, Ricky, I didn't mean to," she cried.

My stomach knotted.

Dad was here.

I pushed myself up from my mattress and hurried into the space. Dad was buff and had more gray hair than black, more frowns than smiles, and more hate than love. He always dressed in suits too. Really expensive-looking suits, with ties and alligator shoes. Everyone in the neighborhood knew to keep their heads down when walking past him, because even looking him in the eye could've been dangerous. He was the biggest bully to walk the streets, and I hated him to my core. Everything about him disgusted me, but what I hated most was that I had his eyes.

Whenever I looked at him, I always saw a piece of myself.

Ma shivered in a corner, holding her cheek, which had his hand-print on it. I watched as he went to smack her again, and I stepped in his way, taking the hit to my face. "Let her be," I said, trying to act like his slap didn't burn.

"This ain't got nothing to do with you, Logan," he said. "Get out of the way. Your mother owes me money."

"I—I'll have it, I swear. I just need time. I got an interview at a grocery store down the street this week," she lied. Ma hadn't applied for a job in years, yet somehow she always had these mysterious interviews that never turned into anything.

"I thought she paid you that money already," I said. "She gave you two hundred last weekend."

"And she took three hundred two days ago."

"Why would you even give her the money? You know she can't pay it back."

He grabbed my arm, digging his fingers into my skin, making me flinch. My body was yanked as he pulled me to the other side of the room and hovered over me. "Who the fuck do you think you are, talking back to me like that, huh?"

"I just thought…"

He slapped me against the back of my head. "You didn't think. Now this conversation is between your mom and me. Don't interrupt." He hit me again, harder. His hand formed a fist, and when it met my eye, I whimpered in pain. Dad started in her direction again, and like an idiot, I stepped in front of her again. "Do you have a death wish, Logan?"

"I'll pay it," I said, trying to stand tall, even though he made me feel tiny whenever I was around him. "One second." I hurried into my bedroom, reached under my mattress, and pulled out my college funds. I could feel my eye swelling as I counted out the money.

Twenty-three dollars left.

"Here," I said, shoving the money into Dad's hands. He narrowed his eyes at me before he began to count it. Under his breath, he muttered something, but I didn't care. As long as he'd leave, that would be good enough for me.

The money went into his back pocket. "You both should know how lucky you are to have me. But don't think I'm going to keep paying your rent like I have been."

We don't need you, I wanted to say. *Leave and never come back*, I dreamed of shouting. But I kept my mouth shut.

His steps moved toward Ma, and I watched her flinch as he caressed his hand against her cheek. "You know I love you, right, Julie?" he asked.

She nodded slow. "I know."

"And I just want us to be happy. Don't you?"

She nodded slower. "Yeah."

He bent down and kissed her lips, and I wanted to set him on fire. I wanted to watch him burn and scream out in pain from the way he used, belittled, and pretty much spit on her soul.

But I also wanted to shout at Ma, because she definitely kissed him back. When they pulled apart, she looked at him as if he was her god, when really he was just Satan in an expensive suit.

"Logan," he said as he walked toward the front door to leave. "If you ever need a real job, a real man's job, I'm sure I can always get you in on the family business. This chump money you're making isn't going to get you anywhere."

"Not interested."

His sinister smirk attached to his lips at my reply. It was the same reply I gave him every time, but each time, he smiled as if he knew a secret and was keeping me on the outside. When he left the apartment, I released the weighted sigh from my mouth.

"What's the matter with you?!" Ma cried, charging at me, hitting me against the chest. I grabbed her tiny wrists in confusion. She kept yelling. "Are you trying to ruin everything for me?"

"I just stopped him from attacking you!"

"You don't know what you're talking about. He wasn't really going to hurt me."

"You're delusional. He *was* hurting you."

"Let me go," she whined, trying to loosen my grip on her arms. I dropped her. Within a second, her hand swung up and slapped me— *hard*. "Don't you ever interfere with my life again. You hear me?"

"Yeah," I muttered.

She pointed a finger at my face, a stern look in her eyes. "Do. You. Hear. Me?!" she questioned again.

"Yeah!" I shouted. "I hear you."

But I was lying straight to her face, because if I ever saw my father with his hands anywhere near her, I would stand up for her. I would fight for her. I would be her voice, even if it meant I lost my own. Because I knew it was because of him that her own sounds went mute. It was because of him that the fire within her had fizzled out.

Ma, come back to me.

When did I lose her? Would she forever be gone?

If I had a time machine, I'd go back and fix whatever mistake made her become the way she was. I'd direct her to go left instead of right. I'd beg for her to never smoke the pipe for the first time. I'd remind her that she was beautiful even if a man told her differently. I'd fix her heart that was so painfully damaged.

I headed to my bedroom and tried to erase the memories of my father, but whenever he came around, they all came back. All my hatred, all my anger, all my pain. It all flooded back to my brain, filling my head up with so much noise that I needed to shut it up.

You'll be dead by twenty-five.

My heart was panicking, my eye throbbing with pain, and I was seconds away from allowing the demons back in. They mocked me, hurt me, slowly poisoned my mind. I stared at my nightstand where my needle slept each night, feeling it whispering my name, asking me to feed the demons until they went away.

I wanted to win that night. I wanted to be strong, but I wasn't. I've never been strong enough, and I never would be.

Just give in.

You'll be dead by twenty-five.

I took a breath, my hands shaking. I took a breath, my heart breaking. I took a breath, and I did the only thing that I knew how to do.

I opened the drawer, seconds away from allowing the darkness inside, seconds away from fading from the light, but then, my phone dinged.

Alyssa: What are you doing?

Alyssa texted me exactly when I needed her to, even though I was offended that she waited until eleven at night to write me. The only person I heard from for my birthday was Kellan, who took me out to dinner. All Dad gave me was a black eye, and all Ma gave me was disappointment.

Alyssa was the one I was counting on, though. She was my best friend, and she hadn't said a word all day.

Me: Lying in bed.
Alyssa: Okay.

Dots.

Alyssa: Come downstairs.

Sitting up a little, I reread her messages. With haste, I tossed on my tennis shoes, a pair of sunglasses, and my red hoodie and hurried out of the apartment. Parked right in front of the building was Alyssa, smiling at me. I glanced around the streets at people drinking and smoking.

God. I hate it when you come here. Especially at night.

I climbed into the passenger seat of her car and locked the doors the moment I was inside. "What are you doing, Alyssa?"

"Why are you wearing sunglasses?" she asked.

"No reason."

She reached across to me and took them off.

"Oh, Logan…" she whispered, slightly touching my bruised eye.

I snickered and recoiled. "You think that's bad? You should see the other guy."

She didn't laugh. "Your dad?"

"Yeah. It's fine, though."

"It's not fine. I've never hated someone so much in my life. Is your mom okay?"

"She's far from okay, but she's okay." I watched as Alyssa's eyes began to water, but I quickly stopped her. "Everything's okay. I promise. Let's just go wherever we are going so I can forget for a while."

"Okay."

"And, Alyssa?"

"Yes, Logan?"

My fingers wiped her tears away, and I allowed my touch to linger against her cheeks. "Smile."

She gave me a huge cheesy, fake smile. It was good enough for me.

She put the car in drive and kept driving for a long, long time. We didn't talk the whole way, and I wasn't sure what exactly she was up to. When the car pulled over to the side of an abandoned road, my confusion grew.

"Seriously. What are we doing?"

"Come on," she said, hurrying out of the car and running down the road. This girl was going to be the death of me—and by *death* I meant *life*. Because of her coming into my life, I somehow found freedom from my life's restraints each day.

I followed after her, because whenever she moved, I wondered where she was going.

She stood in front of a ladder leading up to a billboard. "Ta-da!" she screamed, dancing with excitement.

"Umm?"

"It's your birthday present, silly!"

"My present is…a billboard ladder?"

She rolled her eyes and dramatically sighed. "Follow me," she said, climbing up the ladder. I did as she told me.

We climbed up the highest ladder I'd ever come across. The large billboard that we sat in front of read, "2 for 5 Burgers from Hungry Harry's Diner." I could tell Alyssa was a bit afraid of heights, because she kept trying her best to avoid looking down. There was a railing that wrapped around the billboard to keep us from falling, but still, it seemed too high for her liking.

"You're a little scared?" I asked, learning something new.

"Um, maybe? I think heights are one of those things you don't know you're terrified of until you're…up high. Anyway." She slowly walked around to the side of the billboard and pulled out a picnic basket and wrapped gifts. "Here you go. Open the gifts first."

I did as she told me, and I almost broke down when I saw the presents.

"I wasn't sure which one it was that you watched with your grandpa, so I got all the DVDs I could find," she explained.

I held over twelve DVDs on the galaxy, and the documentary that I watched with Grandpa was among the pile.

"Jesus," I murmured, pinching the bridge of my nose.

"And"—she waved up to the sky—"this is the best view I could find for seeing the stars at night. I drove around town for days trying to find a spot. I know it's probably dumb, but I thought you'd enjoy the view." She frowned. "It's dumb, isn't it? I should have done something better. The past two years, I did so well, and I just thought that this would be…"

I grabbed her hand.

She went silent.

"Thank you," I whispered, brushing my free hand against my eyes. I sniffled a bit and nodded. "Thank you."

"You love it?"

"I love it."

I'm falling in love with you.

Shaking my head, I tried to run that thought off.

I couldn't love her. Love meant pain. And she was one of the only two good things in my life.

I looked back to the sky. "If you look out there, you can see the Scorpius constellation. Each month, you can see some constellations better than others. It starts with that lower star, curves up, and then splits off into five points, making it look kind of like a dandelion. Antares is the brightest star in the constellation. Grandpa used to tell me it was the heart of the scorpion. Do you see it?" I asked, pointing. She nodded. "The myth behind it is that Orion, the hunter, was boasting that he could kill all the animals on the planet. He was defeated by a scorpion, and Zeus noticed the battle take place. Therefore, he raised the scorpion to the night sky for eternity."

"It's beautiful."

"Yeah," I whispered, staring at her staring up. "It is."

"That's beautiful too," she said.

"What's beautiful?"

Her lips turned up as she kept watching the stars. "The way you stare at me when you think I'm not looking."

My heart skipped once. She noticed me staring?

"Do you ever stare my way?"

She nodded slow. "And then when we aren't together, I close my eyes, and I see you in my mind. That's the moment when I never feel alone."

I'm falling in love with you.

I wanted to open my mouth and tell her those words. I wanted to let her into my soul and tell her the stories of how I daydreamed about her. Then I remembered who she was and who I was and why I couldn't say those words.

The awkward silence stayed until Alyssa helped move it along.

"Oh! I also made a late-late-night dinner for us," she exclaimed, reaching for the picnic basket. "Now, I don't want you to be offended by how amazing my food is. I know you're used to being the best chef in town, but I think I might have topped you with this one." She reached into the basket and pulled out a container holding peanut butter and jelly sandwiches.

I laughed. "No way! You made this?"

"Fully from scratch. Except for the peanut butter, jam, and bread. That was all from the grocery store."

My best friend, folks.

I bit into the sandwich. "Mixed berry jam?"

"Mixed berry jam."

"Well, aren't you fancy?"

She smiled. And I died a little.

"For dessert, I have a container of raspberries and these." She pulled out a package of Oreos. "I went all out, didn't I? Here." She picked up a cookie, untwisted it, placed a raspberry inside, and put it back together. Then, she proceeded to fly it around like an airplane to my mouth. I opened wide, took a bite, and moaned. She cocked an eyebrow, pleased. "Are you moaning over my cookies?"

"I'm definitely moaning over your cookies."

She shimmied and sighed dramatically. "If I had a dollar for every time a guy told me that."

"You'd have one dollar and zero cents."

She flipped me off, and I fell more for her. I couldn't decide what I wanted more: her lips against mine or her words. The idea of both entertained me more than I ever thought they could.

Words. Go with words. "What's your biggest dream?" I asked, tossing a few raspberries into my mouth before throwing a few into hers.

"Biggest dream?"

"Yeah. What do you want to be or do in the future?"

She bit her bottom lip. "I want to play the piano and make people smile. Make people happy. I know it sounds little to a lot of people, like my mom. And I know it sounds like a stupid goal, but that's what I want. I want my music to inspire people."

"You can do it, Alyssa. You are already doing it." I believed in her dream more than I could ever say. Whenever I heard her play the piano, it was as if all the terrible parts of life kind of melted away. Her sounds made me find a few moments of peace.

"What about you?" she asked, placing a raspberry between my lips.

I wasn't really in a life situation where I'd ever been able to dream, but when I was with Alyssa, all that seemed a little more possible.

"I want to be a chef. I want people to come in grumpy and leave happy because of what I put on their plate. I want people to feel good eating my food and forget all the bullshit stuff going on in their real lives for a few minutes."

"I love that. We should open a restaurant, toss a piano inside, and call it the AlyLo."

"Or LoAly," I smirked.

"AlyLo sounds much, much better. Plus, it was my idea."

"Well, let's do it. Let's open AlyLo and make amazing food and play amazing music and live happily ever after."

"The end?"

"The end."

"Pinky?" she asked, extending her finger toward me.

I wrapped my pinky with hers. "Pinky." Our hands kind of clasped together after that.

"What's another dream of yours?" she asked.

I debated if I should tell her, because it seemed a little corny, but if there was anyone I trusted to not judge me, it was her. "I want to be a dad. I know that sounds stupid, but I really do. All my life, I grew up with parents who didn't know what it meant to love. But if I were a dad, I'd love them more than words could say. I'd show up to their baseball games, their dance recitals, and love them, regardless of whether they wanted to be a lawyer or a garbageman. I'd be better than my parents."

"I know you would, Lo. You would be a great dad."

I don't know why, but her saying that made my eyes tear up.

We stayed up there for a while, not speaking one word but solely looking up.

It was still so peaceful up there. I couldn't imagine anywhere else I'd rather be. We hadn't stopped holding hands. Did she like holding my hand? Did her heart flip every few seconds? Was she kind of, sort of falling in love with me too? I held her hand tighter. I wasn't sure if I'd be able to let go.

"What's your biggest fear?" she asked softly.

I pulled out my lighter and started flicking it on and off with my free hand. "Biggest fear? I don't know. Something happening to the few people I care about. Kellan. You. My mom. What about you?"

"Losing my dad. I know it sounds stupid, but each day, when the doorbell rings, I wonder if it's him. Each time my phone goes off, my heart stops, hoping he's calling me. I know these past few months, he's been a bit MIA, but I know he's coming back. He always does. But the idea of losing him forever kind of breaks my heart."

We listened to each other's darkness and showed each other our light.

"Tell me a beautiful memory about your mom," she said.

"Hmm…" I chewed on my bottom lip. "When I was seven, I walked to and from school each day. One day, I came home and heard music blasting on the front porch of our old apartment building. Ma had a boom box playing oldies music—the Temptations, Journey, Michael Jackson, all these classics. Ma said she got the CD from a neighbor, and it made her want to dance. So she had been dancing in the street, and she only moved to the sidewalk when a car came. She looked so beautiful that day and made me dance with her all night until the moon was high. Kellan came over too. He rode his bike over because he had leftovers of his dinner that he'd bring for Ma and me. When he came, all three of us danced.

"I mean, looking back on it, I'm sure she was on something back then, but I couldn't tell. I just remember laughing and spinning and dancing free with her and Kellan. The sound of her laugh was my favorite part because it was so loud and wild. That's my favorite family memory. That's the memory that I go back to whenever she seems so far gone."

"That's a good one to hold on to, Lo."

"Yeah." I gave her a tight smile, never really letting anyone know how much I missed my mom but knowing that she understood, because she missed her dad too. "What's a beautiful memory about your dad?"

"You know the vinyl record player in my bedroom?"

"Yeah."

"He got me that one year for Christmas, and we started the tradition that every night, we'd listen and sing a song before I went to bed. Then, in the morning, we'd wake up and sing a song too. Modern music, oldies, anything. It was our thing. Sometimes my sister, Erika, would come in and sing with us. Sometimes Mom would yell for us to turn down the sound, but we always laughed and smiled."

"Is that why there's always music playing at night when I come to see you?"

"Yeah. It's funny how I play all the same songs that he and I used to, but now the lyrics all seem so different."

We kept the conversation going all night long.

I fed her raspberries while she fed me her dreams.

She fed me raspberries while I fed her my fears.

We stared out at the night sky, feeling safe and free for a while.

"Do you ever think about how insane people are?" I asked. "There are over three hundred billion stars in the Milky Way galaxy alone.

Three hundred billion specks of light reminding us of all that is out there in the universe. Three hundred billion flames that look so small. Yet they are literally bigger than you could ever imagine. There are all these different galaxies, all these different worlds that we have never and will never discover.

"There's so much wonder in the world, but instead of giving a damn and taking the time to come to the realization that we are all very, very, small in a very, very miniature place, we like to pretend we are the alphas of the whole universe. We like to make ourselves feel big. And we each like to make our way seem like the best way and our hurts seem like the biggest hurts when really, we are nothing more than a tiny burning dot that makes up a part of the giant sky. A tiny dot that no one would even notice was missing. A tiny dot that will soon enough be replaced by another speck that thinks it's more important than it actually is. I just wish people would sometimes stop fighting about stupid mundane things like race, sexual orientation, and reality television. I wish they would remember how small they are and take five minutes a day to look up to the sky and breathe."

"Logan?"

"Yeah?"

"I love your mind."

"Alyssa?"

"Yeah?"

I'm falling in love with you.

"Thanks for tonight. You have no clue how much I needed this. You have no clue how much I needed you." I lightly squeezed her hand. "You're my greatest high."

CHAPTER 5
Logan

Lo! Lo! Lo!" Alyssa screamed a week later, running toward me in the pouring rain.

I was on the highest rung of the ladder, working on cleaning the third-floor windows from the outside. Obviously Ma only asked me to clean them when it was pouring rain outside. Alyssa's voice rattled me, making me send the bucket of water (which was mainly rainwater) crashing to the ground.

"God, Alyssa!" I shouted at her.

She gave me a slight frown, holding a bright yellow polka-dot umbrella over her head. "What are you doing?" she asked.

"Cleaning the windows."

"But it's raining."

No shit, Sherlock, I thought to myself. But then I realized it wasn't Alyssa's fault that I was cleaning the windows, and she didn't deserve my bad attitude. I climbed down the ladder and stared at my friend. She took one large step toward me and held the umbrella over both of us.

"Your mom made you do that?" she questioned with the saddest-looking eyes I'd ever seen.

I didn't reply.

"What are you doing here?" I asked, slightly angered. I didn't live in the kind of place that Alyssa did. I lived in a shit neighborhood, and it wasn't the safest place for anyone, especially someone like Alyssa. There was a basketball court down the street where more drug deals happened than games. There were the individuals who stood on the street corners from morning to night, hustling one another, trying to make an extra buck. There were the prostitutes who walked up and down the streets, strung out. And there were the gunshots that were always heard, but luckily I never saw them hit any targets.

I hated this place. These streets. These people.

And I hated that Alyssa showed up here sometimes.

She blinked a few times as if she'd forgotten her reason for coming over.

"Oh yeah!" she said, her frown turning into a full-blown grin. "Ass-Crack called me! I wanted him to come to my piano recital tonight, but he didn't call me back, remember? Until now! He just called me and said he could make it!" She squeaked.

I blinked, unmoved.

Ass-Crack was known for making these kinds of promises to Alyssa, and he always had a way of backing out at the last minute.

"Don't do that," she said, pointing a finger at me.

"Do what?"

"Don't give me that, *Stop-getting-your-hopes-up-Alyssa* look. It's not like I called *him*, Logan. He called *me*. He wants to be there." She couldn't stop smiling. It actually made me sad for her. I'd never seen someone who was so in need of feeling wanted in all my life.

You're wanted, Alyssa Marie Walters. Promise.

"I wasn't giving you that look," I lied. I was definitely giving her that look.

"Okay. Let's do pros and cons of the situation," she suggested.

Before Alyssa and I graduated high school that past June, we were in a history class where the teacher made us make pro and con lists for all the wars that ever happened. It was so freaking annoying, plus our teacher had the most monotone voice ever. So since then, Alyssa and I started doing pro and con lists for any and everything, using monotone voices of course.

"Pro number one," she said, her voice becoming numbingly bored. "He shows up."

"Con number one, he doesn't," I replied.

She wiggled her nose in annoyance. "Pro number two, he shows up with flowers. He called and asked me what my favorite flower was. You don't do that if you're not bringing someone flowers!"

Daisies. Ass-Crack should've known her favorite flower.

"Con number two, he calls and cancels last minute."

"Pro number three," she said, placing her hand on her hip. "He shows up and tells me how amazing I am. And how proud of me he is. And how much he missed me and loves me." I went to open my mouth, and she shushed me, dropping her monotone sound. "Listen, Lo. No more cons. I need you to look at me and be happy for me, okay? Even if it's a fake happy!" She kept smiling with a high-pitched sound of excitement in her voice, but her eyes and hiccups always told how Alyssa was really feeling. She was nervous, scared that he'd let her down again.

So I put on a smile for her, because I didn't want her to be nervous or scared. I wanted her to actually feel as happy as she pretended to be. "This is good, Alyssa," I said, lightly nudging her in the arm. "He's coming!"

A deep exhale left her and she nodded. "He's totally going to be there."

"Of course he is," I said with fake confidence. "Because if there's anyone in the world worth showing up for, it's Alyssa Fucking Walters!"

Her cheeks reddened and she nodded. "That's me! Alyssa Fucking Walters!" She dug into her back pocket and pulled out a ticket that was in a ziplock baggie. "Okay. So I need your help. I'm paranoid about Mom finding out I've been trying to talk to Dad. I don't want him anywhere near our house. So I told him he could pick up the ticket from you here." Alyssa looked at me with hopeful eyes that her plan was okay. It didn't go unnoticed to me that she was now calling him Dad again instead of Ass-Crack. That made me sadder for her.

I really freaking hoped he showed up.

"I'll do it," I said.

Her eyes filled with tears, and she handed me the umbrella to hold so she could wipe her tears away. "You're the best friend a girl could ever have." She leaned in and kissed my cheek a total of six times.

And I pretended not to notice how my heart flipped six times too.

She didn't notice it, did she? She didn't notice how she sparked my heart each time she stood near me.

CHAPTER 6
Alyssa

How was your rehearsal?" Mom asked when I came back from Logan's house.

Instead of going to rehearsal, I drove over to his place and begged him to give a ticket to Dad. I couldn't tell Mom that, though—she wouldn't understand. She sat inside her office, typing away at her computer, doing what she did best: working. She had a glass of wine sitting next to her along with the whole bottle beside the glass. She didn't look up toward me, and before I could reply, she said, "Toss any of your dirty clothes into the laundry basket in the bathroom. Then if you could, wash them and fold the load in the dryer."

"Okay," I said.

"And I made a lasagna if you want to toss that into the oven at four forty-five for an hour."

"Okay."

"And please, Alyssa." She stopped typing and turned my way, pinching the bridge of her nose. "Can you stop leaving your shoes in the front hall? It's honestly two steps to the left to put them in the closet."

I glanced down the hallway at my Converse shoes lying tossed in the hallway. "I put them in the closet."

She gave me a *bullcrap* frown. "Put them in the closet, please."

I put them in the closet.

When dinner came along, Mom and I sat at the dining room table, her looking down at her cell phone, answering emails, and me looking down at my cell phone, commenting on Facebook posts.

"The lasagna tastes different," I said, poking my fork around it.

"I used egg white omelets instead of pasta."

"But isn't it lasagna because of the noodles? Like, the name of the noodle is legit called lasagna. Without it, we are just eating eggs, sauce, and cheese."

"This way, it has fewer carbs, and you know how I told you that you should be watching your carbs before you go off to college. The freshman fifteen weight gain is a real thing, and I read an article about how those who are already overweight tend to gain more weight than normal people."

"'Than normal people? Are you saying I'm not normal?" I felt my chest tighten a bit.

Mom dramatically rolled her eyes. "You're overly sensitive, Alyssa. I wish you could be more stable like your sister, Erika. Plus, her eating habits are ten times better than yours. I'm merely stating the facts. You need to watch what you're eating more, that's all." She quickly changed the subject. "You never told me how your rehearsal was," she said, taking a bite of her dinner.

"It was fine," I replied. "You know, the piano and me, same ol' same ol'."

She huffed. "Yeah, I know. Sorry I can't make it to the recital thing tonight. I have too much work."

Over-the-top, dramatic eye roll from me, which she didn't notice. She never made it to any of my recitals, because she always thought music was a hobby, not a life choice. When she found out I was going to college to study music therapy, she almost refused to help pay for my schooling, until Erika talked her out of it. Even though my sister was just like my mom when it came to being realistic, she still believed in my music. Maybe because her boyfriend, Kellan, was a musician, and she loved him and the depth of an artist.

Sometimes I closed my eyes and tried to remember a time when Mom wasn't so harsh, wasn't so ruthless. In my memories, I sort of remembered her smiling. But maybe those moments were just my imagination, wishing for something beautiful to hold on to. Did she become cold the day Dad walked out? Or did his warmth just hide her icy soul for a while?

"I think I'm going to head to the music hall to get ready for tonight. Thanks for dinner, Mom," I said as she poured herself some more wine.

"Yup."

As I tossed on my light jacket, my Converse, and my handcrafted purse, which Dad bought me when he traveled to South America for a concert, Mom called after me.

"Alyssa!"

"Yes, Mom?"

"Start the dishwasher before you go. And go dry that load of clothes. And pick me up a pint of ice cream from Sally's Ice Cream Shop. Make sure to skip getting some for yourself, though. You know, freshman fifteen and all."

I felt like my chest was on fire.

Seat 4A was empty still when I peeked out from behind the stage. *He is coming,* I promised myself. *He called me. He said he would be here,* I thought. *With daisies.*

I loved daisies, they were my favorite flowers, and Dad knew that and was going to bring them to me. Because he promised he would.

"You're up next, Alyssa," my instructor said.

I could feel my heart pounding against my rib cage. It felt as if I were falling apart with every step I took toward the piano. I was suffocating, knowing that he wasn't sitting out there, light-headed knowing that everything out of his mouth was nothing but lies. Lies. Hurtful, useless lies.

And then I looked up.

Pro.

Seat 4A was filled.

He came.

I relaxed against the piano bench and allowed myself to get lost in the keys. My fingers connected to the piano, making magic happen, making the sounds of my soul fill the space. I didn't mean to cry, but a few tears fell as I played. When I finished, I stood and took a bow. The audience wasn't supposed to applaud until after everyone performed, so the bad players wouldn't feel terrible when they didn't receive the loud roars of the room. But the boy in seat 4A was standing with a single daisy in his hands, clapping like crazy, hooting and hollering.

I smiled at the boy with a suit too big for him.

Quick, without thought, I ran into the audience and wrapped him in a hug. "The ticket was for you anyway," I lied into his shoulder.

That was when he held me tighter.

Who needed Ass-Crack anyway? I had Logan Francis Silverstone.

That was good enough for me.

CHAPTER 7
Logan

Y our suit is too big," she said, tugging at the sleeves that hung past my fingertips. The single daisy I gave her had sat behind her left ear since we left the recital.

"It's Kellan's," I explained. "He drove out to drop it off when I realized Ass-Crack wasn't going to make it."

"You're swimming in it," Alyssa joked. "But you still look hand-some. I've never seen you dressed up before. Did you like the recital? It wasn't my best performance."

"It was perfect."

"Thanks, Lo. I think we should do something fun tonight. Don't you think? I think we should, oh I don't know…do something wild!" She was talking and talking and talking, something she was very good at. As she walked, she spun in circles, smiling and talking, talking and smiling.

But I wasn't completely listening to her, because my mind was somewhere else.

I wanted to keep telling Alyssa how amazing she was at the piano recital, how she was better than everyone else who performed. How she made me feel alive just from how her fingers played the keys. How she made my eyes never falter from her the whole time. How when she hugged me, I wanted to never let her go. How I sometimes thought about her when I was doing random things like brushing my teeth or combing my hair or searching for clean socks. I wanted to tell her everything I was thinking because all my thoughts were *her*.

I wanted to tell her how I felt about her. I wanted to tell her how I was falling for her. I wanted to tell her how I loved her wild hair and loved her mouth, which was always chattering about something or another.

I wanted to…

"Logan," she whispered, frozen still on the sidewalk.

My hands somehow landed against her lower back, and I guided her closer to me. My breaths were falling from my lips as they hovered inches away from her mouth. Her hot exhales were mixing deep with my heavy inhales as both of our bodies shook in each other's hold.

"What are you doing?"

What was I doing? Why were our lips so close? Why were our bodies pressed against each other? Why could I not break my stare? Why was I falling in love with my best friend?

"Truth or lie?" I asked.

"Lie," she whispered.

"I'm fixing the flower in your hair," I said, combing her curls behind her ear. "Now ask me again."

"What are you doing?" she asked as I moved closer, feeling her words brush against my lips.

"Truth or lie?"

"Truth."

"I can't stop thinking about you," I told her. "Not even just now, I mean all the time. Morning, afternoon, night, you're on my mind. I can't stop thinking about kissing you either. I can't stop thinking about kissing you slow. It *has* to be slow, though. Because the slower it goes, the longer it will last. And I want it to last."

"That's the truth?" she asked softly, staring at my lips as she hiccupped once.

"That's the truth. But if you don't want me to kiss you, I won't. If you want me to lie, I'll lie."

Her eyes locked with mine, and her hands fell against my chest. My heartbeats hammered against her fingertips as she inched closer to me. She bit her bottom lip, and a tiny smile found its way to her. "You're my best friend," she whispered, tugging on the bottom of her polka-dot dress. "You're the first person I think of when I wake up. You're the one that I miss when you're not lying in bed with me. You're the only thing that ever felt right to me, Lo. And if I were honest, I'd say that I wanted you to kiss me. Not just once but a lot."

Our bodies wrapped together, and I felt her nerves racing through her as she kept hiccupping.

"Nervous?" I asked.

"Nervous," she replied.

It was awkward but at the same time felt exactly how I'd always hoped it would. Like we were meant to be.

I shrugged.

She shrugged.

I laughed.

She laughed.

I parted my lips.

She parted her lips.

I leaned in.

She leaned in.

And my life changed forever.

My hands wrapped tighter around her back as she kissed me. She kissed me harder and harder each passing second, almost as if she was trying to decide if this was real or not.

Was it real?

Maybe my twisted mind was making up fantasies as we stood against each other. Maybe in reality, I was merely dreaming. Maybe Alyssa Walters never even existed; maybe she was just someone I made up in my head to get me through my shitty days.

But if that was true, why did it feel so real?

We pulled our lips away from each other for a split second. Our eyes locked, and we stared as if we were both wondering if we could keep the dream alive or if we should quit before we ruined the small, safe haven of our friendship.

Her face inched closer to mine as she ran her shaking hands through my hair. "Please," she whispered into me. My lips grazed across hers, and her eyes faded shut before our mouths crashed together. Alyssa's hands pulled me closer to her. She leaned in more and slid her tongue between my lips. I kissed her back harder than she kissed me. We fell against the closest building, and I lifted her up against the chilled stones. I wanted her more than she could've ever wanted me. Our kisses deepened, our tongues meeting each other as my mind made fake promises of allowing me to feel Alyssa against me forever.

I wasn't making this up. Her lips, the same lips I'd imagined against mine for so long, the same lips that always made smiles that brightened my days, they were kissing me.

I kissed my best friend, and she kissed me back.

She kissed me like she meant it, and I kissed her like she meant the world.

She does.

She is my world.

When we stopped kissing, both of our breaths were heavy. I lowered her feet back down to the ground.

She stepped backward.

I did the same. Our bodies both trembled as we stood, unsure what to do next.

I shrugged.

She shrugged.

I laughed.

She laughed.

I parted my lips.

She parted her lips.

I leaned in.

She leaned in.

Then we started all over again.

CHAPTER 8
Alyssa

We were quiet.

There were only a few sounds in my bedroom that I chose to notice. The sound of the ceiling fan rotating round and round overhead as we lay beside each other on my bed. There was the sound of the vinyl record playing on top of the dresser, a record that hiccupped every few seconds as if it were damaged, yet somehow it also sounded as if it were completely whole. An automatic air freshener sent off a hiss of rose scent every few minutes, the smells dancing across our noses. And last there were our small inhales and exhales.

My heart was pounding in such a violent way because it was scared, I was certain of that. Each day that we spent together, the more I started to fall for him. Tonight we kissed. We kissed for what felt like forever but still not long enough.

And now, I was afraid.

His heart was as afraid as mine, I thought. *It has to be.*

"Lo?" I said, my throat dry, making my voice crack.

"Yes, High?" He started calling me High the moment we left the billboard—after he called me his greatest high.

I loved it more than he'd ever know.

I snuggled closer to him, falling into the curve of his side. He always made me feel as if he were my security blanket, the place that always wrapped me up when life grew a bit cold. He'd always held me, even when he himself felt so, so lost. "You're going to break my heart, aren't you?" I whispered against his ear.

He nodded, guilt in his eyes. "I might."

"And then what will happen?"

He didn't reply, but I saw it in his eyes—the fear that he might hurt me. He loved me. He never said the words, but it was there.

There was something to be said about the way Logan loved a person. It was quiet, almost secretive.

He was afraid of letting anyone know of his love, because if life had taught him anything, it was that love wasn't a prize, it was a weapon. And he was so tired of being hurt.

If only he knew that his love was the only thing that kept my heart beating… Oh, how I wished he'd love me out loud.

We were quiet once more.

"High?" he whispered, inching a little closer.

"Yes?"

"I'm falling in love with you," he said softly, his words a mirror to my mind.

My heart skipped.

I sensed the fear and the excitement in the tones of his voice. The fear was much stronger, but the undercurrent of bliss was still alive too.

Nodding slowly, I reached for his hand, which he allowed me to hold. I held it tight, because I knew this was it. This was the moment that changed everything. The moment when we couldn't go back. We'd been doing this now for a few months, having these feelings that we felt yet understood nothing about. Loving your best friend was weird. But somehow it was right. Before that night, he never came close to saying the word *love* to me. I wasn't certain that there was space in Logan's heart for such a feeling. Everything about his life existed in the realm of darkness. So for him to say those words meant more than anyone would ever understand.

"It scares you," I said.

He held my hand tighter. "It scares me a lot."

I used to wonder how one knew they were falling in love. What were the signs? The clues? Did it take time, or was it one full sweep? Did a person wake one morning, drink their coffee, and then stare at the person sitting across from them and surrender completely to the free fall?

But now I knew. A person didn't fall in love. They dissolved into it. One day, you were ice, the next day, a puddle.

I wanted that to be the end of the conversation. I wanted to lean in, wrap my arms around him, lie back down, and fall asleep in the bed. My head would rest against his chest, and he would lay his hands against my heart, feeling the beats that were made by his love. He would softly kiss my chin and tell me that I was perfect the way I was. He'd say that my quirks were what made me beautiful. He'd hold me as if he was holding himself, his touch filled with care and protection. I wanted to wake up feeling the warmth of this damaged boy beside me, the boy I was dissolving into.

Yet what one wanted wasn't always what they received.

"I don't know if this is a good idea," he said. His words hurt me more than I'd ever show. "You're my best friend, High."

"You're my best friend, Lo," I replied.

"And I can't lose that. I don't have many people… I trust two people in my life: you and my brother. And I would fuck us up. I know I would. I can't allow myself to do that. I'll hurt you. I hurt and ruin everything." He turned to me, and our foreheads pressed against each other. His pupils were dilated, and as my hand lay against his chest, I could feel how his words hurt him. He parted his mouth and moved in close, whispering against my lips. "I'm not good enough for you, High."

Liar.

He was everything good in my life.

"We can do this, Logan."

"But…I'll hurt you. I don't want to, but I will somehow."

"Kiss me once," I said, and he listened.

His mouth found mine, and he kissed me slow, pulling away even slower. My body tingled as he ran his fingers through my curls.

"Kiss me twice."

He listened once more, lifting himself slightly so he hovered over my body. Our eyes locked, and he stared at me as if he were trying to promise me forever, even though we only had our now. The second kiss was harder, hotter, more real.

"Kiss me three times."

His lips traveled down to my neck, where he massaged me with his tongue, sucking it slowly, making me push my hips up in his direction.

"Logan, I…" My voice was shaky as we lay in the darkened room. "I've never…" My cheeks heated up, and I couldn't say the words. But he already knew.

"I know."

My stomach fluttered as I bit my lip. "I want you to be my first."

"You're nervous?"

"I'm nervous."

He grimaced slightly. "If you don't want to—"

"But I do."

"You're beautiful." His fingers combed my hair behind my ear.

"Still a little nervous."

"Do you trust me?" he asked.

I nodded.

"Okay. Close your eyes."

I did as he told me, my heart beating faster and faster each second. What was going to happen first? Would it hurt? Would he hate it? Would I cry?

Tears were already forming in the backs of my eyes.

I'd cry.

His mouth kissed the edge of my lips. "You're safe, High," he promised me. His hands slowly started to lift my oversize pajama T-shirt, and my body stiffened up. "You're safe," he whispered against my earlobe, sucking it gently. "Do you trust me?" he asked once more.

My body relaxed, and I began to cry, not because I was nervous anymore but because I'd never felt so safe. "I do. I trust you."

Each time a tear fell, he kissed it away.

He lifted the shirt off of my body inch by inch, tossing it to the side of the room. His mouth started high, and he worked his way down, licking my neck, sucking my chest, his tongue outlining the curve of my bra, kissing every inch of my bare skin. "Alyssa," he whispered before reaching the edge of my panties.

My breaths were heavy, and my hips arched up, needing him to keep touching me. My hands fell against my chest, feeling the way he controlled my heartbeats.

His voice filled with concern. "Tell me to stop, okay? If you need me to stop—"

"No... Please..."

He edged my panties down my legs, and each inch they moved, the faster my heart raced. "Alyssa," he said once more. He looked up to me, locking eyes with me for a split second before spreading my legs wide on the bed and allowing his head to lower.

When his tongue found me, I gasped out from the bliss of it all. My fingers twisted the sheets into my palms, and his tongue slid in and out of me. My mind was spinning. My heart somehow found a way to both speed up and completely stop beating. It was as if every few seconds, I'd die, and his lips, his tongue, his soul resuscitated me. I'd never known something so simple could feel so...

Logan...

"Please..." I panted, twisting and turning as he slid two fingers inside me, thrusting them in slow and pulling them out slower. Then, they thrust harder, faster, deeper...

Lo...

I was seconds away from exploding as I twisted my hands in my sheets. I was seconds away from begging him to take me to the edge and allow me to free-fall. "I want you, Logan. Please." My breaths sawed in and out, my body becoming accustomed to the pleasure he brought to me.

"Not yet," he said, pulling away, removing his fingers from me.

Our eyes locked, and the way he looked at me made me feel as if I'd never be alone.

"Alyssa," he said. "I love you." His voice was shaky, and his eyes watered, yet the tears fell from my eyes.

You're my best friend, Lo, I thought.

We were closer than I ever knew any people to ever be. He was a part of me in every way possible, our lives twining together as if we were one flame burning together in the dark of the night.

When he felt like crying, the tears always came from my eyes first.

When his heart wanted to break, mine shattered.

You're my best friend.

He bent forward and kissed me. He kissed me with promises that we never made to each other. He kissed me with apologies for things he never did. He kissed me with all that he was, and I kissed him back with everything that existed within me.

He stood up and removed his pants and boxers, and even though I felt safe, the butterflies still formed in my gut.

"You can change your mind, High," he swore. "You can always change your mind."

I held my hands out to him, and he took mine in his. He came back to me and climbed on top, widening my knees. When his hips brushed against my upper thigh, I let out a light moan, my legs tingling with desire, with fear, with passion, with love.

"I love you," I whispered, making him pause. His lips parted but no words came out. He seemed surprised that someone could love him. "I love you," I repeated, watching a softness come to his eyes. "I love you."

"I love you," he whispered, placing his lips against mine. Tears fell from his eyes and intermixed with my own.

I knew how hard those words were for him. I knew how scared he was to expose himself like that. But I also knew how much I loved him.

"Tell me to stop if I hurt you," he said.

But I didn't need to. The pain was there, but the want was more. He was my security blanket, my safe haven, my most beautiful Lo. He rocked his hips against mine, sliding himself deeper into me.

"I love you," he whispered.

He thrust once.

"I love you," he said once more.

Twice.

"I love you," he murmured.

Three times.

"Logan… I…I'm going to…"

Once, twice, three times, four…

High.

Low.

Heaven.

Hell.

Him.

Me.

Us.

We released, shaking against each other, falling apart yet somehow becoming whole. Losing ourselves but finding each other.

I loved him.

I loved him to my core, and he loved me back.

He kept his promise. He made me feel safe the whole time. He was the person I went to each and every time anything hurt or whenever I felt afraid.

Like home.

Logan was home to me.

"Alyssa, that was…" he sighed, lying beside me, out of breath. "Amazing."

I grinned, turning my head away from him. My fingers wiped away the tears that still fell, and I tried my best to laugh away the feeling of bliss that held an ounce of worry. What would happen next? "If I had a dollar for every time I heard that."

He narrowed his eyes, knowing that my joke was to hide my nerves, before pulling me closer to him. "Are you okay, High?"

"I'm okay." I nodded, meeting his stare. He bent down and kissed the few tears away. "I'm better than okay."

"I want this to be us. For always, I want this."

"Me too. Me too."

"For always, High?" he whispered.

"For always, Lo."

He took a deep breath in, and his eyes smiled along with his lips. "I'm so happy right now." Those were his last words of the night, and I thought they perfectly described my entire being that evening.

The ceiling fan rotated round and round overhead as we lay beside each other in my bed. The vinyl record played on top of the dresser, hiccupping every few seconds yet also sounding completely whole. The scent of rose refreshed every few minutes, and we inhaled and exhaled.

We were quiet.

CHAPTER 9
Alyssa

Logan and I had officially been in love out loud for two months now. I didn't know our friendship could grow stronger just by us falling in love, but somehow it did. He made me laugh on the sad days, which meant the world to me.

When you found someone who could make you laugh when your heart wanted to cry—hold on to them. They will be the ones who will change your life for the better.

I'd been planning out a lot of details too. In three weeks, I was off to live on the campus of my college, but I planned out Logan's visits. We'd stay just as close as we were now, and we'd fall more in love. He said he loved the idea, which was great, because I loved him to my core.

I'd been floating on a cloud for weeks now, and when I came home from work, Mom was there, ready to bring me back down to solid earth.

"Alyssa!" she called after me right as I walked into the house. I tossed my shoes in the foyer, paused, and picked them up, placing them in the front closet.

"I already picked them up!" I hollered in her direction.

"That's not what I was going to say," she replied from her office. Walking toward the sound of her voice, I glanced into the room. Her eyes were glued to her computer, and a wineglass was in her hand. "I made a meatless meat loaf using protein powder and tofu. Toss that into the oven for me."

That's not a meat loaf, Mom. "Okay."

"And your father wrote you a letter."

My eyes widened, a burst of excitement hitting me. "What?"

"He wrote you a letter. It's on the kitchen counter."

Dad wrote me a letter today.

Dad wrote me a letter today!

My excitement built more and more as I raced to the kitchen, snatched the envelope, which wasn't sealed shut, and pulled out the paper.

Sweet Aly.

Already off to a promising start.

My eyes danced across the pages from the left to the right, taking in each word, each note, wanting nothing more than a line that mentioned how much he missed me, how much he loved me, how much he cared. There were so many words, so many pages. Pages filled front to back, pages filled with some words that were long, others short. There were periods, question marks, and exclamation points.

He had wonderful handwriting that was sometimes hard to read.

My chest was on fire with each letter I came across, letters building words, words building sentences, sentences building apologies, apologies that felt fake, because who could do this for real?

I won't be around much.

I took a sharp breath, reaching the final paragraph.

My music is taking off. I'm the lead of this new band.

Another sharp breath.

Focused on my career…

My thumb fell between my lips. When I hit the final page of the letter, I set it down, staring at five pieces of paper completely filled with words front and back.

I won't be around much, Sweet Aly. I hope you understand. Keep the music alive.

My father *broke up with me* through five pages of paper, and when the meatless meat loaf was ready that night, Mom said, "I told you so."

I couldn't eat. I spent most of the night in the bathroom, throwing up my insides. I couldn't believe a person could do something so heartless. He wrote the words as if they actually made sense to him too, which made me even sicker.

I spent the rest of the night on the bathroom floor, debating what I did wrong and wondering why my father didn't love me anymore.

"He broke up with you through a five-page letter?" Logan asked, shocked.

I had spent the past five days away from him, feeling embarrassed by the letter. Each day, I could hardly keep anything in my stomach without it coming back up. What bothered me the most was how pleased Mom seemed that Dad let me down. She always seemed happy that I was hurting.

I sat with Logan at the billboard, knowing the five-page paper by heart. "Technically he broke up with me through ten pages since they are front and back."

"Give me the envelope," he ordered. His nostrils were flaring, his face red with anger. I didn't know he'd get so upset by the letter, but he seemed on the edge of snapping.

"Why?"

"The address he sent the letter from, that's probably where he lives. We can go there. We can confront him. We can—"

"There wasn't an address on the envelope. He dropped it at the house I think, in the mailbox."

His hands ran over his face. A weighted sigh left him. He began flipping through the pages once more. "What about the name of the band he's in? Did he say?"

"No."

"This is bullshit."

"It's okay." I said. It hadn't hit me yet. A big part of me still thought he was coming back. Hope was dangerous when you were relying on unreliable people. "I'm over it." I wasn't though. I was far from over it.

"Well, I'm not!" he shouted, standing up, pacing back and forth. "It's not fair. What have we ever done to these people? Your parents. My parents. What have we done wrong?"

I didn't have an answer for him. Many people probably couldn't understand why Logan and I connected. We were different in so many ways, except for the one that was the biggest fire that burned in us: we both longed to be loved by our parents.

"You're a good thing, Alyssa. You've done everything to be a good daughter to him. You went above and beyond with this dick, and then he doesn't even have the balls to break up with you in person?! I mean, come on. Who breaks up with their daughter via snail mail?" he hollered. "What kind of parent breaks up with their kid at all?"

"You see why I told you to break up with Shay in person instead of via text?" I tried to joke. He didn't laugh. "Logan, come on. It's okay."

"You know what? Screw him, High. You're going to do great things. You're going to change the world without him. You're going to succeed beyond his wildest expectations. You don't need him."

"Why are you so upset?"

"Because how could he do that? How could he turn his back on you? On you, High. You're the most beautiful, genuine, gentle person I've ever met. And he left you. For what? For music? For money? Fame? It's crap, because none of that adds up." He sat back down beside me, his breaths still heavy with irritation. "I'm just trying to understand, that's all," he said, hanging his legs off the edge of the billboard as we stared out into the distance.

"Understand what?"

"How anyone could ever give you up."

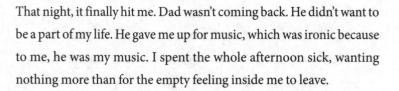

That night, it finally hit me. Dad wasn't coming back. He didn't want to be a part of my life. He gave me up for music, which was ironic because to me, he was my music. I spent the whole afternoon sick, wanting nothing more than for the empty feeling inside me to leave.

Me: Can you come over?

Logan showed up to my house around eleven that night. I gave him a tight smile as he stared my way, wrapping me in a tight hug.

"Are you okay?" he asked.

"I'm fine."

He narrowed his eyes. "Lie?"

"Lie."

"Truth?"

I shrugged, my eyes watering over. "Can you just hold me?"

He grew extremely concerned, pulling back a little to study every inch of me. "High... What's going on?"

"He really left me." I swallowed hard. "He didn't want me."

He led me to my bedroom, closing the door behind us. As I climbed into bed, he moved over to my vinyl record collection and thumbed through each record. When he found one, he put it on, making my eyes water even more.

As Sam Smith's song "Life Support" began to play, Logan shut off the light and crawled into the bed and wrapped his arms around me. As he pulled me closer, making me curve into him, I began to shake as he softly sang the lyrics into my ear.

I began to cry. As he continued to sing, my body kept trembling against his. He pulled me closer, holding me tighter. The song played on a loop, over and over again. He kept singing against me, into my soul, taming the wildfire, making me ache.

His voice put me to sleep. His arms kept me safe.

When I woke in the middle of the night, crying from a nightmare, Logan was fast asleep. His arms had fallen to his sides, his breaths fell through his mouth, and I stared at him, tears still falling down my cheeks.

"Lo," I whispered. He stirred.

"Yeah?"

"I had a bad dream. Can you hold me?"

He didn't hesitate. He pulled me close once more, allowing me to rest my head against his chest, feeling his heartbeats.

"You're okay, Alyssa Marie Walters," he sighed against my skin.

I cried more, pulling him closer. "I'm okay, Logan Francis Silverstone."

CHAPTER 10
Alyssa

When it rained, it poured.

My mom always said those words whenever she was in the middle of a court case and bad news came rolling in. When one bad thing happened, something worse wasn't that far behind. I never truly believed in that saying, because I was the optimist of the family, the glass-half-full girl. But lately, it seemed true. It was only a week since Dad broke up with me, and I hadn't had time to process that event before the world came crashing down on me once again. I could hear Mom's words playing on repeat in my head.

"When it rains, it pours, Alyssa. That's just the truth about the world."

"So," Erika sighed, standing beside me in a grocery store aisle. "How many should we get?"

It'd been two weeks since I'd started throwing up each day. What I thought was created from nerves was now a bigger fear as we stood in front of the pregnancy tests. I didn't know who else to call other than my sister, and when she heard the tremble in my voice, she was parked right outside the house forty-five minutes later. Even though Erika was realistic and driven like our mom, she wasn't so heartless. She loved me for my creative ways and quirky personality, and I knew she'd do anything to help me.

"Maybe two?" I whispered, my body shaky.

She placed a comforting hand on my shoulder. "We'll do five. Just in case." We walked up to the cashier, and they looked at us as if we were crazy for having so many tests. She grabbed a jug of water too. As I was about to run out of the store humiliated, feeling the judgment coming through the cashier's eyes, Erika huffed. "Didn't anyone ever tell you that it's rude to stare?"

They rang up our items, not looking at us once.

My phone dinged as we were walking out of the store.

Logan: Where are you? I need to see you.

I couldn't answer. My phone dinged from him four more times before we got home. I shut it off.

We sat in my bathroom with the door locked. Mom wasn't home yet, and all five pregnancy tests were unwrapped, sitting on the sink, waiting for me to pee on each one. I'd drank a whole jug of water, and as I started to feel the urge to use it, Erika made sure to coach me through it.

"You have to pee a little on a stick, then hold it, then another stick, then hold, then another—"

"I get it," I sassed, annoyed. Not at her but at myself for being in the current situation. I was supposed to be off to college next weekend, not peeing on five sticks.

Once the deed was done, we waited ten minutes. The packs said they'd only take two minutes, but I felt as if ten minutes would've been more accurate.

"What does a pink line mean on this one?" I asked, picking up the first stick.

"Pregnant," Erika whispered.

I picked up the second. "And a plus sign?"

"Pregnant."

My stomach tightened. "And two pink lines?"

She frowned.

Vomit rose to my throat. "And another plus sign?"

"Alyssa…" Her voice shook.

"And this one that says pregnant? What does that mean?" Tears were falling down my cheeks, and I wasn't certain how to make them stop. My breaths sawed in and out, and my heartbeats became erratic. I didn't know what to think about first. Logan? College? Mom? My tears?

"Aly, it's okay. We'll figure this out. Don't panic." Erika's hand on my leg was the only thing keeping me from falling to the ground and rocking back and forth in a corner.

"I start college next weekend."

"And you still will. We just need to figure out—"

"Alyssa!" Mom hollered, walking into the house. "What did I tell you about leaving your shoes in the foyer! Come get these now!"

My hands started shaking uncontrollably as Erika helped me stand up, swiping all the pregnancy tests into a bag before she shoved them into her oversize purse. "Come on," she said, washing her hands, forcing me to wash my hands, and then nudging her head toward the door. "Let's go."

"No," I whisper-shouted. "I can't. I can't see her right now. I can't go out there."

"You can't just hide in here," she said, wiping my eyes. "Don't worry. We won't say anything to her. Just breathe."

She walked out of the bathroom first, and I followed behind her.

"Erika? What are you doing here?" Mom asked with a heightened voice.

"I just thought I'd stop by to visit. Maybe have dinner with you both."

"It's rude to just show up for dinner without calling. What if I didn't get enough food for you? Besides, I was ordering in tonight. Alyssa has to finish packing all her boxes in her room, even though I told her she should've had it done last weekend. And—"

"I'm pregnant."

Mom's eyes shot up to me as Erika's jaw shot to the ground. "What did you just say?"

The moment I said the word once more, the yelling began. She told me what a disappointment I'd become. She screamed her disgust toward me. She said she knew I'd screw up somehow and called Logan a deadbeat.

"You'll have an abortion," she said matter-of-factly. "That's all there is to it. We'll go to a clinic this week, handle this mishap, and then you'll leave for college."

My mind hadn't even wrapped around the fact that I was pregnant, yet she was already telling me to make it disappear.

"Mom, come on. Let's not be so irrational," Erika said, standing up for me, because words weren't able to escape my closed-up throat.

"Irrational?" Mom folded her arms across her chest. She raised an eyebrow with a glassy stare. "No, what's irrational is getting pregnant five days before starting college. What's irrational is dating a loser with no life plans. What's irrational is Alyssa having a child when she hasn't even grown up herself."

"He's not a loser," I swore about Logan. He was so far from being a loser.

Mom rolled her eyes and started off toward her office. "I have a case tomorrow, but then we are going to the clinic. Otherwise, you can figure out a way to pay for college yourself. I will not put my money into you going to a school for a fake major when you'll end up dropping out and becoming nothing," she ordered. "You're just like your father."

I inhaled sharply, and the knife in my heart dug deeper.

Erika stayed at our place that night, moving furniture around the living room. Rearranging things was how she always got her frustration out. Other times, she broke plates and glasses from her frustration. "She's being unreasonable, Aly. You don't have to listen to her, you know. And if she threatens you, don't take it to heart. I'll help you figure it out."

I smiled, then frowned. "I have to tell Logan. He's been texting me all afternoon, and I haven't texted back. I don't know what to say."

Erika frowned, then frowned some more. "That's going to be a tough talk, but it should happen sooner rather than later."

I swallowed hard, knowing that it had to happen that night.

"I'm worried, though, Alyssa. I've known Logan for a long time, and he's not always the most stable person."

Erika wasn't the biggest fan of Logan, and I couldn't blame her. He was the boy who almost burned down her and Kellan's apartment a year ago after going on a bender with drugs due to his parents belittling and hitting him.

"That's only five percent," I murmured.

"What?"

"He's there ninety-five percent of the time, Erika. Ninety-five percent of the time, he's gentle. He's kind. But sometimes that five percent slips in, and he's not himself. He loses the battle between his truths and the lies that his parents feed him. But you can't judge him on those moments."

"Why not?" she asked.

"Because if you judge him solely on his few moments of lows, then you miss out on his beautiful highs."

When it rained, it poured and poured and poured.

I'd seen Logan's low points quite a few times within the past two years. Whenever it happened, he turned into a person I didn't recognize. His words slurred, his body wavered, and his voice was always so loud. He was angry and somewhat mean whenever he used drugs other than smoking pot. I knew it mostly happened when his parents hurt him, though, when they left abusive scars on his heart. The bruises on one's heart were always the hardest ones to heal; they seemed to last the longest. When those low moments happened, I knew it was best to just let them pass, because afterward, he always found his way back to the Logan I loved and adored.

Five percent low, ninety-five percent high.

When I finally turned my phone back on that night, I had fifteen missed text messages from Logan.

Logan: Where are you, High?

Logan: I need you.

Logan: Please. I'm falling apart. My dad just left, and I'm not in a good place.

Logan: Alyssa? High?

Logan: Never mind.

Oh no. He was having a low moment. Those were the ones that scared me the most.

Me: I'm here.

He didn't reply until three in the morning. When he called, I heard it in his voice, how he was so far away.

"I'm on your porch," he said.

When I opened the front door, I gasped. His left eye was swollen shut, his lip busted open. Black and blue took over his normally tan skin tone.

"Lo," I breathed, reaching for his face.

He cringed, stepping backward.

"Your dad?"

He didn't reply as I took him in.

I noticed the twitching first, followed by his impaired coordination. He frantically scratched at his skin and kept licking his lips.

How far into the shadows did you drive tonight, Logan?

"Can I shower or somethin'? I couldn't go home tonight." He sniffled as he tried to widen his left eye, but it wouldn't budge open.

"Yeah, yeah, of course. Come on."

I led him to my bathroom as he stumbled beside me. Once we made it, I shut the door behind us. I reached for a small cloth, soaking it in warm water as he sat on top of the toilet. As I started pressing it to his face, he hissed.

"It's fine," he argued, pulling away.

"No. It's not. You can't open your eye."

"But I can still see you." His mouth hung open slightly before he went back to licking his lips. "Were you busy earlier?"

I blinked, not looking into his one open eye. I soaked the towel more. "Yeah."

"Too busy to text?"

"Yeah, Lo. I'm sorry." My breaths quickened as I eyed the exit. I needed a moment away.

"Hey," he whispered, placing his finger under my chin, raising my stare to meet his one eye. "I'm okay."

"Are you high?"

He hesitated before laughing. "Fuck you for asking that, High. Look at my face. What do you think?"

I flinched. He never spoke to me in such a way except for when he was almost completely down the rabbit hole. I should've answered his texts.

"I'm going to get some ice for your eye, okay? You can start the shower." I stood up to leave, but he called after me.

"High?"

"Lo?"

He swallowed hard, and one tear fell from his eye, which was shut. "I'm so fucking sorry. I don't know why I said that to you."

I gave him a tight smile and hurried away.

My hands were shaking as I went to grab a baggie to put ice in for Logan. I'd never seen him so beaten up or out of it before. *What did your father do to you?* Why was he such a monster?

"High?"

I leaped at the sound of Logan's voice behind me. Hairs stood up on my arms as I turned to see him holding something in his hand.

"What's this?"

"Oh my gosh. Logan, I wanted to talk to you about that." I stared at the pregnancy test in his hand, one that must've been left behind in the bathroom earlier that afternoon.

"What do two pink lines mean?" he asked, hardly able to hold himself up, and he swayed.

You're too far gone for this talk tonight. "We should talk tomorrow," I offered, approaching him to place my hand on his shoulder.

He yanked himself away. "No, we should talk about this now," he said loudly.

"Lo, can you keep it down? My mom's sleeping."

"I don't give a damn. Are you pregnant?"

"We shouldn't do this tonight."

"What's going on?" was asked behind me. I cringed, seeing Mom walk into the kitchen wearing her robe. When her tired eyes locked with Logan's, she grew fully awake. "What are you doing here? You need to leave, now."

"Mom, come on," I begged, seeing the hate in her eyes.

"Jesus Christ. Can't you see we're h-h-having a fucking t-t-talk?" Logan slurred.

That wasn't helping the situation.

Mom hurried over to him, grabbing his arm. "You are trespassing. Leave before I call the cops."

He yanked his arm away from her, stumbling backward, hitting the fridge. "Don't touch me. I'm talking to your daughter."

Mom's eyes shot over to me. "And this is exactly why we are going to have the abortion. He's a mess."

Logan stood up as straight as he could, his eyes wide with disgust. "Abortion? You're having an abortion?"

My body was shaking, my eyes glassed over. "No. Wait. Mom, stop. You're not helping."

"You really spoke about an abortion?" Logan asked again.

"We are getting it on Thursday. I already called to set it up," Mom said, which was a lie. I was eighteen and had the right to do what I wanted with my body, not what my mother found fit.

Logan let out a low breath. "Wow. So you were gonna do this without talking to me? You don't think I'd be a good dad or something?"

Mom laughed sarcastically.

Again, not helping.

"That's not what I said, Lo."

"That is what you said! That's what you meant!" he hollered, his eyes dull, as if the light I loved so much in him had been sucked from his entire existence.

"You're not listening to me because you're high, Logan."

"Which isn't anything new," Mom muttered under her breath, disgust stinging her words.

"Mom, will you stop?" I begged.

"No. She's right. I'm always high, right? That's all you people think of me," he said, gesturing toward Mom and me. "You and all your fucking money in your big-ass house with no fucking struggles." As he stumbled around, he accidentally knocked over our knife set, sending them across the floor. Both Mom and I jumped out of fright.

Oh, Lo. Come back…

"You need to leave. Now." Mom grabbed her cell phone and held it up. "I'm calling the cops."

"Mom, don't. Please."

"No. I'm leaving. You can have this all," he hissed. "Your money. Your house. Your life. Your abortion. What the hell ever. I'm gone."

He hurried away, and tears fell down my cheeks as I stared at Mom. "What's wrong with you?!"

"*Me?*" she screeched, shocked. "He's a disaster waiting to happen. I knew you were naïve, Alyssa Marie, but I didn't know how extremely stupid you could be. He's an addict. He's sick, and he's not going to get better. He'll drag you down into the flames before you bring him fresh air. You should give up on him. He's a lost cause. Kellan and you both are his enablers. You're allowing this to keep happening, and it's only going to get worse."

I took a deep breath before racing after Logan.

He was walking toward the gate to climb back over it. "Logan, wait!" I cried.

He turned around to see me, his chest rising and falling heavily. "I let you in," he said, his voice harsh.

My voice was the complete opposite. Weak. Pained. Scared. "I know."

"I let you in, even though I told you it wasn't a good thing. I'm not someone who loves, Alyssa. But you fucking made me love you."

"I know."

"So you made me love you. And I loved you hard, because I don't know any other way. I loved you to my core, because you made this life seem a little bit more worth living. And then, out of nowhere, you turn on me. What did I do? Why would you…? I told you my dreams. I told you everything." He stepped closer to me, his voice lowering, shaking. When our eyes locked, he shook his head once, stepping backward. "Stop looking at me like that."

"Like what?" I asked, bewildered.

"I'm not my mother," he snapped.

"I know you're not."

"Then why the hell are you looking at me like I am?"

"Logan…please just hear me out."

He walked over to me, and our bodies melted together as they always did. His forehead fell against mine, his tears brushing against my skin as my hands rested on his chest. We wrapped our arms around each other, both of our bodies heated from the inside out, burning to know the reasons why life had to be so hard. His lips fell against my ear, and his hot breath brushed against my skin as he said the words that scorned my soul.

"I never want to see you again."

He disappeared that night.

He disappeared from my life in a blink of an eye. The late-night calls vanished. His gentle voice was gone. Each night, I wondered where he was, if he was safe. Whenever I stopped by his apartment, he wasn't there. Whenever I called him, it went straight to voicemail. Kellan said he hadn't heard from his brother either. He hadn't seen him, and he was just as terrified as me.

When I told Mom I wasn't going to give up the baby, she screamed at me and went ahead with her threats and cancelled her payment plan for my college. Erika and Kellan let me move into their small apartment as I tried to find my footing.

Each night, Kellan and I came back to town, and we'd drive around to the different places that Logan might've been. We spoke to his friends but always seemed a minute too late.

He was at parties but seemed to always vanish. His friend Jacob told us Logan had been using a lot lately, but he hadn't been able to talk to him.

"I'll keep an eye out for him," he swore. "If I run into him again, I'll let you know."

I felt a knot in my stomach.

What if Logan crossed a line?

What if he couldn't come back from this hurt he was feeling?

It was all my fault.

CHAPTER 11
Alyssa

I hated receiving phone calls during the middle of the night. They always shook my nerves. No good news came at three or four in the morning. Unfortunately, I'd had way too many of those calls during the past few months, all because of one boy who set my heart on fire. Whenever the phone rang, my mind went to the worst possible situations—an illness, an accident, death. Some nights, I'd stay up with heavy eyes, waiting for the phone calls. When I didn't get them, sometimes I'd dial his number just to hear his voice, just to make sure he was okay.

"I'm okay, Alyssa Marie Walters," he'd say.

"You're okay, Logan Francis Silverstone," I'd reply before falling asleep to the sound of his breathing.

But lately, we weren't talking.

When I worried, I couldn't call him.

When I was scared, his sound weren't on the other line.

So that night when the phone rang, I was more afraid than ever before.

"Alyssa?" a voice said into my cell phone, not Logan's, even though his name was the one that appeared on my screen.

"Who is this?" I asked, sleep still stinging my eyelids.

"It's Jacob…Logan's friend. I…" He hesitated. "Look, I'm at this party, and I found Logan. He's not doing too well. I didn't know who to call."

I sat up in bed, wide awake within seconds. "Where is he?" Jacob gave me all the information, and I scrambled out of the bed, searching for a pen and paper to scribble it all down. "Thanks, Jacob. I'll be there soon."

"Yeah okay. Listen, you might want to bring Kellan too."

I hurried to Kellan and Erika's bedroom and banged on the door. My heart pounded against my rib cage, and I bit my tongue to keep from crying. My body wouldn't stop shaking as I waited to hear Kellan's voice. When he opened the door and spoke, I took in a pained breath. He sounded so much like Logan, it almost knocked me backward. It'd been a few weeks since Logan stopped talking to me. All I wanted to do was hear his voice again.

"Alyssa? What's wrong?" Kellan asked, alarm and alertness filling his tones. He knew just as I did that a late-night call when Logan was using again could've always been the call that we each feared the most. "Is he…?"

"I don't know," I replied. I told him everything I knew, though, and we were out the door within minutes.

When we arrived at the party, Jacob was standing on the front porch of some broken-down house while Logan lay on a bench. His eyes were hardly open, and he was drooling out of the left side of his mouth.

"Jesus," Kellan muttered, walking up to his brother.

"He's not that responsive."

"What did he take?" Kellan asked.

"He was shooting up some heroin, and I think he did blow earlier. I don't know what else, though."

"Why didn't you call the cops?!" I screamed. I rushed over to Logan and tried to lift his body. He cringed at the movement and started to throw up on the porch.

"I don't know, man. Listen, normally Logan can handle this shit. But these past few weeks, he's been getting into some deep shit. I couldn't call the cops because… Look. I didn't know what to do, so I called you guys."

I'd known Jacob for a while. Logan didn't have many people he called *friend*, but Jacob was one of the rare few that he spoke about in a good light. But I disagreed that night. A real friend—a true friend—would never let someone fall so deeply and not even reach out a hand.

"You should've called an ambulance," I hissed, angered. Scared. Angered and scared.

"Help me get him to the car," Kellan ordered Jacob. They laid him in the back seat, and I climbed back there with him. "He might throw up again, Alyssa. You might want to sit up front."

"I'm fine here," I replied.

Kellan thanked Jacob, and we drove off toward the hospital to get Logan checked out. I'd never seen him like that, and I was seconds away from losing my mind.

"Keep him awake, okay?" Kellan said.

I nodded as my tears fell against Logan's cheeks. "You have to stay awake, okay? Keep your eyes open, Lo." He laid his head in my lap in the back seat of Kellan's car, and I was terrified that if he closed his eyes, they wouldn't open back up. His whole body was soaked from his own sweat, and every inhale he took looked painful, every exhale exhausting.

He laughed. "Hi."

My lips turned down. "Hi, Logan."

His head shook back and forth, and he sat up on his elbows. "No. Not hi. *High.* H-I-G-H."

I hated when he talked about being high. I hated the way he lost himself in something that changed him from my best friend into my greatest fear. *What happened to you tonight, Logan?* What made him go so deeply toward the darkness?

I paused, knowing the answer.

It was me.

I did this to him.

I made him chase his shadows.

I'm sorry, Logan.

My mom's words rang in my ears and mind as I stared down into his slitted eyes. *He's an addict. He's sick, and he's not going to get better. He'll drag you down into the flames before you bring him fresh air. You should give up on him. He's a lost cause. Kellan and you both are his enablers. You're allowing this to keep happening, and it's only going to get worse...*

"You're high," Logan whispered, falling back down.

"What?"

"You call me Lo, which makes sense because I am low. I'm the bottom of the fucking pit. But you?" He chuckled and closed his eyes. "You're my High. And you broke my fucking heart."

Tears filled my eyes as I held him in my arms. "Keep your eyes open, Lo. Okay? Just keep your eyes open." I glanced at the front of the car, where Kellan was wiping at his face. I knew seeing his brother in the shape he was in had to be the hardest thing ever.

I knew Kellan's heart had to be breaking like mine was.

"Take me back," Logan muttered, trying to push himself up from the back seat.

"Chill out, Logan. Everything's okay," Kellan said.

"No. Take me back," Logan hollered, leaping up from my lap and diving at the wheel, making Kellan swerve the car. "Take me back!"

We both tried to stop him, to get him to control himself, to get him to calm down, but before we could, Kellan lost control.

The car took a sharp left.

And everything went black.

CHAPTER 12
Logan

When my eyes opened, I was in a hospital bed, and sunlight was shining through my window. I tried to turn away, but everything hurt. "Shit," I muttered.

"You okay?" a voice said. I twisted my head around to see Kellan sitting in a chair with pamphlets in his hand and a large bandage on his forehead. He was wearing a hoodie and sweatpants and missing the smile that was always on his face.

"No. I feel like I've been hit by a semitruck."

"Or maybe like you hit a freaking building," someone else murmured. I turned to my left to see Erika. Her arms were crossed and her stare harsh. Beside her was a man in a bow tie holding a notepad, and Jacob was in the far corner, sitting on the countertop.

What happened? Why is Jacob with Kellan?

"You don't remember?" Kellan asked, sounding somewhat short with me.

"Remember what?"

"Driving into a freaking building!" Erika exclaimed, her voice shaky. The man beside her put a comforting hand on her shoulder.

I closed my eyes, trying to remember what happened, but everything seemed a blur.

"Logan." Kellan pinched the bridge of his nose. "We found you passed out on a front porch. Then when we were trying to bring you to the hospital to get you checked out, you panicked and took control of the wheel, making us hit a building."

"What?" My throat was dry. "Are you okay?"

He nodded, but Erika disagreed. "Show him your side, Kellan."

"Stop, Erika."

"No. He needs to see this. He needs to see what he's done."

Kellan lowered his head, staring at his shoes. "Drop it, Erika."

"Show me," I ordered.

He rubbed the back of his neck as he pulled up his hoodie, showing his whole left side, which was black, blue, and shades of purple from top to bottom.

"Holy shit. I did that?"

"It's fine," Kellan said.

"It's not," Erika snapped.

She's right. It's not.

"Kel, I'm so sorry. I didn't mean to…"

"That's not even the worst of it! You almost killed my sister!" she shouted.

My heart dropped to my gut.

Alyssa.

High.

My greatest high.

"What happened to Alyssa? Where is she?" I barked, trying to sit up but failing from the pain that shot through my back.

"Logan, relax. The doctors are helping Alyssa. But right now is about you. We brought someone here to help you," Kellan said.

"Help me what? I don't need anyone's help. What happened to Alyssa?" I felt the walls in the room closing in. What was I doing here? Why was everyone looking at me as if I were damaged goods? *Why won't they tell me about Alyssa?*

"We're all here because we love you," Kellan tried to explain.

Then it clicked in my head. I realized why the bow tie man was standing in the room. I read one of the pamphlets in Kellan's hands, and I closed my eyes tight. *They're having an intervention for me. In a hospital room.*

"Love?" I hissed, my voice filled with bitterness as I slowly realized what was going on. "Bullshit."

"Come on, Logan. That's not fair," Kellan said.

I turned to meet Kellan's heavy eyes as he looked at me with fear, worry. "Don't 'come on, Logan,' me, Kellan. So what?" I looked up from my fidgeting hands. "This is an intervention? You all think I'm so fucked up that you had to gather in a hospital room and embarrass the living shit out of me because you think I'm dangerous? You have to bring in people who don't give two shits about me? I made one mistake last night." I gestured toward Jacob. "It's pretty hypocritical to have the asshole who got high with me last week here, don't you think? Jacob, I'm almost positive you're fucked up right now."

Jacob frowned. "Come on, Logan…"

"No. And, Erika, I don't know why the hell you're even here. You can't stand me," I said.

"I don't hate you, Logan." She swallowed hard. "Come on. That's harsh."

"I really fucking wish you guys would stop saying *come on* as if you're better than me. You're not better than me." I laughed sarcastically, trying to sit up a bit. I was growing defensive, because deep inside me, I knew they were right. "It's comical, actually. Because here we are talking about me being screwed up in the head when we are sitting in a room filled with people who are just as fucked up, if not more, than I am. Kellan here can't even stand up to his dick of a father to let him know that he wants to be a musician instead of a lawyer. Jacob has an addiction to weird damn porn that involves forks and shit. Erika breaks one plate and buys fifty to replace them, just in fucking case the new one shatters too. Does no one else find her break-and-buy lifestyle insane?"

"I think we all just want you to get better, Logan," Kellan said.

I wondered if Kellan's heartbeats were as frantic as mine currently were.

"I can only imagine what you've been through with staying with Ma. I doubt she makes it easy to stay clean."

"You must be feeling pretty good," I said, brushing my finger beneath my nose. "Because you're Kellan, the golden child. The one with the rich father. The one with a future. The one with a full ride to a top college to become a top lawyer. And I'm just the fucked-up brother with a crackhead mother and a drug-dealing father. Well, congratulations, Kellan. You're the winner. You are Mom's better son who made something of himself, and I'm just a pathetic piece-of-shit kid who will probably be dead by twenty-five."

Kellan took in a pained breath. "Why would you ever even say that kind of shit?" His nose flared as he paced the hospital room. "What's wrong with you, Logan? Wake up. *Wake up.* We're all trying to help you, and you're yelling at us as if we are the enemy, when in reality, the enemy is your own mind. You're killing yourself. You're fucking killing yourself, and you don't care," he shouted. Kellan never raised his voice—never.

I went to say something, but Kellan's stare stopped me. He narrowed his eyes at me, and I swore for a second I saw a glimpse of hatred.

His hands rubbed against his face over and over again as he tried to calm himself. When he spoke, he sniffled to hold back his own emotion. He tossed the pamphlets toward me, and when they landed in my lap, I read the words over and over again.

St. Michael's Health and Rehabilitation Clinic
Waterloo, Iowa

"Rehab?" I said. "You think I need rehab? You all think I need rehab? I'm fine."

"You drove a car into a building," Erika recited again for the hundredth time.

"It was an accident, Erika! Haven't you ever made a mistake?!"

"Yes, Logan. But not one that almost killed my boyfriend and sister. You're a complete mess, and if you don't get help, you'll hurt more people than you already have."

Where's High?

"Listen, we are getting off track. Logan. We want to help. My dad will pay for your stay in Iowa. It's one of the best facilities in the country. I think you could really get the help you need," Kellan explained.

I opened my mouth to say something again, but Kellan caught my action. He narrowed his eyes at me, and I swore for a second I saw a glimpse of love.

A glimpse of hope.

A glimpse of pleading.

"Can I talk to my brother alone?" I whispered, closing my eyes.

Everyone else in the room left, closing the door behind them.

"I'm sorry, Kel," I said, fiddling with my fingers. "I didn't mean to cause the accident. I didn't mean to. But after Alyssa said she was having an abortion—"

"What?" Kellan cut in.

"You didn't know? Alyssa was pregnant. But she had an abortion a few weeks ago. Her mom took her, and it fucked with my mind, Kel. I know that I've been off these past few weeks, but my mind is messed up."

"Logan…" Kellan moved in closer, pulling a chair up to the side of my bed. "She didn't have an abortion."

"What?" My heart started racing, and my fingers gripped the railing on the bed frame. "But her mom said—"

"Her mom kicked her out when Alyssa told her she was going to keep the baby. She wanted to tell you, but you freaking disappeared."

I sat up, in pain but filled with hope. "She didn't do it?"

His stare fell to his hands, which were clasped together. "No."

"So…" I choked on the emotions running through me. "I'm going to be a dad?"

"Logan," Kellan said, shaking his head. His mouth parted, but he didn't say anything for a moment. He brushed his hands against his temple. "During the car accident, she wasn't wearing her seat belt. When you went to grab the wheel, she went to grab you. When the collision happened, she flew up and out the back window when it shattered."

"No." I shook my head.

"She's okay, but…"

"Don't, Kellan."

"Logan. She lost the baby."

My thumbs pressed against my eyes to hold back the tears. "Don't say that, Kel. Don't say that." I shoved him. "Don't say that to me."

"I'm so sorry, Logan."

I began to sob into the palms of my hands, shaking hysterically. *I did it. I caused the accident. I did this. It's all my fault.* Kellan wrapped his arms around me as I fell apart, unable to speak any words, unable to stop the hurt, unable to breathe. Each inhale felt painful, each exhale a chore.

CHAPTER 13
Alyssa

H ey," Logan whispered, walking into my hospital room. He was in his regular clothes, and the few bruises on his face didn't seem that bad. I hoped he knew how lucky he was to walk away from that accident.

"Hi." For the past day, I sat in the hospital bed debating what I'd say to him. My emotions traveled up and down, going back and forth between grief and rage for a long time. I wanted to scream at him nonstop. I wanted to tell him how much I blamed him, how much resentment I held for him to even question my motives with the baby. I knew his dreams, and I knew his heart. I knew we could've found a way to make it work. But he disappeared. I wanted to hate him for a little while, but the moment I saw him, everything inside me switched.

I was simply heartbroken.

He opened his mouth but shut it fast. His fingers ruffled through his hair, and he wouldn't make eye contact. Everything felt like a dream—how close we stood but how far away we still felt. It was a dream that I couldn't shake, and I wanted Logan to be the one to wake me.

I wanted him to promise me that this was simply a dream that had somehow turned into a vile nightmare but that when dawn came, I'd wake up.

I wanted to wake up. Please, God…wake me up.

I sat on the right side of the bed, and my knees bent up to my chest. I choked on each breath I took. The air in the room was stuffy, toxic, dead. My need to cry grew heavier and heavier as my body shook. Just looking at Logan broke my heart into a million pieces, but I didn't shed a tear. "I'm fine," I finally said, feeling in every bone of my body that I wasn't.

"Can I hold you?" he asked.

"No," I said coldly.

"Okay," he replied.

I looked down to my shaky hands, my mind jumbled. "Yes."

"Yes?" he asked, his voice heightening a bit.

"Yes."

His hand landed on my shoulder before he climbed into the hospital bed and wrapped me up in his hold. I shivered when I felt his fingers touch my skin for the first time in a long time as his fingers wrapped around me. "I'm sorry, High."

His touch was so warm…

You came back to me.

The tears fell down my cheeks. My body was shaking uncontrollably as Logan held on strong, refusing to let go of me any time soon. Our foreheads fell against each other, and his warm tears intermixed with mine. "I'm so fucking sorry, High." We stayed wrapped together, feeling the world on our shoulders, until we both fell asleep.

He came back.

When I awakened to find him still holding me as if I were his lifeline, I turned my body to face him. He was sleeping, his inhales and exhales almost a whisper. My hands moved to his hands, and I locked our fingers together. He stirred a bit before opening his eyes.

"Alyssa, I don't know what to say. I didn't know you were—I didn't…"

I'd never heard such vulnerability in his voice. The Logan who left my house weeks ago was so detached from me, from his emotions. But now, hearing him cry as he wrapped his hands around my face made the little bit of my heart that was still beating shatter.

"I shouldn't have gone off the deep end. I should've stayed. I should've talked to you. But now, because of me—because of me…" He buried his head in my shoulder as he lost himself. "I killed him," he said, speaking of the baby. "It's my fault."

I took my hands and cradled his face the way he held mine. "Logan. Don't do this to yourself." I could almost feel the blame he felt as his eyes spilled with emotion. I nestled my head against his neck, and my hot breath melted against his skin. My hooded eyes were exhausted, and I blinked a few times before closing them and muttering against his ear. "Don't do this to yourself." I couldn't hate him. No matter what happened, hating Logan wasn't something I'd ever be able to do, but loving him? That love was always going to be there. We'd figure out how to move on from the terrible tragic accident together. It was us against the world. We'd stand together.

"I'm leaving," he said, pulling himself together, wiping his eyes dry.

I sat up, alarmed. "What?"

"I'm leaving. I'm going to a rehab clinic in Iowa."

My eyes lit up with anticipation. Earlier, Kellan told me about the rehabilitation clinic, and we both really hoped Logan would take the ninety-day course. It wouldn't take away the pain that we were both suffering through, but it would help him learn to handle it in a better way. "This is good, Lo. This is good news. And then when you come back, we can start over again. We can be us again," I swore.

He frowned, shaking his head. "I'm not coming back, High."

"What?"

"When I leave True Falls, I'm not coming back. I'm never coming back to Wisconsin, ever, and I'm never coming back here."

I slightly pushed away from him. "Stop it."

"I'm not coming back. I always end up hurting people. I ruin lives, High. And I can't keep messing up yours or Kellan's. I need to disappear."

"Shut up, Logan!" I yelled. "Stop saying that."

"I've seen how these things happen. We'd get in a routine, on a hamster wheel where we go round and round and I keep screwing up your life. I can't do that to you. I won't." He pulled himself up from the bed; then he stuffed his hands deep into his pockets. He shrugged once, giving me a broken smile. "I'm sorry, High."

"Don't do this, Lo. Don't leave me like this," I begged, taking his hands and pulling him closer to me. "Don't leave me again. Don't run. Please. I need you." I couldn't get through this without him. I needed him to help me learn to stand again. I needed his voice late at night. I needed his love early in the morning. I needed the one person who had lost what I lost to mourn with me. I needed my most painful low to stay by my side.

His lips kissed my forehead once, and then he whispered against my ear before turning around and leaving me shouting his name.

The last thing he said to me were words that played over and over again in my head. Words that cut me deeper than anything else could've.

"I would've been shitty," he whispered against my ear, sending chills down my spine. "I would've been a shitty father. But you?" He swallowed hard. "You would've been the best mother. Our child would've been honored to be loved by you."

And he was gone.

With those simple words and his fading footsteps, I found out what it meant for a heart to truly break.

PART 2

From the ashes, they rose,
And burned once again.

He never forgot her glow,
And she never forgot him.

Message #1

———————

*Hey, Logan, it's Alyssa. I'm just calling to see how you're doing. I just...
I hate how we left things. I hate how the last times we were near each
other weren't the best. I hate how I miss you. I hate how much this hurts.*

*I'm going to call you, though, every day, even if you don't answer.
I want you to know that you're not in this alone. No matter how bad it
gets. I want you to know you're not alone.*

I'll see you soon, Lo.

Message #5

Hey, it's me.

You've been at the clinic for five days now, and I wish I could hear your voice. Kellan said he spoke with you and that you're doing okay. Are you doing okay? I really hope so. I miss you, Logan. So, so much.

I'm glad you're working on yourself.

You deserve it.

I'll see you soon, Lo.

Message #14

_____

Two weeks. You've been there two weeks, and Kellan said you're doing okay. He said you're struggling a bit with withdrawal, but I know you're stronger than your biggest demons.

I lay in bed last night, listening to the record on the vinyl player skip every few seconds, and it reminded me of you. Remember the first time we...?

Never mind.

I just miss you, that's all. Some days are harder than others.

I'll see you soon, Lo.

Message #45

You're halfway through the program. How are you? Are you eating enough? Is your mind staying clear? I hope they have documentary DVDs there for you to watch. If you want, maybe I can come out there and bring you some DVDs. I saw a new documentary on the Beatles that I thought you might like.

Do you want me to bring it?

Because I will.

Just say the word.

I've been leaving you voicemails every day for the past forty-five days, and I'll keep leaving the messages. I just wish I could hear your voice. I wish you'd answer the phone.

Lo...

Please.

Gosh. I miss you.

I'll see you soon, Lo.

Message #93

Hey, it's Alyssa.

You finished the program, and I can't help but want to cry. I'm so, so proud of you. This is good. This is the best...

Kellan said you're doing okay. That you're healthy and in good spirits.

He also said he took you some DVDs. Why didn't you ask me? Why will you answer his calls but not mine? What did I do wrong?

I would've brought them to you, Logan—the DVDs. I would've brought them to you.

That doesn't matter, though.

I'll see you soon, Lo.

Message #112

_____

He said you're not coming back to True Falls. He said you're staying in Iowa. I didn't believe you when you told me. I didn't want to believe you.

He said you found a small studio apartment and a job...

This is good. If you need anything, furniture, food...company.

I just miss you, that's all.

I can't believe you're not coming back.

This is good, though. This is good for you.

I love you.

I'll see you soon, Lo.

Message #270

_____

Do you know this month the baby would've been born? I'd be in the hospital, and you would've held my hand. I know it probably sounds like I'm crying, but I'm not.

I'm just sad tonight. It doesn't take much to make me sad lately. A friend took me out to help me clear my mind.

Hearing your voice would help even more.

But you haven't called me.

Maybe this isn't your number anymore.

Maybe you've moved on.

Maybe you don't fucking care anymore. I don't even care that you don't fucking care!

It doesn't matter.

Fuck you for not calling me, Logan. Not once. You haven't called me. Sorry.

I'm just sad tonight.

I'll see you soon, Lo.

Message #435

What do you do during the night when it rains?
I lie in bed and think of your voice.
I'll see you soon, Lo.

Message #756

I decided that I hate you. I hate everything about you.
But still, I hope I'll see you soon, Lo.

Message #1090

I'm waving the white flag, Logan. I'm tired, and I give up. I'll stop now.

Five years.

I'll stop with the messages.

I love you.

I miss you.

I wish you the best.

Message #1123

_____

Logan, it's Kellan. Listen, I know you've made your life out in Iowa, and things are going well for you. And I wouldn't ask you to ever come back to this crappy town unless I really needed you and…

Erika and I are getting married. But I can't get married without my brother. I can't stand at the altar without the only family I have beside me.

I know this is asking a lot.

But I promise to never ask for anything else.

Plus, I bought you the documentary on NASA that we spoke about a few weeks ago.

You only get it if you're my best fucking man.

Yes. I am trying to buy your love, and I don't feel guilty at all.

Chat soon.

CHAPTER 14
Logan

FIVE YEARS LATER

Each night, I lit a cigarette and set it on my windowsill. As it burned, I allowed myself to remember my past. I allowed myself to hurt and mourn up until the moment the flames hit the filter. Then I shut my brain off and allowed myself to forget, because the pain was too much to swallow. When my brain was shut down, I kept busy, making sure memories wouldn't slip in. I watched documentaries, I worked dead-end jobs, I worked out—I did everything possible to keep from remembering.

But now, my brother had called me back to the one place that I'd spent the past five years running from.

The moment I made it back to True Falls, I sat in the train station, debating if I should've found a way to collect money to get a one-way ticket straight back to Iowa.

"Coming or going?" a woman sitting two seats away from me asked.

I turned to her, somewhat taken aback by her intense green eyes. She gave me a small smile and chewed on her thumbnail.

"Not sure yet," I replied. "What about you?"

"Coming. Staying, I think." She kept smiling, but the more she did, the sadder she appeared. I didn't know smiling could look so heartbreakingly sad. "I'm just trying to waste some time before I head back to my life."

I could understand that.

I sat back in my chair, trying to keep from remembering the life I'd left behind all those years ago.

"I even booked a hotel for tonight," she said, biting her bottom lip. "Just so I could have a few more hours to forget, you know? Before I returned to the real world."

I nodded once.

She slid two chairs closer to me, her leg brushing against mine. "You don't remember me, do you?" Tilting my head her way, she gave me that sad grin again and combed her fingers through her long hair.

"Am I supposed to?"

Her head shook back and forth. "Probably not. My name's Sadie." She blinked once, almost as if knowing her name was supposed to mean something to me. Her lips curved down. "Anyway. You seem like a guy who'd like to forget for a while too. If you want, you're welcome to come to the motel with me."

I should've told her no. I should've ignored her invite. But there was something about how sad she looked, how her pained soul seemed to burn like mine. So I grabbed my duffel bag, tossed it over my shoulder, and followed Sadie to the land of forgetting.

"We attended the same schools for years," Sadie said as we lay in some piece-of-shit motel room.

I'd been in the motel before, many moons ago, passed out in a filthy bathtub. Being there didn't bring back the best memories, but I figured since I returned to Wisconsin after five years, everything would be covered in crap recollections.

Her wine-stained lips moved as she stridently smacked on her gum. "Senior year, you copied my test for every math exam. I was legit the reason you graduated." She pushed herself up on her elbows. "I wrote four of your English essays. You can speak Spanish because of me! Sadie? Sadie Lincoln?"

Not a clue.

"I can't speak Spanish."

"Well, you could. You really don't remember me?"

Her eyes were saddened by this, but she shouldn't have been sad. It was nothing personal. There was plenty that I didn't remember.

Then there was everything I wished I could forget.

"To be fair, I spent most of my high school career fucked up."

That wasn't a lie.

"Or with that Alyssa Walters girl," she remarked.

My chest tightened right along with my jaw. Just hearing her name made my mind flood with memories.

"Is she still in town?" I asked, trying to sound nonchalant. Alyssa stopped leaving me messages months ago, and whenever Kellan called me, we didn't speak on the subject.

Sadie nodded. "Working at Hungry Harry's Diner. I saw her working at Sam's Furniture store too. She plays piano at some bars. I don't know. She's been all over the place. I'm surprised you didn't know that. You two were pretty much glued to each other, which was weird because you had nothing in common."

"We had plenty in common."

A sarcastic chuckle fell from her. "Really? The straight A music kid and the straight D—thanks to me—druggie with a crackhead mother had a lot in common?"

"Stop talking like you know shit," I hissed, growing annoyed. Back then, Alyssa and I had more in common than any two people on this earth. Plus, Sadie didn't know a damn thing about my mother. Screw her for thinking that she did.

I should've walked out of the motel room. I should've told her to piss off and find another person to harass, but I really hated being alone. I'd spent the past five years alone, except for the occasional mouse that came to visit every now and then.

Sadie stayed quiet as long as she could, which wasn't long at all. She didn't know what peaceful silence was. "So was it true? That you were in rehab?"

She was talking more than I was comfortable with. I hated talking about rehab because half the time, I wished I was back at the clinic. The other half of the time, I wished I was back in the alleyway with a line or two on a garbage can. It'd been so long since I'd used, and I still thought about it almost every damn day. Dr. Khan said it would be a tough transition coming back to the real world, but she believed I could handle it. I promised her whenever I felt like using, I'd snap the red rubber band she gave me against my skin as a reminder that the choices I made were real, just like the sting against my skin.

The band read, "strength," which was weird because I felt like I had none.

I'd been snapping the band against my arm since Sadie began speaking.

"There was a bet going around town that you were dead. I think your mom started that one," she said.

"Do you know how beautiful your eyes are?" I asked, changing the subject. I began kissing her neck, listening to her moan.

"They're just green."

She was wrong. They were a unique shade of celadon, holding a bit of gray and a touch of green to them. "A few years back, I was watching a documentary on Chinese and Korean pottery. Your eyes are the color of the glaze they used to make pottery."

"You watched a Chinese documentary on pottery?" She muttered with a chuckle, trying to catch her breath as my lips moved to the curves of her collarbone. I felt her shiver against me. "You must have been pretty messed up."

I laughed because she had no clue.

"They call it celadon in the West but over there, it's *qing ci*." I pressed my lips against hers. She kissed me back, because that was the main reason we were there in the dirty motel room. We were there to mistake a few moments of touch with the idea of love. We were there to mistake kisses for some kind of passion. We were there to mistake loneliness for wholeness. It was crazy what people would do—who people would do—to avoid feeling so alone.

"Can you stay the night?" she whispered.

"Of course," I sighed, rolling my tongue against her ear.

I wanted to stay the night with her because loneliness sucked. I wanted to stay the night with her because darkness spread. I wanted to stay the night with her because she asked me to. I wanted to stay the night with her because *I wanted to stay the night*.

She slid my shirt over my head, and her fingers rolled against my chest. "Oh my gosh!" she squealed. "You're buff!" Then she giggled.

Fuck. Did I really want to stay the night?

Without replying, I took off her pants and removed my own. As she lay down, I hovered over her, moving my lips from her neck, down to her chest, across her stomach, and pausing at her panty line. As I rubbed my thumb against her panties, she moaned.

"Yes…please…"

God, she was my addiction that night. I felt a little less alone. I even daydreamed about calling her tomorrow, meeting her back at the motel and screwing her again in the crappy bed.

It didn't take long for my boxers to come off and for me to climb on top of her. I tossed on a condom, and right before I slid into her, she yipped.

"No, wait!" A fear shot through those qing ci eyes. Her hands flew over her mouth, and tears welled up in her eyes. "I can't. I can't."

I paused, frozen over her. Guilt sucker punched my stomach. She didn't want to have sex with me. "Oh God. I'm sorry. I thought—"

"I'm in a relationship," she said. "I'm in a relationship."

Wait.

"What?" I asked.

"I have a boyfriend."

Boyfriend?

Crap.

She was a liar.

She was a cheater.

She has a boyfriend.

I removed myself from over her and sat up on the edge of the bed. My hands gripped the sides of the mattress, and I listened to her moving around. The sheet crinkled with her every move.

She said softly, "I'm sorry. I thought I could do it. I thought I could go through with it, but I can't. I thought it would be easy with you, ya know? To let go and let loose. I just thought I could forget for a while."

Not turning to her, I shrugged. "No big deal." Pushing myself up from the mattress, I moved toward the bathroom. "Be right back."

The door closed behind me, and I ran my hands across my face. I removed the condom from my cock and tossed it into the garbage can before I leaned against the door and stroked myself.

It was pathetic.

I'm pathetic.

I thought about cocaine as I jerked myself. The strong rush it used to deliver to warm me up. The feeling of complete peace and bliss. I stroked harder, remembering how it took away all the problems, all the fears, all the struggles. I felt as if I was on top of the world, unstoppable. Euphoria. Jubilation. Love. Euphoria. Jubilation. Love. Euphoria. Jubilation. Love.

Hate. Hate. Hate.

Deep breath.

I released.

I felt empty in every way possible.

Turning on the sink, I washed my hands and stared into the mirror, looking deep into my own eyes. Brown eyes that weren't important. Brown eyes that were sad. Brown eyes that were overshadowed by a vague depression.

I shook off the feeling, dried my hands, and returned to her.

She was getting dressed, wiping her eyes.

"You're leaving?" I asked.

She nodded.

"You—" I cleared my throat. "You can stay the night." I promised. "I'm not some dick who would kick you out at three in the morning. Besides, it's your motel room. I'll leave."

"I told my boyfriend I'd be home after I got back into town," she

said to me, a forced smile on her lips. Wearing only her bra and panties, she moved toward the balcony, opened the door, but didn't step
outside.

It was a deluge, raindrops hammering against the metal cage. The
rain always reminded me of Alyssa and how much she hated sleeping
during a rainstorm. I wondered where her mind was tonight. I wondered how she was dealing with the sounds against her windowsill.

"I can't sleep, Lo. Can you come over?"

Alyssa's voice played like a recording in my mind. Over and over
again, her sound took a voyage in my brain until I pushed her out.

Sadie combed her fingers through her long locks of hair. Her
forced smile fell into a frown. "He probably isn't home yet. I hated
sleeping alone when I was single. And now that I'm in a relationship,
I still feel alone."

"Am I supposed to feel bad for you because you're a cheater?" I
asked.

"He doesn't love me."

"I can tell how much you love him, though," I mocked.

"You don't understand," she stated defensively. "He's controlling.
He's pushed everyone I ever cared about away from me. I used to be
clean, like you are right now. I used to never fuck with drugs until I
ran into him. He trapped me, and now when he does come home, he'll
smell like a perfume that I don't own. He'll climb into bed and not even
touch me once."

Thoughts started running through my head that I knew were a
bad idea.

Stay with me tonight.

Stay with me in the morning.

Stay with me.

Loneliness was the voice in the back of your head that made you make bad decisions based solely on a broken heart.

"Does it feel weird? Being back here?" she asked, changing the subject. Smart move. A slow turn of her body, and we were staring into each other's eyes again. A crimson color affected her cheeks, and I swore I felt my heart break with the mere idea of her being alone.

"A little."

"Did you see Kellan yet?"

"You know my brother?"

"He plays at open mics around town. He's really good too."

I didn't know he'd been playing music again.

She arched an eyebrow, curious. "Are you two close?"

"I've been in Iowa for five years, and he's been here in Wisconsin." She nodded in understanding.

I cleared my throat. "Yeah, we're close."

"Best friends?"

"Only friend."

"I'm really freakin' shocked about your friendship with Alyssa not lasting. I thought you would've had her knocked up or something by now."

There was a time when I thought that too.

Stop talking about Alyssa. Stop thinking about Alyssa.

Maybe if I stayed the night tonight with Sadie, I wouldn't let Alyssa fill my mind. Maybe if I fell asleep with her in my arms, I wouldn't overthink being back in the same place where the one girl who I'd ever loved still resided. Stepping closer to Sadie, I brushed my hand over my chin. "Look, you can—"

"I shouldn't," she sighed, cutting me off. She was strange. Our stare

broke as she looked to the ground. "He's never cheated on me. He's...
He loves me." Her sudden confession made my mind race.

She was a liar.

She was a cheater.

She's leaving.

"Just stay," I requested, sounding more desperate than I wanted
to. "I'll sleep on the couch." It wasn't exactly a couch but more of a
broken-down futon that had more stains than cushion. To be honest,
I'd probably be more comfortable on the dirty carpeted floor. Or I
could've called Kellan and slept at his place.

But I wasn't ready for that.

The moment I saw someone from my past—someone I actually
remembered—I knew I'd fall back into the old world. The world I ran
from. The world that almost killed me. I wasn't ready. How could one
be ready to look their past in the eye and pretend that all the hurt and
pain was gone?

She slipped into her dress and glanced over her left shoulder
toward me, eyes filled with compassionate sorrow. "Zip me?"

It only took three footsteps before I was standing behind her, zip-
ping up her dress, which hugged every curve of her body. My hands
rested against her waist, and she leaned back against me.

"Can you call me a cab?"

I could and I did. The moment she left, she thanked me and told
me that I could stay the night at the motel—she had already paid and
it shouldn't go to waste. I took her up on the offer, but I wasn't sure
why she thanked me. I didn't do anything for her. If anything, I made
her a cheater.

No.

A first-time cheater probably felt some kind of guilt.

She just felt empty.

I hoped I never saw her again, because being around other empty individuals was draining.

After she left, I paced the motel room for an hour. Were there other people out there like me? Other people who felt so alone that they would rather spend meaningless nights with meaningless people just to have a few hours of staring into someone else's eyes?

I hated being alone, because when I was alone, I was reminded of all the things I hated about myself. I remembered all my past mistakes that brought me to the point where instead of living, I simply existed. If I truly lived life, I'd end up hurting anyone who came near me, and I couldn't do that anymore. That meant I had to be alone.

In the past, I was never alone when I had my drugs—my silent, deadly, destructive friends. I was never alone when I had my greatest high.

Alyssa…

Shit.

My mind was messing with me, the palms of my hands itching. I tried to watch television, but there was only reality garbage on the screen. I tried to draw for a while, but the pen in the room had no ink. I tried to shut off my brain, but I kept thinking about the best high I ever had.

When would I see her?

Would I see her at all?

Of course. Her sister's marrying my brother.

Did I want to see her?

No.

I didn't.

God.

I did.

I wanted to hold her yet at the same time never touch her again.

I wanted to kiss her yet at the same time never remember her curves.

I wanted to…

Shut up, brain.

Lifting my cell phone, I held down the number two. The voice was different that time, but the greeting was the same. They thanked me for calling the drug and alcohol hotline. They welcomed me to talk about my current struggles and urges in a confidential setting.

I hung up, like always.

Because people like me, with a past like mine, didn't deserve help. They deserved seclusion.

My steps moved to the balcony, and I lit a cigarette, resting it against a dry spot on the ground. I listened to the rain hammer against the town of True Falls, and my eyes shut. I took a deep breath and allowed myself to hurt for the short period that the cigarette burned.

I thought about Alyssa. I thought about Ma. I thought about all the drugs.

Then, I always ended up thinking about the child that I could've held if it weren't for the demons inside me.

Sometimes the cigarette burned for eight minutes. Other times, ten.

One thing that never changed, no matter how long the cigarette lasted, was how my shattered heart still found ways to break into even smaller pieces.

CHAPTER 15
Alyssa

Each day I carpooled to work with my neighbor, a seventy-year-old waitress named Lori. We both worked the morning shift at Hungry Harry's Diner and hated every single moment of it. Lori had been working there for the past twenty-five years and told me that her escape plan was to marry one of those Chris boys. Evans, Hemsworth, or Pratt, she wasn't picky. Every day, we'd drive over, and Lori always complained about being five minutes early, stating that the worst place you could ever arrive early was your place of employment. I didn't blame her.

I'd been working at Hungry Harry's for the past five years. The worst thing about the job was I'd go in smelling like rose perfume and peach shampoo, and I'd walk out smelling like fried burgers and hash browns—every single day. The only thing that kept me going was knowing that every hour I worked put me closer to my dream of opening a piano bar.

"You can do it, young'un," Lori said as we pulled up to the diner. "You're still cool and hip. You got plenty of time to make that vision become a reality. The key is to not listen to the outside noise from those around you. People always have opinions on lives that they don't live. Just keep your head up high, and avoid listening to their bullshit."

"Good advice," I said and smiled, knowing she was only talking to keep us from having to walk into the building a second earlier than our punch-in time.

"You know what my mama would say to me when I was being bullied as a kid?"

"What's that?"

"'One day at a time.' That's all it takes to get through anything. Don't think too much about the future or keep your brain running on the past treadmill. Just stay in the now. Be here now. That's the best way to live life. In the moment. One day at a time."

One day at a time. One day at a time.

I repeated those words in my mind when a rude customer screamed at me about their eggs being too scrambled, or when a baby threw a plate of food on the floor and the parents blamed me, or when a drunk dude threw up on my shoes.

I hated the food service industry. But then again, it was good to see the ins and outs of such a place, because when I had the piano bar, such a big part of it would be about running the kitchen.

Just one day at a time.

"Do you always shake your hips like that after you're done taking someone's order?" a voice mocked, making me smile when I realized the source.

"Only when I know they'll be good tippers." I smiled, turning around to see Dan standing behind me, his hands filled with files. He looked so handsome in his navy-blue slacks and light-blue button-down shirt with his sleeves rolled up. His smile was big and bright as always, and he was giving that grin to me. Stuffing my pad of paper and pen into my apron, I walked over to him. "What brings you around this early?"

"I was looking into the property we've been talking about getting."

"Yeah?"

"Yeah. I love it, I really do, but there's a termite issue. Do you have a minute to go over some things? I brought a few more floor plans of other places that we could check out."

I frowned, glancing around the diner. "I think my boss would fire me if I stopped working to look at piano bars."

Dan was a friend I had crossed paths with a few years ago at a piano bar. He was currently working for one of the best Realtors in the state, and when I told him my idea about opening a piano bar, he jumped at the idea of helping me look into places, even though I told him it would be a long while before that day came to life.

"Oh no, of course. I was just in the neighborhood and thought I'd stop in for some hash browns and coffee. I'm on my way to work anyway."

I smiled wide and he smiled wider. "We can look over them tomorrow night if that works?"

"Yeah, yeah!" he exclaimed, excitement overtaking him. "I can bring them to your place. We can order Chinese food, and I can bring wine. I could even cook steak or something for you…" His voice faded as he grew a bit too joyful. He ran his hands through his hair, shrugging. "You know, or whatever."

"That sounds like a plan. Just a heads-up, though, my house is still a piece of work. And with the rain, there's been a few leaks through the roof."

"My offer still stands about you crashing at my place until you finish updating your house. I know that stuff can be a headache."

"Thanks, but I think I'll pioneer my way through the complication that is my home."

"Okay. Well, I better get going to work, but I'll meet you tomorrow at your place to go over these." He shook the files in the air and winked my way.

"Wait. I thought you came in for coffee and hash browns?"

"Oh yeah. I did, but I just realized…" He was a bit flustered, and I couldn't help but smile. "I should really get to work a bit early to look some things over for my boss."

"Then tomorrow it is. I'll supply the alcohol; you supply the properties."

With that, he disappeared. I let out a sigh. Dan had had the same crush on me for the last three years, virtually since we met, but I never felt that kind of connection to him. He was an important person in my life, though, and I always hoped he'd be okay with just being friends.

"I swear, he brings you properties, has a solid job, lies about wanting hash browns just to see you, has that screw-me-sideways kind of smile, and offers to cook you steak. But you can't even take up the offer to stay with him for a while?" Lori said, carrying a tray with scrambled eggs, hash browns, and sausage links.

I laughed. "My house is fine. I've spent all these years saving up to buy my dream home, and now that I have it, I'm not ready to let it go. It just needs a few Band-Aids, that's all."

"Honey. Your house needs a bit more than Band-Aids." She smirked, placing the plates of food down on table five before she headed back over to me with a hand on her hip and sass in her lips. "I'm just saying. If I had Dan offering me a bed, I'd move in with him and have him show me his floor plans on every inch of my body in every inch of the house."

"Lori!" I shushed her, my cheeks heating up.

"I'm just saying. You're working three jobs to pay for a house that you need to fix up anyway in order to prove that you can be an independent woman. You could fix up the house *and* live with Dan, you know."

"The house isn't that much of a fixer-upper," I argued.

"Aly." She moaned, slapping her hand against her face. "The last time I came over to share a bottle of wine, I used your bathroom and I didn't close the door when I used it. You know why? *Because there wasn't a bathroom door.*"

I laughed. "Okay. I get it. So it's a fixer-upper. But I like the challenge."

"Hm. You must be a really good lay for Dan to stick around the way he does."

"What? Dan and I haven't slept together."

"Seriously?" she exclaimed. "You mean he's drooling over you, and you two have never done the deed?"

"Never."

"But…that smile!"

I giggled. "I know. But he's a good friend. I have a big rule for my relationships, and it includes never dating any of my friends. Ever." I'd been down that road before and was never planning to travel down it again. To this day, I still thought about Logan and mourned the friendship I loved and lost.

We would've been better off never falling in love.

"You know, Charles and I were best friends before we decided to date. He was the love of my life, and no one has ever compared. He used to make me laugh so hard before I even knew what love was. Some of the best things in life come from the strongest kinds of friendships," Lori explained. Her head lowered, and she gripped the locket hanging from her necklace, which held their wedding photo inside it. "Boy, oh boy, do I miss that man madly." She hardly ever spoke about Charles, her late husband, but whenever she did, there was a twinkle in her eyes as if her mind was traveling back to the day she first fell in love with him.

Our boss told us to stop chatting so much and get back to work, which we did. We were always busy in the mornings, serving more people than seemed humanly possible, but the busier we were, the less time I had to think about things.

"Are you good on coffee?" I asked a woman sitting near the window. I held the coffeepot in my grip as I made my way around to all my tables for refills.

"Yeah, I'm good. Thank you."

I smiled wide, and when I glanced up out of the window, my heart caught in my chest. My fingers landed against the glass, trying to reach out and touch the figure across the way. When I blinked once more, what I thought I saw was gone. A shiver ran down my spine, and I stood up straight.

Lori glanced up in my direction. "You okay, Alyssa? You look like you saw a—"

"Ghost?" I said, finishing her sentence.

"Exactly." She came over and looked out the window. "What is it?"

A ghost.

"Nothing. It was nothing," I said, taking my coffeepot to the next table.

It was my imagination, that's all.

Nothing more, nothing less.

CHAPTER 16
Logan

My stare was trained on Alyssa as she walked around the diner, helping customers. I sat in a back corner, unable to be seen from her location. *I shouldn't be here.* My mind knew all the reasons I shouldn't have walked into the diner that day, but my heart felt a tug in her direction.

She still smiled the same. That made me happy and sad all at once. How many smiles had I missed? Who did she smile for nowadays?

"Here's your omelet," my waitress said, setting the plate in front of me. Her face was somewhat pale, and sweat was dripping from her forehead. She rocked back and forth, trying to force a smile. "Anything else I can get you?" she questioned.

"Orange juice would be great," I said.

She nodded in reply, walking away.

I picked up the saltshaker and started to add some to my omelet. A loud chuckle escaped the diner, and I took a deep breath. Alyssa's laugh. It hadn't changed. I shut my eyes, feeling my chest tighten. Memories flooded me like a hurricane, knocking me backward as I envisioned all the times I lay beside her, listening to her laugh ripple through my soul.

"If you wanted a plate of salt with an omelet on the side, you could've just asked," a voice offered, snapping my mind from the past. My stare fell to the omelet that I'd been mindlessly shaking salt onto for the past five minutes.

"Sorry," I muttered, placing the saltshaker onto the table.

"No need to be sorry. We all have our preferences," the voice promised. "Anyway, the wait staff is being hammered, Jenny was just sent home with the flu, and I was ordered to bring you an orange juice and take over your table."

My eyes moved to the girl speaking. She had full rose-colored lips and blue eyes that were more than familiar to me; they were the one thing amazing about that town. Those eyes had a talent of being able to smile all on their own. Her blond hair was straight, and she had bangs that fell over her eyebrows.

She kept staring.

I wouldn't look away.

Alyssa.

High.

My greatest high.

She looked beautiful, but that wasn't surprising. There wasn't one day I remembered where she wasn't beautiful. Even on the days when I was too far gone to open my eyes, I remembered the beauty of her soft words begging me to come back to her, to keep breathing.

"Logan," she whispered, placing the glass of orange juice onto the table.

I stood up from my chair as she stepped forward toward me. At first, I thought she was going to hug me, embrace me, forgive me for being me and never returning her calls. But in reality, she wasn't going to hug me. Her palm was open, and I knew right when I saw it, she was going to slap me. *Hard.* Whenever Alyssa did anything, she did it with full force. Nothing was ever half-assed.

Her arm rose, came at me swiftly, and I was ready for the sting that I deserved. I closed my eyes in anticipation, but I never felt her touch. God, how I wanted to feel her touch. Opening my eyes, I watched her shaky hand hovering in the air, centimeters from my cheek. Our eyes locked, and I saw the tears burning in the backs of her eyes, the confusion, the heartbreak.

"Hi, Alyssa," I said softly.

She cringed and closed her eyes. Her hand stayed in the air, and I took it in my own, laying her fingers against my cheek. A small whimper of pain escaped her lips as her skin lay against mine. I pulled her closer into a hug, and it felt just like yesterday. Her skin was so cold, like always, and my body heated hers up. Her fingers moved from my cheek, and she wrapped both arms around my neck, holding on to me as if she forgave me for all the missed calls and silence.

Her fingers clung to me, almost digging into my flesh as if she thought I was some kind of mirage that would disappear if she didn't keep hold. I didn't blame her—I'd disappeared before.

I inhaled her hair.

Peaches.

God, I hated peaches until that day.

She smelled like the days when summer went to sleep and awakened as fall. Soft, sweet, perfect.

My fucking High.

"I missed…" she said against my ear.

"I know," I replied.

"You left…" she started.

"I know," I replied.

"How dare you…" she began.

"I know," I replied.

Her body tensed up, and she yanked away from me. The sadness in her eyes was gone. Only anger remained.

That seems right.

"You know?" she hissed, standing tall but still so small. Her arms crossed, and she bit her bottom lip. The small crinkles in the corners of her eyes deepened, and it was clear that she wasn't that same girl I left behind years ago. She was a grown woman now, and she had a fire burning deep in her soul. "I called you."

"I know."

Her brow furrowed. "No. I called you, Logan. I called you and left you over five hundred messages."

One thousand and ninety messages.

I didn't want to correct her.

"You disappeared. You left me. Us. Kellan. You left us all," she said. "I understand you needing your space, but you left me. After everything we'd been through—after what happened—you left me alone with that."

"I was getting better. I was working through the shit with my mom, the shit with you, and yeah, I was a mess, but I just needed time."

"I gave you space, and you still stayed gone."

"You called me every day, Alyssa. That's not giving me space."

"Kellan and I saved your life, and we thought you'd come back.

I called you every day to let you know I was here, waiting. I thought you'd come back for me. For us."

"You can't save people's lives, and you can't expect people to come back for you, Alyssa. You should've known that after what happened with—" I bit my tongue, stopping my speech, but I knew I couldn't take back my words. She knew what I was going to say. *You should've known that after what happened with your father.*

"That was mean."

"I didn't say anything."

Her head shook back and forth. "For someone who said nothing, it sure communicated plenty." Her voice cracked. "Over five hundred messages, and not one reply."

One thousand and ninety messages.

Still didn't correct her.

"I didn't have anything to say to you," I lied. I was building the wall that I knew I had to build coming into town. I had to keep my emotions and mind at bay to keep me from falling back into Alyssa's life. Last time I was in her life, I ruined it. I couldn't allow myself to do that to her again. So I had to be cold, harsh even.

Because she deserved better than to be waiting by her phone for someone like me to call her back.

"Nothing?" She stepped back, flabbergasted. "Not one thing? Not even hello?"

"I was always better at goodbyes."

"Wow." She blew out a sharp breath.

Every emotion I felt toward her throughout the years was coming back to me, stronger than ever. I was mad at myself for not calling her. I was sad. I was happy. I was confused. I was in love. I was everything that Alyssa ever made me feel.

My mind was seconds away from exploding.

"You know what?" She cleared her throat and gave me a tight smile. "We aren't going to do this."

"Do what?"

"Fight. Argue. Because if we do that, you know what it means? It would mean you and I have some kind of relationship, which we don't. You became a stranger the moment you disappeared into the cornfields of Iowa."

My lips parted, but before I could speak, she'd turned on her heel and stormed off to help another table. She had a fake smile pasted to her face while she spoke to the customers. Her foot tapped nonstop against the checkered floor, and there was a slight rock back and forth to her body.

Her eyes shot over to me as she spoke to the individuals.

"Well, I think I'll have the eggs over easy and"—one customer said but was cut off by Alyssa storming back over to me—"bacon."

"Does Kellan even know that you're here?! Or were you just going to surprise attack him at his job too?" Her hands hit her hips, and she cocked an eyebrow.

I cocked a brow back at her. "Yeah. He's the reason I'm here. For the wedding."

"What?" she asked, flustered.

"The wedding… You know, how my brother is marrying your sister."

"But…" She paused, her irritation dropping. "The wedding isn't for another month. You came back a month early just to help with that?"

"Kellan said it was this weekend."

"Well, that would definitely be news to me. But with everything that's happening, I wouldn't be shocked."

"What does that mean? What's happening?"

Her mouth opened, but no words came out. She tried again, nibbling on her bottom lip. "Are you using, Logan?"

"What?" I asked defensively. "What the hell does that mean?"

"You know what it means. I just…" She started shaking, her nerves taking ahold of her. "I need to know if you're clean. If you've been using anything."

"That's none of your business. Seeing as how if I told you anything, that would mean we had some kind of relationship, and as you stated earlier, we—"

"Lo," she whispered.

The nickname falling from her lips made me rethink my annoyance and my defensive approach.

Her eyes.

Her lips.

Alyssa.

High.

My greatest high.

"Yeah?" I whispered back.

"Are you using?"

"No."

"Not even weed?"

"Only weed," I replied.

A heavy sigh fell from her lips.

"Come on, Alyssa. Give me a break. Weed is legal in some states."

"Not in Iowa."

She was starting to sound like she was worried, which meant she kind of still cared, which meant hope. What did I care about hope though? *The keep Alyssa out* wall was built, and I wouldn't be knocking it down any time soon. I'd be on the next train out of this place if a wedding wasn't happening.

"Only weed though?"

"Only weed."

"Promise?"

"Promise."

She stepped back once before stepping forward twice. She held out her pinky in my direction. "Pinky?"

I stared at her pinky for a while, remembering all the promises we used to make when we were younger, locking our fingers together.

My pinky wrapped around hers, the small touch filling me up. "Pinky."

When we released our hold, she stepped back twice before stepping forward once. Her hands stretched out toward me, and without any thought, I took her hold. She pulled me from my seat and wrapped her arms around me. The way she held on so tight told my gut that something was wrong.

"High, what is it?"

She pulled me closer, holding on while I refused to let go. Her lips pressed against my ear, her hot breaths dancing against my skin. "Nothing. It's nothing." When we parted, she put her hands in prayer position and pressed them against her lips, tilting her head slightly. "Lo…"

My fingers ran through my hair and I nodded. "High…"

"Welcome home," she said.

"It's not home. I'm just stopping in before leaving again."

She shrugged. "Home is always home. Even when you don't want it to be. And, Logan?" she said, slightly rocking back and forth on her heels.

"Yeah?"

She didn't say anything else, but I heard her loud and clear.

I missed you too, High.

CHAPTER 17
Logan

I dropped my duffel bag on Kellan and Erika's front porch before knocking. My stomach knotted, not knowing how it'd be seeing both of them after so long. Time had a way of changing people, and I wondered how much it had changed them. I let a few more seconds pass before building up the courage to knock.

When the door opened, a weighted sigh left me. Kellan gave me his big brother grin seconds before pulling me tight into a hug. "Your train was supposed to get in yesterday. You get lost, brother?"

I laughed. "I took the long way."

"All right, let me look at you." He stood back, crossed his arms, and chuckled. "You look buff or something. You legit left town as Peter Parker and came back as Spider-Man."

"Those radioactive spiders in Iowa aren't fucking around, man. And look at you!" I jokingly punched at his gut. "You look like a peanut. Maybe now I can kick your ass instead of vice versa."

"Ha, don't count on it. Still deep conditioning your hair like a woman, I see," he said, messing up my perfect hair.

"Envy is one of the seven deadly sins, brother."

"I'll keep that in mind," he snickered. Damn. It was good to see him. He looked just as great as he always did. You never realized how much you could miss a person until they were standing right in front of you after so long.

"Kellan, who's at the door?" Erika said, walking out of the bathroom, drying her hair with a towel. When she saw me, shock filled her up. "What are you doing here?"

"Good to see you too, Erika."

"What are you doing here?" she asked again.

My eyes darted from Kellan to Erika and back to Kellan. "I'm starting to wonder the same thing. What's going on, Kel? I ran into Alyssa earlier and—"

"You ran into Alyssa?!" Erika exclaimed.

It was funny…how little I missed her overly dramatic self.

"That's what I just said. Anyway, she said the wedding wasn't this weekend?"

"Next month," she corrected. "It's next month. Why do you have a duffel bag with you?"

"Uh, I was told I would be staying with you two? For the wedding that doesn't seem to be happening."

"It's next month!" she echoed once more. "It's next month. I didn't even know you were coming. Staying with us?" She started itching at her neck, her pale skin growing red with irritation. She looked so much like her sister, yet their personalities were so different that they could've been strangers. "Babe, can I talk to you in the bedroom for a minute?"

I stepped forward to follow her, making Kellan smirk as Erika growled with annoyance. "Oh? Sorry. When you said *babe*, I assumed you were talking to me. But now I see it was directed toward my brother. My bad."

Kellan chuckled. "Don't be a dick."

"Can't help it. I have one, so I am one."

The two hurried into the bedroom, where the door slammed. I sat down on the sofa, and right as I reached into my pocket, the bedroom door flew open.

"Logan?" Erika said.

"Yes?"

"Don't touch anything."

I tossed my hands up in defeat, and she reentered the bedroom with another loud slam.

"I *cannot* believe you didn't tell me he was coming, Kellan!" echoed through the house, and I couldn't help but chuckle. Even though I had no clue why I was currently back in the town that created all my demons, it always felt like home to get under Erika's skin.

Reaching into my pocket, I pulled out my pack of cigarettes and then lit one with my lighter. Glancing around the house, I was reminded of how much of a neat freak Erika was, and I couldn't for a second understand how Kellan could put up with her. I was certain each day was filled with nagging.

When ashes began to form at the end of the cigarette, I panicked, knowing Erika would freak out if I got any on her probably overpriced coffee table. I hurried toward the dining room table that was set as if there were a big dinner party taking place and grabbed a saucer, dropping the ashes onto that. I took the saucer back to the sofa and relaxed a bit.

"Kellan, I just…we are already under so much stress. You have so much going on with work. I'm working on my master's degree. Plus, we are trying to tie everything together for the wedding. Do you think having Logan here is a good idea?" she asked him as I listened through the thin walls.

"He's my brother."

"You're... We... I don't know if this is a good idea."

"He's my brother."

"But you know how he is. He'll drag you into his crazy life. He always does."

"Erika, he's clean. He's been clean for years now."

I could hear the irritation in Kellan's voice, and a bit of disappointment overtook me. He was always one of the few to actually believe in me ever getting clean. Him and Alyssa. Everyone else considered me a lost cause.

Her voice held the same kind of aggression. "Or so he says. Seriously, how many times have we heard that from him? You have this need to parent him and your mom. You aren't in charge of their lives, babe. And you're not Logan's father. Gosh, he's not even your full brother! He's your half brother."

I heard a loud slam, and my gut tightened up. Standing from the sofa, I was seconds away from going to check on them. The saucer full of ashes stayed in my grip as I walked toward the bedroom, yet I paused when I heard Kellan's voice.

"If you ever say something like that again, I will walk out of this place and have a hard time looking back. Yeah, Logan has fucked up in the past. He's burned bridges between you and tons of other people. To many, he's unforgiveable. But he's my brother. None of that 'half' shit. One hundred percent, he's my brother. I will look after him, and I will never give up on him. I will never burn that bridge, Erika. So if that bothers you, well, that's probably going to be an issue."

Their voices lowered, and I had to listen very closely to hear Erika apologize, followed by the exchanges of *I love you*s and more apologies.

When the door opened, I stood with my cigarette hanging between my lips. The two stared at me, shocked to see me so nearby. "Listen, you guys," I started.

"Are you smoking in the house?" Erika gasped, ripping the cigarette from between my lips. "And are you putting ashes on my good china?!" she whined, snatching the saucer from my hands. "Oh my gosh. My mom is going to be here in a few hours, and now the place smells like smoke!"

Erika's mom. The only person on the earth who was more dramatic and annoying than Erika herself. *How was Alyssa related to these people?*

She hurried over to the sink where she drowned my cigarette, sending it through the garbage disposal. She muttered to herself as she began to scrub the plate over and over again.

An awkward silence took over the room as Kellan and I stared at his fiancée, who seemed to be level five hundred crazy that day.

"So…" Kellan said, rocking back and forth. "Want to go check out Jacob's restaurant?" he asked.

"Yup," I replied, faster than the speed of light. Jacob was an old friend who I hadn't spoken to since I snapped on him about his porn collection. I wasn't certain how the reunion would go, but I was hopeful that it would be better than the reunification with Erika.

We hurried out the door before Erika could grow any angrier.

"You think she's still not over me almost burning down her last apartment?" I asked with a smirk on my face.

"Oh, she's definitely not over you almost burning down her apartment," Kellan laughed.

"Give me a break. It was a mistake."

"That cost her four thousand dollars, yeah. An expensive mistake. But she'll get over it, no worries."

"Kellan, why am I here?"

Before he could reply, the front door opened. "You can stay in one of the guest rooms," Erika said, nodding toward Kellan. Her eyes locked with mine, and she seemed calmer than before. Maybe the intense cleaning session balanced out her mojo. "I'll put your bag in there."

"Thanks, Erika. It means a lot to me," I replied.

"We'll be back in time for dinner," Kellan said, kissing her cheek.

"We?" she asked, her voice heightening with concern.

"We," he said, pointing toward himself and me.

She tried her best not to cringe, but she definitely cringed. "Oh, wonderful. I'll just somehow make the meat loaf big enough for four instead of three people. And I'll set an extra placemat." I could feel her annoyance floating in the air, but she smiled and slowly walked back inside and shut the door.

"I think she and I are officially best friends," I laughed.

"The bestest of friends," he agreed. "Speaking of… How was it seeing Alyssa?"

"Fine," I lied. "I just plan on avoiding her the best I can."

"Good," he said, walking down the front porch. "It's probably for the best that those feelings from the past are gone, huh? Maybe you can forgive, forget, and both move on now."

"Yeah. I felt nothing being around her actually. So that's good." That was the truth too. And by *truth*, I meant the ugliest lie. I remembered the words Alyssa said earlier at the diner.

"Home is always home. Even when you don't want it to be."

After all the time that passed, after all the distance, Alyssa Marie Walters still somehow felt like home to me.

I wasn't certain how to handle that fact, which was exactly why I needed a one-way ticket away from True Falls, Wisconsin.

Fast.

CHAPTER 18
Alyssa

"On a scale of one to ten, how long did you know Logan was in town before you figured you should call me? One being you had no clue, ten being 'I secretly hate my sister,'" I asked Erika through the phone, juggling my keys as I tried to get into my house. Ever since Logan and I crossed paths at the restaurant, my nerves had been shot. I couldn't think straight. I felt nauseous. I felt anger. I felt…relief?

A big part of me sometimes doubted that Logan was still alive, even though Kellan would give me updates every now and then.

"Trust me, I had no clue," Erika said.

I finally opened my front door, and within seconds, I was flopped on my sofa.

"Kellan sent out an SOS for him I guess. It's a mess. He's supposed to be staying with us for a while."

"A while?" I asked, perking up. "How long is a while? Is he there now?" I debated walking over to her house just to see his face. Just to make sure he was real.

"Aly," she scolded, her voice sounding a lot like Mom's when she'd discipline us as kids. "Don't."

"Don't what?"

"Don't go back down that road. Logan Silverstone is out of your life. And I think it's best if we keep it that way."

How is he supposed to stay out of my life if he's literally blocks away from me, staying with my sister?

"I was just curious, Erika. Seriously." I paused, listening to the noise coming through the phone. She was rearranging her whole house; I just knew it. I could hear her pushing the furniture around. Whenever Erika was nervous or upset, she rearranged things or accidentally broke items, which she would quickly run to the store to replace. It was a weird quirk about her, but I left a boy a message each day for almost five years—everyone had their weird quirks. "Wow, he must have really gotten under your skin," I said, pulling out a tube of lipstick and applying it over and over again. "I can hear you moving things around."

"Can you blame me? It's like the Ghost of Christmas Past showing up and saying, 'Oh? Are you under some stress? Well, let me come screw things up a little more for you.'"

"How many plates have you broken so far?"

"Only one, thankfully," she sighed. "I had extras in the storage closet, though." Of course she did. She was always ready for almost any kind of incident. "He was smoking and leaving ashes on my saucer, Alyssa! Who does that?"

I snickered. "Better than on your five-hundred-dollar coffee table."

"Do you think that's funny?"

A little.

"No, it's not funny. Sorry. Look, I'm sure after a few days, things will get back to normal. You probably won't even know that Logan's there."

"Do you think he's still using?" she whispered through the phone. "Kellan's in denial, but I don't know. I think this is a terrible, terrible idea. The timing couldn't be worse."

"He looked good," I said, walking to my bathroom, staring in the mirror at my messy lips with too much ruby-red color to them. I picked up a wet wipe and started wiping the lipstick away, thinking about Logan's eyes, which reminded me so much of yesterday. "He actually looked really great. Healthy."

"You don't worry, though? That he'll relapse? Being back in this place where all his trouble started can't be good."

"I think that we shouldn't overthink everything. One day at a time. One broken plate at a time, Erika."

She snickered. "Are you sure you don't want to come over to join us for dinner? Mom will be here to greet Logan."

Oh no. Poor Logan.

My mom was far from his biggest fan. And the last time Logan saw her, he called her a belittling monster.

"As much as I would love to be a part of that train wreck, I think I'll have to pass." Seeing Logan earlier made my mind dizzy. I wasn't certain that I could've handled seeing him again. Even if a big part of my heart wanted to stare at him, just to make sure he was real. "Anyway, have fun tonight, and text me all the disastrous details."

"Will do. And, Alyssa?"

"Yeah?"

"Don't fall back down the Logan rabbit hole. No good comes from that."

"I won't. And, Erika?"

"Yes?"

"Don't break a freaking lamp."

"Deal."

I pulled out the box.

The box that was supposed to be destroyed years ago. The box that Erika thought I got rid of because I let him go after the million voice messages I'd left him. But it was packed under my mattress, with all our memories inside.

I took off the lid and went through all the photos of us from when we were younger. I lifted the pressed daisy from when he first kissed me. I pulled out the teddy bear he stole from the amusement park when the guy cheated me out of the main prize.

The ticket stubs from the movies we went to.

The birthday cards he always made me.

His lighter.

"Why did you have to do this to me?" I whispered, lifting the red hoodie that he gave me the first time we hung out. I smelled it and could almost still smell the cigarette smoke traces that he left in the fabric. "Why did you have to come back?"

In the bottom of the box was a framed silver fork. I closed my eyes as I held it in my hands. I sat in the pile of memories until it was time to pack up the box and put it back under my bed.

I'd get rid of them one day, I was certain of it.

Just not today.

CHAPTER 19
Logan

I was amazed when we walked into Jacob's restaurant, Bro's Bistro. It was so cool to see how Jacob turned his life around. When we were younger, we used to smoke weed and joke about how we both wanted to be chefs and own restaurants. It was cool to see his dream live in action.

"Well, I'll be damned! Look what the cat dragged in," Jacob exclaimed from behind the large bar. "Logan Silverstone. I didn't ever think I'd see you back in these parts of town." His hair was buzzed short, and he had that same big goofy smile that he always showcased in the past.

I smiled. "It's been a long time, man, that's for sure."

"You look good," he said, hurrying over to me, giving me a bear hug. "Healthy."

"Trying man. Trying. This place is amazing, Jacob."

"Yeah, yeah. It's still early," he said. "I'll get a bit of a rush closer to seven or eight. And tomorrow is open mic night, where you'll find your brother performing."

I cocked an eyebrow. "Seriously? I haven't heard you play the guitar and sing in a long-ass time, Kellan."

"Yeah. I'm trying to go back to the things I love, ya know? Life is too short to not do what makes you happy."

"That's the truth. This place is real cool, though, Jacob. It's not every day that someone has a dream and makes it come true," I said as he walked me through the whole place, showing me everything. "You're doing it, though. You're living your dream."

"Trying to," he said and laughed. "Turns out running your own restaurant is really fucking hard."

"Just thinking about it is tiring."

"Rumor has it you got your culinary degree while you've been in Iowa?" he asked, leading Kellan and I to the bar.

"I did indeed. I didn't think I could, but..." *Alyssa always knew.* "But I did it."

He smiled wide. "Shit. That's awesome, man. Who would've thought two fucked-up kids like us would've made it to college? What can I get you two? Beer? Girly martinis?" Jacob asked, wiping down the bar.

"I'll have a water," Kellan said.

I laughed. "Still the wild party animal that I knew you to be, brother. I'll have a water, too," I told Jacob.

Kellan arched a brow. "I see you're just as wild and crazy as I am."

Jacob grabbed the drinks and set them in front of us before he placed his elbows on the countertop. He clasped his fingers together, resting his head on his fists. "So Iowa, huh? What the hell is there to do in Iowa?"

"Absolutely what you think there would be to do. Nothing. Work, sleep, women, and weed. Wash, rinse, repeat."

Kellan grimaced at the mention of weed the same way Alyssa did.

"Give me a break, Kellan. I'm not using anything else. Just a little pot here and there. It's California sober."

"I just don't want you to slip up, that's all."

"I haven't in years. I'm good." I cleared my throat. "By the way, thanks for helping me with last month's rent. And the month before that…" My words faded off into a whisper. "And the month before that…" Even though I had a degree, finding a real job had been quite the struggle.

"Anytime," he said, knowing I was changing the subject, but he allowed it. "But let's make sure we never mention that to Erika, all right?"

Jacob laughed. "That must be weird, Kellan."

"What's that?" he asked.

"Having your balls gripped that tight by a woman."

I snickered. "I'm surprised that he still has any balls."

"Fuck you guys. So Erika is a bit of a…" Kellan scrunched up his nose, looking for the right word.

"Control freak?" Jacob offered.

"Pushy?" I said.

"Dramatic?"

"Extremely dramatic?!"

"Mothering?"

"Belittling?" I joked.

"Stable," Kellan said, drinking his water. "Erika is stable. She's everything that keeps me grounded. She's a handful, yeah, but I would choose her hand to hold any day because she's strong. She's my anchor."

Jacob and I went silent, a bit stunned.

"Wow." Jacob breathed out a heavy sigh. "That's just…" His eyes watered up. "That's just so fucking cheesy."

I laughed. "The ultimate cheese."

"It's like gouda and brie had a baby and Kellan popped out." Jacob smirked.

"Screw off. I wouldn't expect two single dumbasses to understand anything about relationships," Kellan said. "So you like the place?"

"Like it? It's amazing. I bet the food tastes just as good as it looks here. If I lived here, I'd be in this place every day."

A wicked grin found its way to Kellan's face, and it wasn't long before Jacob's face had the same look of pleasure. "It's funny you should mention that, because Jacob and I were talking… If you were to stay in town, you'd have a built-in job. He's looking for a chef," Kellan offered.

"It pays well. I mean, the head boss man is a total dick, but it's a good job," Jacob added.

I laughed, because it was a ridiculous idea. I stopped laughing when I saw how serious they both were. "No offense, Kellan, but seeing how there's no wedding happening any time soon, I'm on the first train back to Iowa."

"Yeah? Can you afford a train ticket back?" Kellan asked me.

I cocked an eyebrow. "What? You said you would cover the ticket."

"Not true. I told you I'd get your ticket out here. I didn't say anything about sending you back."

"Fuck off," I huffed once. I turned to face my brother, confusion in my stare. "You're serious, aren't you?" I glanced at Jacob. "He's freaking serious, isn't he?"

"I'm just saying, brother. This is your home. And you're always welcome home."

"You're holding me hostage," I replied, bewildered.

"We're offering you a job," he replied. "Listen, if you really want a one-way ticket back to Iowa, I'll buy it in the morning. But the offer is always there for you."

Kellan was really pushing the idea of me staying, and for the life of me, I couldn't understand why. True Falls wasn't a place I considered home anymore. It was just the past demons of my life.

"I'll take the one-way ticket. No offense, Kellan. I love you, I do. But this town? I can't stay here and stay sane. I just can't."

He nodded in understanding. "I get it. Just thought I'd offer."

I thanked him.

"So you ran into Alyssa earlier? What's your plan of attack if that happens again?" Kellan asked.

"I'm going to ignore her and push her away. She and I can't go backward. I can't go down that road anymore, and she is definitely better off without me. But," I said, changing the subject, "it's good to see that you got clean, Jacob."

He nodded. "It wasn't that long after you left town, actually. One day, I woke up and just couldn't do it anymore. I didn't go to rehab, but I did the church thing for a while, which helped. I haven't been to church in years now, but it did affect me enough that I became an ordained minister."

I chuckled. "No way."

He smirked, pointing his thumbs at his chest. "If you're ever looking to get married, keep this handsome dude in mind." Out of nowhere, Jacob leaned forward with the most solemn expression I'd ever seen him have before. "Logan, on a serious note, I do have to ask you something really important…"

I sighed, knowing I couldn't avoid the questions that a lot of people probably had for me. The same kinds of questions Sadie shot my way at the motel. *How was rehab? Have you slipped up? Do you still think about using?* "Yeah, Jacob?"

"How the everlasting fuck do you keep your hair so perfect? It's shinier than anything I've ever seen. And that volume! Shit. I have a damn receding hairline and had to buzz cut it just to look half-decent."

"Oh my God," Kellan moaned, rolling his eyes. "Don't get him started on his hair."

"I told you, Kel, that envy is a sin." I snickered. "Once a month, deep condition with egg yolks and avocados."

"For real?"

"For real. But when you wash it out after forty-five minutes, don't use hot water. Otherwise, you'll have scrambled eggs in your hair and you'll be picking the pieces out for a week. Plus, the splash of cold water is good for your hair follicles, helping them grow in healthier and stronger. I can make you a list of all the products I use if you want."

"No shit? You'll do that?"

"Sure, no biggie."

"I can't believe this conversation is seriously happening right now," Kellan sighed, rolling his eyes so hard I thought they'd get stuck in the back of his head. He might've had a better life than I did growing up, but the joke was on him nowadays, because at least my hair was fucking amazing while his was ceasing to exist.

We stayed at the restaurant for a while longer, not talking about the past, not talking about the future, but just enjoying the current moment.

"I hate to break this reunion up, but we better get back to help Erika set up for the dinner," Kellan said.

I stood up from the booth and held my hand out toward Jacob, and he gripped my hold. "Good to see you, Jacob."

"You too, Logan. You look good. Really good, man."

"You too. And, um, I never was able to say this, but I'm sorry about what I said so long ago. About your porn addiction and the fork comment."

He laughed. "I forgive you, buddy. Even though it wasn't a fork, it was a chilled spoon. And hey! Don't forget to get me that list of hair products!"

I didn't know if that made it more normal or more awkward, but either way, it was good to be around a familiar face.

CHAPTER 20
Logan

"Y ou guys are late!" Erika whined as we walked into the house—which looked completely different than when we left. Everything was moved around: the dining room table, the sofas, the television. I felt as if I'd walked into the twilight zone. "Mom will be here soon."

"I'm going to go shower before dinner," I said.

"Good. I left a set of towels and extra items that you might need in the guest room." Erika gestured her head to the back room. "Now, Kellan, come taste the mashed potatoes I made."

"Wait, time out. Erika is cooking dinner?" I asked, fear in my throat. I felt another stab in my side from Kellan, but I couldn't hold this one in. "Last time I ate food that she made, the chicken was still clucking, Kellan!"

"Dude. Just…go shower."

As I walked away into my room, I snickered hearing Erika say she'd work really hard on not killing me. Sitting on the bed was a box containing clean towels, a toothbrush, floss, Q-tips, safety pins, body wash, deodorant, and everything else a person might need.

I knew she hadn't gone to the store, so she legit just had this stuff lying around. Sometimes being a bit crazy came in handy.

The shower water ran over me nice and hot. I shampooed and conditioned my hair as my mind tried to replay each and every moment of running into Alyssa. Her smells, her touches, her smiles, her frowns.

The idea of staying in town solely for the purpose of maybe running into her crossed my mind. But a lot could change in five years, especially after all the missed calls I received from her.

I should've called her back. I should've answered the phone.

After a few minutes, I was snapped back from my thoughts when I heard knocking at the front door. I shut off the shower, toweled off, and tossed on a pair of jeans and a white T-shirt.

"Was someone smoking in here?" Erika's mom, Lauren, asked loudly, her voice traveling down the halls.

"What? No. Come on in, Mom."

"It smells like smoke," Lauren said, her voice filled with disappointment.

In the other room, Lauren muttered, shocked once she heard about my return to town. I took a deep breath and snapped the band on my wrist. *It doesn't matter what people think of me. I'm not the same person I was when I left.* Their opinions didn't define me.

It was all mumbo jumbo that Dr. Khan told me when I was in the rehab clinic, but in that moment, that mumbo jumbo gave me the strength to exit the bathroom and face more individuals from my past.

"Is he still on drugs?" Lauren wondered out loud as I turned the corner.

"Not today," I replied, putting on a bright, fake smile. *Fake it till you make it, Lo. Just one dinner and then you're on a train back to Iowa.*

"Lauren, it's good to see you." I extended my hand to her for a shake, but she refused it, pulling her purse closer to her side.

"I thought it was just going to be us for dinner," Lauren said, her voice heightened with annoyance. "And I thought we were going to a restaurant to eat?" Lauren frowned a lot more than she smiled, and even though she had Alyssa's eyes, she didn't have her kind spirit.

"We just thought it would be better to have a small dinner without all the noise of the restaurant. Come on in. There's already wine bottles open on the table, and Erika cooked up a great meal," Kellan replied with a big smile. I wondered if his grin was as fake as mine.

Before we could sit down to eat, there was another knock at the door. When Erika opened it, my gut tightened seeing Alyssa standing there, holding two bottles of wine.

Whenever she entered a room, my mind melted a little. *Keep the wall up, Logan.*

"Do you still have room for one more?" she asked, smiling.

"Yeah, definitely, we can make room," Erika said, rushing to make another place setting.

Lauren huffed. "It's extremely rude to just show up to someone's house and ask for an extra seat at the dinner table."

"It's good to see you too, Mom," Alyssa sassed.

My stare stayed on Alyssa, and her eyes found mine. She gave me a small smile, and I had to break the stare before I got lost in my mind. Being back here, being near her, was so much harder than anything I'd ever had to do.

And I'd done a ton of hard shit.

We all sat down to eat, my seat right next to Lauren's, who seemed more nervous than not. Kellan poured everyone wine. I was quick to lift my glass and take a big gulp.

"Should you be drinking?" Lauren asked.

"No, probably not," I said, finishing my first glass and pouring another. We all started eating Erika's disgusting food, which I had to chew five times more than normal just to swallow down, but I didn't complain.

"How are they treating you at the law firm, Kellan?" Lauren asked. The girls' mom was a lawyer, and one of her favorite things about Kellan was that he studied law and found a successful job where he made good money and hated his soul.

Kellan cleared his throat, wiping his mouth with a napkin. "I actually quit over a month ago."

I cocked an eyebrow, shocked. "No shit?"

"What?" Lauren asked, surprised. She turned to Erika. "You didn't tell me that. Why didn't you tell me that?"

"It didn't really seem my place, Mom."

"But why? Why did you quit?" she questioned.

"It wasn't a part of my heart, I guess," Kellan said, squeezing Erika's hand. They smiled at each other, and for a moment, I saw it—the love that Kellan said he always felt. Those two really did care for each other. "Leaving the firm gives me a chance to pursue my other passions."

"Like what?" Lauren asked.

"My music. Playing my guitar."

"That's a hobby, not a job." Lauren frowned. She was one negative Nancy.

"Mom. You do know that I work at a piano bar for a living, right?" Alyssa mentioned.

"Oh, honey." Lauren frowned. "You work at a diner and a furniture store and play a piano in dirty bars at night. That's not really something you want to be broadcasting to the world as some kind of accomplishment."

Still a bitch, I see.

"I think music is really important," Kellan said, chiming in. "It's fun. The gigs I've been getting pay good money too. It's something I love. And life is too short to not do what you love."

"Hear, hear!" I mocked, drinking more wine. "That's why I drink so much wine," I smirked, winking at Lauren, loving how uncomfortable I made her.

"You'll see the show tomorrow. My friend's having me play at his restaurant."

"What? You said we were going to the theater tomorrow," Lauren said, turning to Erika.

"No…I said we were going to a show," her daughter replied. The two were so much alike it was almost impossible to see how Alyssa fit into that equation.

"No worries, really. It will all be fun. Plus, after the show, we can swing by the reception hall for the wedding next month," Kellan explained.

"What?" Lauren questioned.

Erika started coughing harshly, trying to clear her throat. "Anyone want more wine?"

"What do you mean the wedding is next month?"

"You didn't tell her?" Kellan asked, frowning at his fiancée.

"Tell me what?" Lauren asked.

"I forgot," Erika replied.

Wow. I felt like I was watching a bad sitcom unfold in front of me.

"We moved the wedding up to next month. But don't worry! You don't have to do anything but show up."

"No. The wedding is next year. I thought we were waiting until you finished your master's degree, Erika. Plus, I'm the one paying for the wedding. Didn't you think I had a right to know this? We already made down payments on the reception hall! And now you're saying you found a new location?"

"We'll pay you back the down payment. It was a last-minute change."

"Last-minute change? Give me a reason. One good reason why we have to rush this. There are so many things to figure out. Flowers, cake, the food. Dresses, invitations, everything. There isn't enough time." Lauren kept whining.

"We don't need all that stuff, Mom. We are just going to keep it simple."

Every now and then, I'd catch Alyssa staring my way, and she'd look away quickly. Every now and then, she'd catch me staring her way, and I'd look away quickly. I hardly wanted to pay attention to the conversation happening at the table. I was much more interested in watching Alyssa and me try to avoid each other.

"You've been planning your dream wedding since you were five, Erika Rose. And now you just don't care about those details? No. We had a plan. We are sticking to the plan. Plus, Kellan doesn't even have a job right now!"

"He has a gig tonight." I jumped into the conversation with a smirk. Alyssa laughed. I died from the sound. Why did she have to be so beautiful? I was really hoping I'd come back to town and she'd look and smell like a skunk.

No luck there.

"I just don't understand the rush. You should hold off until next year like we had planned," her mom offered. "We should stick to the plan."

"Plans change, Mom. It's fine."

"Tell me why. Why now? This is such a radical change. Don't you think you should be more focused on the fact that Kellan is unemployed? How are you even going to make ends meet for this house? Huh? Have you thought about any of this? The property taxes on a home this size in this neighborhood have to be high. I told you both not to buy a place this big, but you wouldn't listen. What's the plan?" Her mom kept asking her again and again.

I felt bad for Erika. Her face was red and her nerves were rocked.

"I love him! I love him, Mom. What does it matter if we get married today or years from now? I want to be with him."

"It's not logical. You're sounding very much like your sister, Erika."

Alyssa blew a small breath from her lips. "I'm right here, Mom."

"Well, it's true. You were always the wild flame that I couldn't extinguish. You were all over the place. You still are, Alyssa. But, Erika, you're the tame one. You're the one with a good head on your shoulders. But now you're acting as if you have no sense."

I watched Alyssa's eyes water, but she bit her tongue. I went to snap at Lauren for talking about her in such a way, but I paused when I saw Alyssa slightly shake her head at me not to.

What did I care anyway? It wasn't my job to fight her battles.

Erika opened her mouth to speak, but Kellan's words came out first, silencing the room. "I have cancer."

Wait.

What?

No.

My heart dropped into my stomach, and I felt acid climbing up my throat as he kept talking.

"We've been dealing with this news for a while, unsure how to handle telling you all. I already had surgery to remove a tumor, and I'll be starting my first chemo treatment soon, but—"

"I'm sorry. Slow down. Back up. What?" I interrupted him. My blood was boiling, and I felt myself on the verge of a breakdown. My fingers dug into the sides of my chair as my body started to shake. What the hell was he talking about? Kellan didn't have cancer. Kellan was healthy. He was always healthy. He was the only one in our family who wasn't a mess. He couldn't be sick. "Are you fucking kidding me?"

No.

No.

Alyssa's eyes looked saddened by the news, and she almost reached out to take my hand, but I shook my head. Kellan went to speak, but I stood up, uninterested in him explaining. I didn't want him to say any fucking thing else, because his words were currently toxic, and they were poisoning my soul. I needed air. Lots of air.

I headed for the patio door and stepped outside. The cool air rushed at my steaming face, and I let out a pained breath. My hands gripped the railing as I stared out into the darkened sky, taking deep breaths, trying my best to not fall apart.

I shut my eyes and snapped the band on my wrist once.

It's not real...

I couldn't open my eyes.

He was fine. He was healthy.

I snapped the band on my wrist twice.

It's not real. It's not real...

The sliding door opened to the balcony, and I listened to the footsteps grow closer. Kellan leaned against the railing beside me.

"You set me up," I said.

"I didn't want to tell you like that. I didn't know how to tell you."

"What kind?"

"Colon."

Shit.

"I…" My voice started but then it trailed off. I felt like I should say something, yet I didn't know what the right words were. Were there any right words in a situation like this one?

My fingers gripped the railing tighter. "We have to go see TJ. I won't believe it until he tells me straight to my face." TJ was the doctor that both Kellan and I always went to as kids. He was a good friend of Kellan's father, so even though I hadn't had any money or health insurance to go to a doctor's office, TJ always checked me out for free. He was a weird guy but a good man and the only doctor I'd trust to tell me the truth about my brother's diagnosis.

"Logan." Kellan's voice softened. "I've already spoken with TJ. Besides, he's not an oncologist."

"I trust him," I said through clenched teeth. "I trust him, Kellan. And only him."

He rubbed the back of his neck. "Okay. We'll go see TJ tomorrow if it will make you feel better."

"It will." I cleared my throat. "Until then, tell me everything you know. What stage are you in? It's curable, right? How do we get rid of it? What can I do? How do I help? How do we fix this?" *How do I fix you?*

"It's stage three."

No. That's not good.

"But for now, we wait. Like I said, I had the surgery to remove the tumor and two lymph nodes. We start chemotherapy in a week, and we have to give it time to see if it works. The chemo will help stop any potential cells that may have spread elsewhere in my system."

"What happens if they spread elsewhere?"

He went quiet.

No.

No.

No.

I bit my tongue. "You should've told me."

"I know."

We turned around to face the house. Erika screamed at her mother as she yelled back at her. Alyssa tried her best to neutralize the situation but had no luck whatsoever.

"You can't marry a person who has cancer, Erika. It makes no sense! You're thinking with your heart instead of your head."

What a fucking awful thing to say to a person.

"God. Their mom is insane. I forgot how insane she is. She actually makes Erika seem…normal?"

"She's a tough one, that's for sure." Kellan dropped his head a little and stared at his shoes. "She's not completely wrong, though."

"What?"

"Erika's in this panic mode. She's rushing to marry me, just in case something happens. Just in case things go wrong. Don't get me wrong, I want to be her husband but…" His words faded off, and he looked back up into his home, which seemed like it was seconds away from exploding.

I wanted to dive deeper into his thoughts on marrying Erika, but I could tell by his body language that he wasn't in the mood.

The conversation going on inside the house must've hit its boiling point, because Lauren went storming off. Erika quickly started clearing the dining room table, breaking plates in the sink, and rearranging chairs while Alyssa stood back watching.

"Uh, should we go help her?" I asked.

He shook his head. "It's part of her process. Just let it happen."

I snapped my band once more. Or twice. Maybe fifteen times.

"You know what's crazy? I smoke and you get cancer."

"What's yours is mine…"

"And what's mine is yours," I replied.

"If it makes you feel better, you can't get colon cancer from smoking. But you should stop smoking."

I huffed at his parenting voice.

But he wasn't wrong.

"Grandpa had colon cancer," I said, my voice cracking. It was what ended his life.

"Yeah." Kellan nodded. "I know."

The only person in my life who loved me like my brother did was my grandfather. Watching his life be sucked away from him was the hardest thing I'd ever had to witness. What was even worse was how fast it happened. One day he was there, and a few months later, he wasn't. I didn't even have a chance to say goodbye, because he lived so far away.

"Listen. Maybe I should move back here for a while. I really had nothing going on back in Iowa."

"Yeah?" he asked, sniffling his nose, placing his hands on the back of his head.

"Yeah. No big deal. I might even go see Ma soon. See how she's been doing."

"It's not good," he said. "I was going to go grab her food stamps card and take her some groceries later this week."

"I can pick it up tomorrow."

He cringed. "I don't know if that's a good idea, Logan. You know… with you being clean and all. Plus, with what you just found out. I don't want you falling back into that world."

"It's fine," I assured him. "I can handle it."

"Are you sure?"

I laughed and shoved him. "Dude. You're the one with cancer, and you're sitting here worrying about me. Stop. You've taken care of Ma and me our whole lives. It's my turn, okay?" When the word *cancer* fell from my lips, I felt like dying.

"Okay," he sighed, crossing his arms. "I have a few things to do tomorrow after we go see TJ, but Erika can drive you."

"She'll do that?"

"If I ask, yeah. But don't be surprised if you have to make a few stops beforehand."

I shrugged my left shoulder.

He shrugged his right.

We watched Erika destroy the house before she put it together again, and I wondered the whole time if I was really strong enough to face my past. I didn't know how it would feel, coming face-to-face with Ma.

I didn't know how strong I was.

CHAPTER 21
Alyssa

L ogan?" I whispered, knocking on his bedroom door. He'd been in his room for the past thirty minutes, and I could only imagine where his mind was traveling to after finding out about Kellan's cancer. I listened to him moving around the room before the door opened. He sniffled a little and ran his hand over his face before narrowing his eyes at me.

"Yeah?"

His eyes were red and slightly puffy. I wanted to reach out to him and wrap my arms around him, pulling him in closer to me, apologizing for his hurts and suffering.

You were crying.

"I just wanted to check in and see how you were doing," I said softly.

"I'm fine."

I stepped into the doorway a little, growing closer to him, knowing he was far from fine. Kellan was Logan's world. When he left for Iowa, he only kept in contact with his brother. When he ignored all my calls, he answered every single one of Kellan's.

"You're not okay."

"I am," he said and nodded, a cold stare in his eyes. "I'm fine. I'm not gonna fall apart and shit, Alyssa. People get cancer every day. And people beat cancer every day. He's fine. I'm fine. Everything's fine."

Any normal person would've missed it, the small tremble in his bottom lip, but not me. I saw it, the way his heart was currently inflamed with pain. "Lo, come on. It's me. You can talk to me."

"And who are you to me, exactly?" he snapped, a bitterness coming through his tone. "How long did you know? How long did you know he was sick?"

My lips parted, but he kept talking.

"So you did know? One thousand and ninety messages, Alyssa. You left me one thousand and ninety messages. You called my phone one thousand and ninety times, but you couldn't take the time to call and leave just one message telling me my brother had cancer, the same cancer that killed our grandfather?" he snapped, lifting his hand and grabbing his doorknob. He slammed the door shut, and I wasn't surprised.

Everything he said was harsh, but it wasn't untrue. I did know about Kellan's cancer for a while, but it wasn't my place to say anything. Kellan made me swear that I wouldn't.

My fingers landed against the door, and I closed my eyes. "I live at the last house on the corner of Cherry Street and Wicker Avenue. It's a yellow house with a piano-shaped flower pot on the front porch. You can stop by if you need to, Logan. If you need to talk to someone. You can come whenever, anytime you need to."

The door swung open, and I gasped lightly as he stepped forward, hovering over me. His face was hard, and where reddened eyes once existed moments ago, they were replaced by an angered stare. "What don't you fucking get?"

He stepped toward me as I stepped back. We kept this up until my back was against the hallway wall, and his body was inches away from mine. Our mouths were so close that if I leaned in, I could've felt the lips I used to always want against mine.

His words fell from his tongue, stabbing me with each syllable. "I don't need you, Alyssa. I. Don't. Need. You. So if you could do me a favor and stop acting like we are friends, that would be great. Because we aren't. We will never be friends again. I don't need you. And I don't need your fucking supportive shoulder."

He walked back to his room and shut the door.

I took a few deep inhales, my nerves shaken. My heart didn't stop pounding destructively against my chest as I walked to the living room to grab my jacket and toss on my tennis shoes.

Who was that?

That wasn't the same boy I knew so many years ago. He wasn't my best friend.

He felt like a complete stranger to me.

"Are you okay?" Erika asked, frowning my way.

I shrugged my shoulders. "Can you just be a bit easy on him, Erika?"

"Seriously?" she huffed, annoyed. "He just snapped at you, literally snapped. And you are asking me to be easy on him? I am two seconds away from telling him to get the heck out of my house."

"No," I quickly said, shaking my head. "No. Don't. He's going through a lot. I mean, I couldn't even imagine… If it were you…" My words faded. I wasn't sure how I'd handle finding out that my sister had cancer. "Just give him a break."

Her posture eased up. "Okay." She gave me a hug and whispered, "It's okay for you to keep your distance from him, Aly. You know that, right? I know seeing him again has to be hurting you."

"It's fine." I shifted my feet around and shrugged. "I'm fine with it."

"Yeah, but it might just be better to keep a safe distance. For both of your hearts."

I agreed. Besides, I didn't see him finding his way to me anytime soon.

CHAPTER 22
Logan

My back stayed against the bedroom door until I heard Alyssa leave. Pushing her away was going to be tough with me staying around town, because such a big part of me always wanted to pull her closer to me.

I sat in my bedroom on my cell phone, with my web browser opened, searching for information about colon cancer. My eyes danced across page after page of information, filling me up with more panic than I thought I could handle. For a while, I read story after story of survivors, but then somehow I traveled into the dark world of the internet where the stories of those who passed away quickly from colon cancer existed.

I found natural remedies. I found common lies. My eyes stayed open until the sun came up, sending the light through my window.

As my eyes grew as heavy as my heart, I shut off my phone.

The only thing I learned that night was that WebMD was the devil, and Kellan probably wouldn't make it through the night.

I pulled out a cigarette and lit it with my lighter. I opened the window, set the cigarette on the ledge, and allowed myself those few moments to hurt.

CHAPTER 23
Logan

Dr. James Petterson's office was cold. Colder than it needed to be. Sure, outside it was probably near the nineties—which was hot for Wisconsin weather—but there was no need for it to be an ice cube in his room. James—or Toothpick Jimmy, or TJ, as everyone around town called him because of his tall skinny body—was the only doctor I'd ever known and trusted. He didn't seem like a normal doctor, though. Half the time, I wondered if TJ was even a real doctor or if he got bored one Saturday night, bought a stethoscope, put on a white coat, and never took it off. He lived in the apartment right above his office too.

His office even looked like it was a fake doctor's office. On the mantel behind his desk was a huge deer head that he swore he shot down with his eyes closed years ago. Beside the deer head was what was supposed to be a black bear's fur, but really it was just a rug he probably found from Walmart on clearance. He pushed the story of how he killed the bear with a beer can in his right hand and a shotgun in his left.

On the corner of his desk, TJ had a jar of jelly beans along with black licorice sitting on the right side. It blew my mind that a doctor was pushing candy into the faces of his patients so much, but for TJ it made sense, seeing as how his wife, Effie, was one of the town's few dentists and she was always looking for new patients.

TJ and his wife should've used more common sense when picking out the candy, though, because nobody in their right mind ate black licorice.

I crossed my arms, pressing them against my body for heat. *Shit*. I was freezing. My eyes moved to the chair right beside me where Kellan sat.

When I looked up to TJ, I saw his lips were still moving pretty quickly. He kept explaining the situation over and over again. At least that was what I thought he was doing. I couldn't be certain, though, because I wasn't listening anymore.

I didn't know the exact moment when I stopped hearing the words flying from his tongue, but for the past five or ten minutes, I was simply watching his mouth move, meaningless sounds flowing from his lips.

My hands gripped the sides of my chair, and I held on tight.

The shock was the worst part, not knowing if I should laugh or cry at the diagnosis. Not knowing if I should get pissed and punch a wall. Not knowing how long I had left with my brother. The overwhelming feeling of isolation took my breaths. The panicked heartbeats that rolled through my system were terrifying yet not unfamiliar. The fear and anger made each moment unbearable.

"Logan," TJ said, pulling me back into the conversation. "This isn't the end for your brother. He's working with the best doctors in the state. He's getting the best treatment out there."

Kellan brushed his fingers against his neck and nodded his head. "This isn't the end for me, Logan. It's just a hiccup." His head nodding paired with his word choice confused me. If it wasn't the end, wouldn't he shake his head instead of nodding?

My right hand brushed against my cheek, and I cleared my throat. "We need a second opinion." I started pacing the small patio porch, and my hands raced through my hair. "And then we want a third opinion. And a fourth."

That was what people did, right? Searched for an answer that was more pleasant? More promising?

We needed a better answer.

"Logan…" TJ grimaced. "Getting second opinions will only slow us down. We are already attacking this head-on, and we are hopeful—"

It happened again. I stopped listening.

The rest of the meeting continued, but I didn't say another word. There wasn't anything to say anymore.

Kellan and I drove in silence the whole way back to his house, and my mind wouldn't shut up, replaying the word *cancer* over and over again.

My brother, my hero, my best friend had cancer.

And I could no longer breathe.

When Kellan told me that Erika wanted to stop somewhere before she dropped me off at Ma's, I wouldn't have imagined us sitting in aisle five of a store for over twenty minutes. It had been a full day since Logan told me the news about his health, and I only thought about using drugs every minute to cope—which was better than every second. Erika had a different kind of addiction that helped her cope with stress, though, called Pottery Barn.

"How long are we going to be here?" I asked Erika as we stood in front of a display of overpriced plates. We'd been standing there for at least twenty minutes as she contemplated which new sets of plates to pick up, seeing as how she broke pretty much all the china in their house.

"Will you hush?" she ordered, her arms crossed, her eyes narrowed, and her mind obviously still completely insane. "This takes time."

"Not really." I gestured toward a set. "Look. Plates. Oh, look, more plates. Gee, what do we have here, Erika? Why, I think it's plates."

"Why do you have to be so difficult all the time? I was really hoping over these five years that you would've grown up a bit."

"Sorry to disappoint. But seriously, can we get going?"

She gave me an annoyed look. "Why are you in such a rush to go see your mother anyway? You've been gone five years, leaving Kellan to handle everything. He had to be there when she fell apart, and you didn't even check in on her. You never called her or anything, so why now?"

"Because my brother has cancer, my mother's an addict, and I feel like a shit son and brother for leaving and never coming back. Is that what you want to hear, Erika? I get it, I'm a fuckup. But if you could honestly just take two seconds to stop throwing it in my face, that would be really freaking nice."

She huffed once, rocking back and forth in her heels. Her stare turned from me to the plates before us, and we went back to our silence.

Five minutes. Ten minutes. Fifteen fucking minutes.

"That one," she said and nodded, pointing in front of her. "I'll take that one. Grab two sets, Logan." Turning on her heels, she headed off in the direction of the cashier, leaving me flabbergasted.

"Why am I getting two sets?!" I shouted.

She didn't bother to answer me. She just hurried off.

Juggling the two sets in my arms, I staggered to the front of the shop, setting the boxes down in front of the cashier. Erika and I remained quiet until the cashier told us the final price of the plates.

"One hundred and eight dollars and twenty-three cents."

"You have got to be shitting me," I choked out. "You're going to pay over one hundred bucks for plates?"

"It's none of your business what I do with my money."

"Yeah, but come on, Erika. You could easily buy some cheap plates from a dollar store or something, seeing how you'll probably break them tomorrow anyway."

"I don't question what Kellan spends his money on, or should I say *who* he spends it on. So I'd rather you not question my spending choices."

"You knew Kellan was giving me money?"

"Of course I knew, Logan. If there's one thing Kellan is, it's a bad liar. I don't care that he's giving you the money but…" She sighed, and her eyes softened as she turned my way. For the first time since I returned, she looked defeated. "Don't let him down, Logan. He's tired. He won't act like he is, but he is. He's exhausted. You being back here makes him happy. You're good for him right now. Just stay good, okay? Please don't let him down."

"I swear I'm not using, Erika. That's not just some bullshit that I've been saying. I really am clean."

We each grabbed a box and walked to her car, putting them in the trunk before we hopped into the car and she started driving to Ma's apartment.

She nodded. "I believe you. But we are about to go see your mom, and I know how much a trigger she was for you."

"I'm not the same kid I was."

"Yeah. I hear you. But trust me. Your mom is the same person she was back then. Sometimes I think people don't really change."

"They do," I said. "If they're given a chance, people can change."

She swallowed hard. "I hope you're right."

The moment we made it to Ma's, I asked Erika if she was coming up, and she declined, looking around. "I'll stay here."

"It's safer inside."

"No. It's fine. I don't do too good seeing…that kind of lifestyle."

I didn't blame her. "I'll be down in a few." My eyes darted around the darkened streets, and I saw a few people hanging out on the street corners, just like when I was a kid. Maybe Erika was somewhat right. Maybe some people, things, and places never changed.

But I had to hope that some did.

Otherwise, what exactly was I doing with myself?

"Just don't take forever, okay? Kellan's show is starting in forty-five minutes," Erika said.

"I guess we shouldn't have spent like two hours standing in front of plates, huh?"

She flipped me off. A term of endearment, I bet.

"I'll be out fast. Are you okay out here?"

"I'm fine. Just hurry."

"Hey, Erika?" I said, climbing out of the car.

"Yeah?"

My eyes once again glanced to the people on the corners, looking our way. "Lock your doors."

I didn't know what I was walking into. I knew it would be bad, but I

guess I didn't know how bad off Ma was. Kellan always kept those conversations short, telling me that I had to worry about making myself
better instead of worrying about making sure Ma was good.

Now it was his turn to take his own advice.

But that meant that someone had to step up and check in on her,
and it had to be me. And I couldn't let Kellan down when he needed
me the most.

The front door was unlocked, which worried me enough to make
my gut tighten. The apartment was completely trashed with beer cans,
vodka bottles, empty pill bottles, and dirty clothes all over the place.

"Jesus, Ma…" I murmured to myself, somewhat shocked.

The same broken-down couch sat in front of the same disgusting
coffee table. I'd be lying if I said I didn't spot the baggie of coke on the table.

I snapped my bracelet.

Just breathe.

"Get off!" I heard screamed from the kitchen, Ma's voice loud
and fearful.

My heart dropped to my stomach, and I was back in hell. I hurried
into the room, ready to tear my father away from her, knowing that
whenever she screamed, his fists were finding their way to her soul.

But when I stepped into the room, she was alone, having a panic
attack. She aggressively scratched at her skin, causing it to turn red.
"Get off me! Get off me!" she hollered louder and louder.

I held my hands up and walked in her direction. "Ma. What are
you doing?"

"They're all over me!" she screamed.

"What's all over you?"

"The roaches! They are everywhere! The roaches are all over me.
Help me, Kellan! Get this shit off me!"

"It's me, Ma. Logan."

Her dull eyes looked up in my direction, and for a split second, she reminded me of Sober Ma.

Then she began to scratch again.

"All right, all right. Come on. Let's get you a shower. Okay?"

After a little work, I got her to sit inside the bathtub as the shower rained over her. She kept scrubbing her skin as I sat on top of the closed toilet lid.

"Kellan told me you were going to cut back on using, Ma."

"Yeah." She nodded rapidly. "Definitely. Definitely. Kellan offered to send me off to rehab, but I don't know. I can do it on my own. Plus, that stuff costs a lot of money." She locked eyes with me and smiled, holding her hands out to me. "You came home. I knew you'd come home. Your father said you wouldn't, but I knew. He still sells to me sometimes." She looked down and started washing her feet.

The bruises on her back and legs almost made me gag. I knew they were from my deadbeat father. And the fact that I wasn't there to step in between the two of them made me feel as if I were just as bad a person as he was.

"Do you think I'm pretty?" she whispered. Tears were running down her cheeks, but I didn't even think she knew she was crying.

"You're beautiful, Ma."

"Your father called me an ugly bitch."

My hands formed fists, and I took a few deep breaths. "Screw him. You're better off without him."

"Yeah. Definitely. Definitely." She nodded rapidly again. "I just wish he loved me is all."

Why did we as humans always want love from the people who were incapable of such a feeling?

"Can you shampoo my hair?" she asked.

I agreed. I lightly touched the bruises against her skin, and she didn't seem to react at all. For a while, we sat and listened to the sound of the water. I wasn't sure how to communicate with her. I wasn't even sure if I wanted to, but the silence was too much to bear after some time. "I was going to run to the grocery store for you tomorrow, Ma. You want to get me your food card?"

She closed her eyes and clapped her hands together. "Shoot! Oh shit. I must've left it at my friend's apartment the other night. She lives right down the street from me. I can go get it," she said, trying to stand up, but I stopped her.

"You still have soap in your hair. Wash it out, towel off, and meet me in the living room. We'll figure out the food another day."

I stood up and left. When I hit the living room, my eyes fell to the baggie of cocaine on the table.

"Fuck…" I whispered, snapping my band.

Focus. This isn't your life. This isn't your story.

Dr. Khan said after I left rehab, moments would come up when I'd find myself seconds from stepping back on the hamster wheel of my past, but then she'd say that it wasn't my story anymore.

My hands were sweaty, and I took a seat on the couch. I didn't know when it happened, but somehow the baggie of cocaine was in my hands. I closed my eyes, taking in a few deep breaths. My chest was on fire, my mind wild. Being back in town was too much for me, but leaving Kellan wasn't an option.

How was I going to survive?

"Look, we are going to be late—" Erika came barging into the apartment and paused, seeing me with the cocaine in my grip.

I quickly glanced back and forth between the cocaine and Erika.

She sighed. "Figures." She turned on her heels and hurried out of the room.

Shit. With haste, I followed her, calling her name, but she ignored me the whole way to the car. Once we were inside, she revved up the engine and pulled away from the curb. A few minutes passed with no words exchanged.

"Listen, what you saw up there," I started, but she shook her head.

"Don't talk."

"Erika, it's not what you think."

"I can't do this, Logan. I can't. I can't be the one driving you around to go on these joyrides. I can't watch you disappoint your brother."

"I'm not using."

"You're lying."

Tossing my hands up in defeat, I released a weighted sigh. "I don't even remotely know how to talk to you."

"Then don't."

"Fine. I won't."

Erika's fingers were gripped tightly around the steering wheel, and I watched as her air freshener swung back and forth on her rearview mirror.

"He's sick, and he's trying to not show his worry about you or your mom, but he's terrified. I think we need to face reality, and the reality is I just saw you with drugs in your hand. The last thing Kellan needs is for you to stress him out more."

"What goes on in your head? You make up all these crazy stories and judge people for things that never happened. You are a lot like your messed-up mother, you know that?"

She pulled up to the restaurant and put the car into park. With a harsh tone, she turned to me and said, "And you are a carbon copy of yours."

CHAPTER 24

Logan

I am nothing like my mom!" I whisper-hissed, chasing Erika into Jacob's restaurant.

"I saw you!" she whisper-hissed back, poking me hard in my chest. "I saw you, Logan!"

"You think you saw something, but you didn't. I wasn't going to."

"Don't lie to me, you jerk! How could you?! You promised! You promised!"

Before I could reply, Kellan walked over. "What took you guys so long?" he asked.

Erika had her frown glued to her face but forced it to change direction when she saw the worry in her fiancé's eyes.

"I just had to make a stop on the way," she said, kissing his cheek. "But we are here! And I can't wait to watch you perform!"

Kellan's stare moved over to me, and his worried eyes remained. I slightly shrugged my shoulders, unable to ever truly lie to my brother.

His brows lowered with understanding. He nodded toward the

front door. "You want to go get some air with me, Lo? My set doesn't start for another fifteen minutes."

"Yeah, for sure," I replied. My hands were stuffed into my jeans pockets, still in fists from the way Erika spoke to me in the car minutes before. I couldn't even truly be mad at her about it, though. The person I was when I left town years ago was the only person she ever knew me to be. In her eyes, I was the drug-addicted asshole who screwed up their lives and broke her sister's heart when I never called back. In her eyes, I was the jerk who almost killed Kellan and Alyssa the night I was messed up and took the wheel into my hand. I was the person who was responsible for Alyssa losing our child. In Erika's eyes, I was Alyssa's and Kellan's baggage that they both deserved to unload.

In her eyes, I was the me that I'd tried so hard to never become again.

Kellan and I stepped outside, and the chill of the fall night hit our faces quickly. He leaned against the brick wall of the bar with his left foot resting against the stones and his eyes closed as his head tilted toward the sky. I reached into my pocket for a cigarette and paused.

Shit.

No smoking.

I leaned against the wall beside him. "How are you holding up?" I asked, pulling out my lighter and flicking it on and off.

"Honestly?"

"Yeah."

He opened his eyes, and I saw his fight to hold the tears back. "I was practicing the guitar, and my hand started to tremble. The other day, it happened too, and my hands wouldn't stop shaking. I think it's all in my head, because I'm afraid of the chemotherapy. I've read a lot online about chemo brain. That's where a person kind of loses some cognitive functions. So I might not even be able to play the guitar anymore. Or write lyrics. I mean…" He bit his bottom lip and inhaled deeply. My tough, always strong brother was slowly cracking. And I couldn't do anything about it. "I mean…music…that's me. That's my life. I spent so much time running away from it, though, and now if I can't play the guitar…"

"I'll play for you," I said and meant it.

He snickered. "You don't have a musical bone in your whole freaking body, Logan."

"I can learn. And hell, remember when you learned to cook after my dad broke my hand?"

"When I made the turkey for Thanksgiving that one year?"

I chuckled. "And you yelled, 'Who knew a damn turkey needed to be thawed for more than four hours?!' as you tried to cut into it."

"But seriously! Who knew that?"

"Um, everyone with a brain? I mean, to give you credit, I'd never seen a turkey that was completely burnt on the outside and completely raw inside. That takes talent. What did Ma say about it?" I asked, remembering the few good memories we'd shared.

We spoke in unison, "'What type of fuckery is this?! If you wanted to kill me, you could've used a butcher's knife. It would've been less painful than this damn turkey.'"

Kellan and I both laughed this time. It wasn't even that funny, but we were cracking up, laughing together so hard that our ribs started to ache, tears of memories running down my face.

When we stopped, a cold silence filled the space, but at least this silence wasn't lonely, because my brother was with me.

"How was she today?" Kellan asked about Ma.

"Not your concern, Kel. Seriously. I'm back, so I'll handle her. You have a lot of shit on your plate. It's my turn to help."

He tilted his head in my direction. "Yeah, but what about you? How are you holding up?"

I sighed.

I couldn't tell him how close I was to using.

I couldn't tell him how heartbroken I was to see Ma in the shape she was.

I couldn't fall apart when he needed me the most.

I had to be strong for him, because his whole life was spent being the person who saved me. I wasn't a hero, I wasn't a savior, but I was his brother—and I truly hoped that would be enough.

"I'm good, Kellan," I said. He didn't believe me. "I am, I promise." He knew it was a lie, but he didn't call me out on it.

"I'm really worried about Ma. And I'm not sure how to help her. And if I'm gone…" He paused his words as his inner demons and fears accidentally slipped from between his lips.

Pushing myself off the wall, I stood in front of him. "No. No. You don't get to say that kind of shit, okay? Look, you're here. You're getting the chemotherapy. It's going to work. Okay?"

His doubt was seen fully in his stare.

I lightly shoved him in his shoulder. "You're not dying, Kellan. Okay?"

His jaw trembled, and he slightly nodded. "Okay."

"No, say it like you mean it. You're not dying!" I said, heightening my voice.

"I'm not dying."

"Again!"

"I'm not dying!" he spoke into the cool air.

"Again!"

"I'm not fucking dying!" He shouted it the last time, his arms reaching out in victory, a smile on his lips.

I pulled him into a tight hug and held him close. I hid the tears that started to fall from my face and nodded my head slightly, whispering. "You're not dying."

We headed back inside the restaurant, and I watched him perform, his hands shakier than I wanted to admit, but his music was so much better than I'd ever heard. Erika stared up at him as if she was looking at forever in one guy's soul. She loved him. Which was enough reason for me to love her. Even if she hated my guts, such a big part of me loved her for loving him to her core.

"I have to get back to finish grading my papers," Erika said after Kellan finished his set. We all stood at the bar with drinks in our hands, laughing with Jacob and forgetting for a while about the reality of our days to come.

"I'll head out with you," Kellan told her. He reached into his pocket and tossed me his car keys. "You can drive my car back, Logan."

Those words might not have meant much to anyone else, but it meant he trusted me.

He'd always trusted me—even when I wasn't trustworthy.

"I'll meet you out at your car, Erika. I'm just going to grab my guitar." She nodded and left.

The moment she walked away, Kellan leaned in toward Jacob with the sincerest look in his eyes. "Hey man, I just wanted to let you know. If something happened to me…" He paused, turned my way, and smirked. "Which it won't, because I'm not dying. But if something did happen, I would be okay with you looking after Erika, ya know? I would be fine with that."

Jacob leaned forward, resting both of his elbows on the counter-top. "And this is the moment I tell you to piss off for even thinking something like that."

Kellan chuckled. "No, but really. You'll take care of her?"

"We aren't talking about this," Jacob replied.

"Yeah, Kel. Stop being dramatic," I agreed.

"Dude. I have cancer."

"Don't you fucking play the cancer card on me," Jacob snickered, throwing a rag at him. "I don't give a shit," he said jokingly.

"But promise me you'll take care of her?" Kellan asked one last time.

Jacob sighed, pinching the bridge of his nose. "Even though *nothing* is going to happen to you, if it will make you sleep better at night, Erika will be taken care of. I promise."

Kellan looked visibly lighter, his shoulders relaxing, and he nodded before heading out to join his fiancée.

As I tossed on my coat to leave, I called Jacob over to me. Leaning in close to him, I gripped his white T-shirt and locked eyes with him. "If I ever see you looking any kind of way at Erika, I swear to God I will rip your balls off and feed them to you."

He snorted laughing until he saw the stern look on my face. "Dude. Erika's like a sister to me. That's disgusting. Now, that Alyssa girl on the other hand…" He smirked and wriggled his eyebrows.

"You're a terrible person," I said dryly.

He laughed. "I'm kidding! Come on. That's funny. Trust me, the Walters girls are off-limits."

"Good. I just wanted to make sure we were on the same page."

"We are. Besides, Kellan's not dying."

I nodded in agreement.

Because Kellan wasn't dying.

CHAPTER 25
Logan

I stuffed my hands into my pockets and rocked back and forth on Alyssa's porch. I didn't know how I found myself standing there. I wasn't sure if she would even keep the door open once she noticed it was me.

But I had nowhere else to go. No one to turn to.

She opened the door, and my eyes danced across her body as she stood in a white tank top and tight blue jeans. When I met her eyes, I almost burst into tears because just being near her reminded me of what it felt like not to be alone.

Her arms crossed and she cocked a brow. "What do you want, Logan? Are you still looking to yell at me? To make me feel like crap? Because it's almost one in the morning, and I really don't want to hear it."

The strong stance she held almost made me laugh, but when I opened my mouth to release a chuckle, I choked on the air.

I saw her eyes soften. She stepped out onto the porch.

"What is it?" she asked, alert, the concern that was always in her words loud and clear.

My head shook back and forth. My stomach knotted. "He's…" I cleared my throat. I stuffed my hands deeper into my pockets. My stare fell down to the worn boards of her porch. "He's…"

"Lo. Talk to me." She placed a comforting hand against my chest, over my heart. And without thought, my heart began to speed up from her touch. "What's wrong?"

My body started to shake as I forced the words to leave my tongue. "When I was eleven, my dad made me sit in the pouring rain because I looked at him wrong. I was out there for over four hours, sitting on top of a milk carton, and he'd watch me from his window, making sure I didn't move. And…um…Kellan came over to drop off some things. He was only fifteen, but he knew Ma was going through one of her low points, so each day, he'd stop by to check in on me. Bring me food. Clothes that he outgrew. When he came around the block and saw me sitting there, soaking wet, I saw his face turn red, and his right hand formed a fist.

"I told him it was okay, but he ignored me. He pulled me up to the apartment and started shouting at my dad, calling him a deadbeat this and a deadbeat that. Which is crazy, right, because you know my dad. People don't talk back to him. People don't even look him in the eye. But Kellan did. He puffed out his chest, stared the son of a bitch straight in the eye, and told him if he ever laid a hand on me or made me do some crazy shit again, like stand in the rain, that he'd kill him. He didn't mean it, ya know. Kellan wouldn't hurt a fly. But he stood up to my biggest fear. He fought for me when I couldn't. And my dad hit him." I blew out a low breath, remembering. "He hit him hard too. But Kellan stood up. Over and over again, he stood up. For me. He stood up for me. He's always looked after me, ya know? He's my big brother. He's my…" My head shook back and forth. My stomach knotted, pained. "He's…" I cleared my throat and stuffed my hands deeper into my pockets. My stare fell down to my tattered shoestrings. "He's…he's dying." I nodded my head, realizing that once those words left my lips, they became real. My brother, my hero, my world, was dying. "Kellan's sick. He's dying, High. He's dying." I shook uncontrollably, trying to fight the burning tears sitting in the backs of my eyes. I wanted to shut up, I wanted to stop talking, but I couldn't stop repeating the scariest words in the world. "He's dying. He's dying. Kellan's dying."

"Oh, Logan."

"How long did you know? How long did you know he was sick? Why didn't you call me? Why didn't…? He's dying," I sobbed. Jesus, I was a mess. I was seconds away from slipping away. But then she reached out to me. She held me. Her arms wrapped around me, and she didn't speak. She just held on tight as I lost myself on her front porch that summer night.

For a moment, we were us again. For a moment, she was the fire that kept my cold heart warm at night. For a moment, she was my savior. My safe haven. My bright, beautiful High.

But after the highs always came the lows.

"What's going on?" a deep voice asked from behind Alyssa, coming out of the house. I looked up as he spoke again. "Who's this?"

He stood wearing a button-down shirt with the sleeves rolled up to his elbows, slacks, and expensive-looking shoes. He stepped onto the porch as I stepped away from Alyssa, confused.

"Dan, this is Logan, my…" She hesitated, because she didn't know what we were, with good reason. The truth was we weren't anything. We were the fleeting memories of something that once was. Nothing more, nothing less. "He's an old friend."

An old friend?

I loved you.

An old friend?

You changed me.

An old friend?

I miss you so fucking much.

"Is everything okay?" he asked.

Dan stepped closer to Alyssa with narrowed eyes. His hand sat on her shoulder in a protective manner, and for a split second, I thought about slugging him for touching her, for placing his hand on my girl, but then I remembered.

She wasn't mine.

She hadn't been in years.

She shrugged his hand off her.

I looked away.

"I'm gonna get going," I said and laughed, but nothing was funny. I snapped the band on my wrist, walked down the steps, and listened to Alyssa call after me.

I ignored her.

I ignored the burning inside my soul too.

The world never made promises, but I was certain it was always going to screw me over.

I sat up at the billboard, looking up at the stars shining in the sky. My eyelids were heavy, but I couldn't go back to Kellan's place. I couldn't see him. I needed sleep, and for a while, I'd considered just staying up high in the sky and taking a nap until the sun woke me up. But whenever I closed my eyes, I remembered a few hours earlier when TJ reinforced the worst news of my life.

My heart hurt more than hearts should've been allowed to.

He's my brother.

I couldn't imagine him not being there. And I hated myself in that moment. I hated myself because such a big part of me wanted to run away and find drugs. A big part of me wanted to pull out my cell phone and dial the numbers of the people I never needed to see again to hook me up with some shit. A big part of me wanted to fall into the rabbit hole, because down that rabbit hole, feelings didn't exist. Nothing was real when a person was in the rabbit hole, so the pain of reality never surfaced.

My legs bent, and I wrapped my arms around my knees.

I didn't pray. I didn't believe in God. But for a split second, I considered being the hypocrite who began to that night.

My eyes closed, and I tilted my head up toward the sky.

The footsteps were quiet at first. Then the metal ladder began to slightly rock back and forth as she made her way to the top.

She was carrying a plastic bag, wearing those tight jeans and the tank top, and the worry in her eyes remained.

She shrugged a little, no words needed, but I knew she was asking permission to join me. I shrugged back, and she knew it was a yes. As her footsteps drew closer, I felt my eyes stinging and my heart pounding. She sat on the left side of me, bent her legs, and wrapped her arms around her knees, just as I did. Our heads turned toward each other, and our eyes met.

The plastic bag opened, and she pulled out a package of Oreos, a plastic basket of raspberries, a gallon of two-percent milk, and two red Solo cups.

I listened to the crinkling of the package as she pulled back the seal on the cookies, revealing a small part of our past.

I untwisted the milk top, then poured two cups.

She untwisted a cookie, placed a raspberry inside, then put it back together, handing it my way.

I couldn't remember the last time I had a raspberry Oreo.

Her lips turned into a half smile and she nodded once. I nodded once in reply.

"You're okay, Logan Francis Silverstone," she said.

"I'm okay, Alyssa Marie Walters," I replied.

We turned away from each other, ate two entire sleeves of raspberry cookies, and stared at the firelit sky.

When she felt cold, I gave her my hoodie.

When my heart broke, she held my hand.

CHAPTER 26
Alyssa

Hey, wake up."

I felt a light poke in my side as I rubbed my hands against my eyes. Slowly opening them, I was flooded with the bright sun in my face along with Logan standing over me.

"Hey, get up."

"Geez…what time is it?" I asked, yawning. I had no plans to fall asleep that night. I meant to go home and climb back into my warm bed and pretend that Logan didn't exist in my world anymore, but he looked so broken last night.

"It's time for you to go," he hissed.

I sat up a bit, confused about his attitude.

He tossed all the items I bought back into the plastic bag and shoved them toward me. "Don't come back here, all right?"

"Why are you being so rude?"

"Because I don't want you here. And give me my hoodie."

"Fine," I grumbled, standing up and tossing his hoodie at him. My heart was racing as I walked toward the ladder to leave. Yet instead of climbing down, I swung back around at Logan. "I didn't do anything wrong. You came to me last night. Not the other way around."

"I didn't ask you to come up here. I didn't tell you to bring cookies and shit, like the old days. News flash, we aren't the same people we were. Jesus. Did your boyfriend even know where you were last night?"

I snickered, shocked. "So this is about me having a boyfriend? Logan, Dan isn't—"

He rolled his eyes. "I could give two shits about you having a boyfriend. But I think it says a lot about you that you're so fucking comfortable with the idea of spending the night with another man. Does he even know where you are right now? I mean geez, Alyssa. It makes you look like a real slu—"

I cut him off, stepping in front of him, holding my hand up in front of his mouth before he could say the word. "I get that you're hurting. I get that you're scared and you're taking it out on me because I'm an easy target. That's fine. I'll be your target. Toss all your hate at me. Tell me to never come back here, to the one place that reminds me of you. Tell me to fuck off. But you do *not* get to talk to me like that, Logan Francis Silverstone. I am not the girl you get to belittle because I tried to be there for you. I am not the girl you call a slut."

His face dropped for a moment, slight guilt in his eyes before he huffed in annoyance. "I'm going to be in town for a while, okay? So can we just do our best to avoid each other? It was my fault for ever coming to your house to begin with, but that's over. There's no reason for us to communicate, really. Obviously, we have nothing to say to each other anymore."

"I'm sorry if I made any of this harder for you. I'll stay out of your way. But if you need me, I'll be there too. Okay? Just let me know. And for the record, Dan isn't my boyfriend. Never has been, never will be.

He's just a friend who's helping me look into getting a property. He drank a little too much and ended up crashing on my sofa. I'm not in a relationship. I haven't been in a long time. None of my past relationships have been a good match. And I get it now, why they didn't work out." I took a deep inhale and shut my eyes. "Because I'd been waiting all this time for a boy who I believed once loved me."

"Goddammit, Alyssa, I don't care! I don't care about the stuff happening in your life. And you need to realize something: you and I are never getting back together. We are not a happy ending." His words cut deep as he turned his back on me.

"Do you ever think about us? Do you ever think about me?" I whispered, running my fingers across my neck. "Do you ever think about the baby?"

He didn't turn back to stare my way, but his shoulders drooped. He didn't move another inch. *Say something! Say anything!*

"Just go, Alyssa. And don't come back."

I swallowed hard, my throat dry.

Say anything but that.

CHAPTER 27
Logan

A few weeks had passed since I'd come home to be with Kellan. He'd been through two rounds of chemotherapy and seemed to be himself, although maybe a bit moody. He tended to grow a little annoyed with how Erika helped him with his medicine and checked in with him every second of every day. She was breathing down his neck, and if I were honest, I'd say that I was thankful for it. I knew it annoyed him, her nonstop nagging, but it made me feel some level of peace, knowing he had such good care.

The wedding was supposed to happen last weekend, but they put it off until the coming month. I wondered how often it'd be moved and rearranged. I knew Kellan was the one pushing it off, because of his reservations about his illness.

On Thursday, he gave me money to go buy Ma some groceries. When I went to her house, I brought cleaning supplies with me. The house was trashed. Ma was passed out on the sofa, and I didn't bother to wake her. If she was sleeping, she wasn't using.

It was crazy to me how angelic she looked while she slept. It was as if the demons of her mind went to rest and her true self came out. I stocked the refrigerator and cabinets with food that wouldn't spoil quickly. I wasn't certain how much she'd be eating, but that way she could pick at things without it going bad too fast.

I also made her a lasagna. One of my favorite memories of her was when she decided she wanted to get clean, and she asked me to make her a celebratory dinner before she checked herself into rehab. We laughed, we ate, and we had a moment of what our lives could've been if we both were clean.

When she left the house, she ran into my dad, and rehab became a distant memory for her.

I cleaned the apartment from top to bottom, even getting on my knees to scrub the carpet. I walked all her clothes down to the laundromat, and while they washed, I went back to her apartment and cleaned some more.

She didn't wake until I was back at the apartment, folding her clean clothes while sitting on the floor. As she sat up, she yawned. "I thought it was a dream that you were here the other day."

I gave her half a smile. She gave me the other half as she rubbed her slim arms.

"You cleaned the place?"

"Yeah. I got some food and washed your clothes too."

Her eyes filled with tears and she kept smiling. "You look good, boy." She nodded over and over again, tears falling down her cheeks. She didn't wipe the tears away, allowing them to fall against her chin. "You look so good." Guilt took over as she scratched at her skin. "I knew you could do it, Logan. I knew you could get clean. Sometimes I wish…" Her words faded off.

"It's not too late, you know, Ma. We can get you into a program.

We can get you clean too." I didn't know it still existed in me—that spark of hope I always held for her. I wanted her to get away from this world. There was still a small part of my soul that wanted to get us a house, away from the place that created so much horror for us both.

For a second, it looked like she was considering it too. But then she blinked and started scratching herself again. "I'm old, Logan. I'm old. Come here."

I walked over and sat on the couch beside her.

She took my hands into hers and smiled. "I'm so proud of you."

"Thanks, Ma. Are you hungry?"

"Yeah," she said. I was somewhat surprised.

I tossed the lasagna into the oven, and when it finished, we sat at the dining room table, eating it straight out of the pan. I wished I could lock this moment into my heart and never let it leave.

As she ate, tears kept falling down her face.

"You're crying," I said.

"Am I?" She wiped at her face. She gave me another smile. But it was such a broken grin. "How's Kellan?" she asked.

"Did you know about the…?"

She nodded.

"He's okay. He asked me to come to a therapy meeting with him next week. He's going to beat this, ya know. He's tough."

"Yeah," she murmured, eating more than I'd seen her eat in a long time. "Yeah. He's strong. He's strong." The tears started falling faster down her cheeks, and I wiped them away. "It's my fault, though, you know. I did this to him… I was a shit mother. I wasn't there for you boys."

"Ma. Come on." I wasn't sure what to say, how to make her stop the tears.

"It's true. You know it. I messed up. I did this."

"You didn't give him cancer."

"But I didn't make your lives easy. You went to rehab, Logan. Rehab. I sat with you on your sixteenth birthday, and we did lines of coke. I fed you my addiction." She shook her head back and forth. "I'm so sorry. I'm so sorry."

She was so broken. She was so lost. Truth was she'd been wandering around lost in her mind for as long as I could remember. For so long, I'd been so angry at her. I held so much bitterness for the choices she made, but it wasn't her fault. She was just running round and round on her own hamster wheel, unable to stop repeating all her same mistakes.

"We're all going to be okay, Ma. Don't worry." I took her hand in mine and held on tight.

Just then, the front door flew open, and Ricky came barging in.

It was amazing how much my hatred for him still existed the moment I saw him.

"Julie, what the fuck?" he hissed. He looked much different than when I last saw him five years ago, though. He seemed…broken down? Old. Tired. His fancy suits that he used to wear were replaced with sweatpants and a T-shirt. His fancy shoes were now sneakers. His once-buff arms weren't as strong and defined as they'd been before.

I wondered if he was using the stuff he sold.

"You owe me fifty dollars," he hollered and paused when he saw me. His head tilted to the left, bewilderment in his stare. "Did a ghost just cross my path?"

My chest tightened the same way it always did whenever he came near me. It only took a moment before his confusion turned into a sinister smirk. He seemed pleased by my return, almost as if he knew I'd be back.

"You know," he said as he walked toward me, his chest pushed out, "there were rumors going around saying you were back, but I figured it was just bullshit. Now that you're back, you can come join me in the family business."

"I'm never going to do that. I'm never going down that road again."

His eyes narrowed, and I watched his serious inhales and exhales. Then he laughed. "I love that. I love that you honestly think that you're strong enough to stay clean."

He came nose to nose with me, and instead of backing down, I stood tall. I wasn't afraid of him anymore. I couldn't be afraid.

He pushed my chest with his, trying to make me back down. "But I know you, Logan. I see in your eyes the same weak bitch that resides in your mother. There's no way you'll ever manage to keep away."

I watched tears form in Ma's eyes as he said that. It had to feel like a dagger to her soul, because all her life, all she ever did was love him. She wasted so many years loving a man who loved to control and belittle her.

"Don't talk about my mom," I said, standing up for her because she hadn't a clue how to stand up for herself.

He snickered. "I love your mom. Julie, don't I love you? She's my one and only. You're it for me, baby."

Mom kind of smiled, as if she believed him.

Something I'd never understand.

He made me sick. "You don't love her. You love controlling her because it hides the fact that you yourself are nothing but a fucking rat."

I flinched when I felt his fist contact my eye.

"This fucking rat can still kick your ass, little boy. I'm not going to waste any more time on you, though. Julie, give me my money."

Her voice shook with fear. "Ricky, I don't have it right now. I'll get it, though. I just have to…"

He went to hit her, and I stepped in front of him, this time blocking his hit.

"So what, you went off to some fancy rehab place and come back thinking you can just step back into this place, Logan?" he asked, annoyed. "Trust me, you don't want me as your enemy."

I reached into my pocket and grabbed my wallet, counting out fifty bucks. "Here. Take it and go."

He cocked an eyebrow. "Did I say fifty? I meant seventy."

Asshole. I pulled out another twenty and shoved it at him.

He willingly accepted the bills, stuffing them into his pocket. He bent down in front of the lasagna. "You make this, son?" he asked, knowing that calling me *son* would get under my skin. He took a spoonful of the food, then spit it out, back into the pan, ruining the whole thing. "Tastes like ass."

"Ricky," Ma said, going to defend me, but he shot her a look that shut her up. He stole her voice so long ago, and she had no clue how to find it.

"You act like I don't take care of you, Julie. That's really offensive. Don't forget who was there for you when this boy walked out and left you. And you wonder why it's so hard for me to love you. You betray me every second you get."

Her head lowered.

"And this? Him bringing you food and groceries? That doesn't mean he cares about you, Julie." He opened the cabinets and the refrigerator, grabbing all the food I bought for Ma, opening each item, and dumping them into a pile on the floor. I wanted to stop him, but Ma told me to say quiet. He opened a box of cereal, locked eyes with me, and slowly poured it on top of everything on the ground before opening a gallon of milk and doing the same exact thing. He then walked over it with his sneakers and headed to the front door. "I'm going to handle some business," he said with a smirk. "And, Julie?"

"Yeah?" she whispered, a tremble in her body.

"Clean that shit up before I get back home."

When the door slammed, my heart rate started to go back to normal. "Are you okay, Ma?"

Her body was tense, and she wouldn't look at me. "You did this."

"What?"

"He's right. You left me, and he was there for me. You're the reason he made this mess. You weren't there for me. He took care of me."

"Ma…"

"Get out!" she shouted, tears falling down her cheeks. She started toward me, hitting me, just like she used to when I was young. Blaming me because the devil didn't love her. "Get out! Get out! It's all your fault. It's your fault that he doesn't love me. It's your fault that this mess is here. It's your fault that Kellan's dying. You walked away from us. You left us. You left us. Now leave, Logan. Leave. Leave. Leave!" she shouted, pounding against my chest, her words confusing me, hurting me, burning me. She was hysterical, reminding me too much of the Ma I once knew and hated. Her words were echoing in my mind.

It's your fault. It's your fault that this mess is here. It's your fault that Kellan's dying. You left us. You left us. You left us… Kellan's dying…

My chest scorched as I blinked over and over again, trying not to fall apart. How did I get back here? How did I find myself in exactly the same kind of position that I was in five years ago? How was I back on the hamster wheel I spent so long running away from?

She didn't stop hitting me. She didn't stop blaming me.

So I packed up my things and I left.

LOGAN, ELEVEN YEARS OLD

"Don't you look comfortable?" Dad stumbled into the living room while I sat on the floor watching Cartoon Network. I ignored him the best I could and continued eating my Cap'n Crunch cereal out of a bowl. He was smoking a cigarette and smirked at my attempt to pretend he wasn't there.

It was only four in the afternoon, and he was already stumbling. He was already drunk.

"You deaf, boy?" He moved over to me and ran the back of his hand against my head before he smacked me hard.

I shivered at his touch. But I kept ignoring him. Kellan knew how bad my dad could get, and he said it was best if I didn't respond. Kellan was so lucky that he had another dad. I wished I had another dad too.

I couldn't wait for Mom to get back home. She'd been gone for a few days, but when she called me last weekend, she said I would see her soon. I wished Dad would leave and stay gone forever.

When his hand ran against my shoulder blade, I flinched again, knocking my cereal bowl out of my hands. He laughed wickedly, pleased by my unease. His hand rose, and he slapped me against my ear. "Pick that shit up. And what the hell do you think you're doing eating cereal at four in the afternoon?"

I was hungry, and it was all we had. But I couldn't tell him that. I couldn't tell him anything.

Standing, I shook as I began to put the pieces of the cereal back into the bowl. Dad started whistling a tune from my cartoon, and my heart started pounding. "Hurry the fuck up, kid. Pick that shit up. Making messes in my house like you don't have any damn sense."

My eyes started to tear up, and I hated that I was letting him get to me. An eleven-year-old was supposed to be tougher. I felt weak.

"Pick. It. Up!"

I couldn't take any more of his drunken anger, his apparent displeasure for me. I picked up the cereal bowl and threw it at him. It missed his head and hit the wall, the bowl shattering into a million pieces. "I hate you!" I hissed, tears burning down my cheeks. "I want Mom back! I hate you!"

His eyes widened, and I panicked, regretful of my outburst. Kellan would've been so disappointed. I shouldn't have talked back. I shouldn't have responded. I should've locked myself in my bedroom like always.

But there were no cartoons in my bedroom.

I just wanted to be a kid, if only for one day.

Dad swung around and gripped my arm. "You want to get slick? Huh?" He yanked me across the room, forcing me to trip over my own feet. "You want to break shit?!"

I was dragged through the kitchen where he opened the cabinet under the sink. "No. I'm sorry, Dad! I'm sorry!" I cried, trying to tear away from his grip.

He snickered and pushed me inside the cabinet. "Here's your damn cereal," he said, grabbing the box and dumping it all out on my head. When he shut the cabinet door, I tried my best to open it, but it wouldn't move. He'd placed something in front of it to keep it locked.

"Please, Dad! I'm sorry!" I cried. "Don't leave me."

I'm sorry.

He wasn't listening, though, and after a while, I didn't even hear his footsteps.

I didn't know how much time had passed since I was locked inside the cabinet, but I fell asleep twice and pissed myself. When Mom found me, she looked strung out and shook her head, seeming so disappointed in me.

"Oh, Logan." She sighed and ran her hands through her hair. She lit up a cigarette. "What did you do this time?"

CHAPTER 28
Alyssa

D o you have any idea how much you're confusing me, Logan?" I asked, my arms crossed as he stood on my porch in a black T-shirt with dark jeans. I was chilled by the cool breeze that hit me, seeing how I was only wearing an oversize T-shirt and knee-high socks.

His back was turned to me as he moved over to the edge of the porch and wrapped his fingers around the railing. He stared out into the darkness. His arms were muscular, and I could see every cut to him as he held on to the wooden rail. When we were younger, he was handsome but not built. Now, he looked somewhat like a Greek god who made my legs tingle just by looking at him.

"I know. I just… I don't know where to go."

He turned to face me, and I gasped, seeing his blackened eye. With haste, I hurried over to him, lightly touching it, watching him cringe. "Your dad?"

He nodded. "If I go back to Kellan's like this, he'll freak out."

Oh, Lo…

"Are you okay? Is your mom okay?" I asked, and I paused. It was as if we had traveled back in time, reliving the same routines we used to perform. I wished this wasn't one of the more common memories.

"She's not okay. But she's okay."

Déjà vu.

"Come inside," I said, taking his hand in mine.

He shook his head, pulling his hold away from mine. "You asked me something the last time we spoke, and I didn't reply."

"What?"

"You asked me if I think about the baby." His fingers rubbed the back of his neck. "I think about how at the end of the summer, he or she would've been starting kindergarten. I think about how maybe he'd have your laugh and your eyes. I think about how she'd probably chew on her collar and hiccup when she was nervous. I think about how his heart would beat. How she'd love you. How he'd walk, talk, smile, frown. I think about it. More than I want to. And then…" He cleared his throat. "Then I think about you. I think about your smile. About how when you're nervous, you chew on your shirt collars, and when you're shy, you do the same thing. I think about how when you're angry, you hiccup three times, and every time your mom puts you down, it still stings. I think about where your mind is at night when it storms and if you ever, for a second, still think about me."

"Lo." I sighed. "Come inside."

"Don't invite me in," he muttered under his breath.

"What?"

"I said, don't invite me in."

"You don't want to talk?"

"No." He locked eyes with me. "No. I don't want to *talk*. I want to forget. I want to make my mind stop remembering all the bullshit. I want to… High…" He lost his breath, and his words faltered.

The tremble in his voice would've been missed by someone who didn't know Logan. But I heard it, I knew him, and his mind was traveling to those dark places again. He stepped in closer, and I stood still. I wanted him closer. I missed him being so close. His hand fell against my cheek, and I closed my eyes at his gentle touch.

"I want to talk to you, but I can't. Because then we'll be back to where we were all those years ago, and I can't go back to that, Alyssa. I can't fall back in love with you. I can't hurt you again."

My heart skipped. "Is that why you've been so mean to me?"

He nodded slowly.

"Logan. We can just be friends. We don't have to be in a relationship. Just come inside, and we can talk."

"I can't be your friend. I don't want to talk to you, because when I talk, I hurt. And I don't want to hurt anymore. But…I can't stay away from you. I'm trying to, but I can't. I want you, High."

His words sent chills down my spine and fogged my mind.

"I want to run my hands through your hair," he whispered, taking his fingers and combing my curls behind my ear. "I want to run my tongue across your neck. I want to feel you." His hand ran against my cheek. "I want to taste you," His mouth slowly licked the curve of my neck. "I want to suck you." His lips engulfed my earlobe, sucking it gently. "I want to…fuck…" He sighed, pulling me closer. "I want you, Alyssa. I want you so much. I want you so hard and deep that my mind can't think of anything else. So please, to avoid any more confusion between us," he hissed against my earlobe before sucking it lightly, "don't invite me in."

My heart was racing, and I took a few steps backward until I was pressed up against the wall of my house. He drew closer, his arms boxing me in. His pupils dilated as his eyes locked with mine, filled with need, want, hope…? Or maybe it was my own hope, which I'd prayed still existed within his stare. My thighs quivered, my mind a jumbled mess. A part of me wondered if I was dreaming while a bigger part of me didn't care. I wanted this dream. I missed this dream. I longed for this dream over the past five years. I wanted to feel his body pressed against mine. I wanted to feel how much he missed me. I wanted to lean in closer and kiss him.

I wanted to feel him…

Taste him…

Suck him…

Lo…

"Logan," I murmured, unable to take my stare away from his lips, which were almost touching mine. Logan moved that gorgeous body closer to me, lifting my chin so we stared straight into each other's eyes. His lips reminded me of the summer when we became more than friends. Reminded me of the first boy I'd ever loved and the first and only boy who managed to break my heart. "You're sad tonight." My head tilted to the left, and I studied every part of him. His hair, his mouth, his jawline, his soul. The dark shadows that were always in the depths of his eyes. His breaths were heavy, unsteady like mine.

"I'm sad tonight," he agreed. "I'm sad every night. Alyssa, I never meant to hurt you by not returning your calls."

"It doesn't matter. It was a long time ago. We were kids."

"I'm not that same boy anymore, Alyssa. I swear I'm not."

I nodded. "I know, and I'm not that same girl anymore." But a part of my soul remembered our yesterdays. A part of my soul still felt the fire that Logan and I started to build many years before. And sometimes, in the quiet moments between daylight and night, I swore I still felt its warmth. "That's why I want you to come inside tonight. Because

I'm sad too. No commitment. No promises. Just a few moments to forget, together."

His fingers started lifting my T-shirt, and my eyes closed from the pleasure that simple act brought me. A small moan escaped me as his thumb rolled against the fabric of my panties, and then he pressed harder, sliding his thumb up and down. His tongue danced against my earlobe before he sucked it hard. His right hand gripped my ass as his left moved my panties to the side, allowing him to slide a finger deep inside me.

One finger.

Two fingers.

Three fingers...

My panting was heavy, my needs even stronger. My hips arched in his direction, wanting his hardness inside me. I ground against his fingers, begging for the touch that I missed so much.

"Come inside," I said, quietly moaning, pulling him closer, needing him closer.

"Don't invite me inside."

His fingers deepened. My heartbeats heightened. I felt everything in those moments. Every fear, every want, every need...

Feel.

Taste.

Suck.

Oh my God, Logan...

"Come inside," I ordered, wrapping one leg around his waist.

"No, High."

"Yes, Lo."

"If I come inside, I won't be gentle," he swore. "If I come inside, we don't talk about anything. We don't mention the past, we don't discuss the present, and we don't talk about the tomorrows. If I come inside, I fuck you. I fuck you hard. I fuck you wild. I fuck you to shut off my brain, and you fuck me to quiet yours. And then I leave."

"Logan."

"Alyssa."

"Lo…"

"High…"

I blinked once, and when I reopened my eyes, I promised myself not to look away from him again. "Come inside."

We didn't make it past the piano in the living room. As his mouth found my lips, he kissed me like I'd never been kissed before. It was hard, rough, ugly, and sad. *So fucking sad.* The fire in my chest was burning hot as I kissed him back harder, wanting him more than he could've ever wanted me. We tore off each other's clothing, knowing this was a life time-out. This was a chance to silence our minds and screw the hurt out of each other. He wrapped his arms around me and lifted me up, placing my back against the piano.

He took my hand and slid it over his hardness. I stroked him as he fingered me, our stares never faltering from each other.

Feel.

Taste.

Suck.

Yes…

Reaching into his pocket, he pulled out a condom and slid it on before spreading my knees wider. As he slid into me, I cried out in bliss, in pleasure, in the deepest kinds of ache. His fingers dug into my skin as mine clutched onto his back. My arms gripped him tight as he thrust deep into me, making my body tremble beneath his body weight. We rocked against the piano keys, the sounds matching our wants, our needs, our confusion, our fears. He rolled in and out of me, and I begged him not to let go. We were so broken. We were so worn out from the lives that we lived. But tonight we made love with the broken pieces.

It was intense. It was sacred. It was heartbreaking.

It had its lows. It had its highs.

Oh God. It felt so wrong yet always right.

I missed him.

I missed us.

I missed us so much.

When he left, he didn't say a single word.

When he left, I hoped he'd come back tomorrow.

CHAPTER 29
Logan

I'd been cooking since the age of five. Ma used to leave me at home with nothing but a can of soup, so I had to learn how to use a can opener and the stove to heat it up all on my own. When I turned nine, I was making personal-size pizzas with homemade dough, using ketchup and Kraft cheese slices as toppings. By the time I was thirteen, I knew how to stuff and roast a whole chicken.

So the fact that Jacob sat frowning across from me was troubling. We sat at a booth in Bro's Bistro as I placed my dish of mushroom and sausage risotto in front of him. The restaurant was still closed, and it was the second time he'd made me sit across from him with an entrée.

"Hmm…" he murmured, taking his spoon and scooping up a large bite of risotto. I watched him chew really slowly, not showing any emotion in his face as he debated his opinion of whether my food was good enough to allow me to work in his kitchen.

"No," he flatly said. "This isn't it."

"Are you kidding me?" I asked, baffled and insulted. "That dish got me through culinary school. It was my final meal."

"Well, your teachers failed you then. I don't know how they do things in Iowa, but here in Wisconsin, we like food that actually tastes good."

"Screw you, Jacob."

He smiled. "Bring me another dish next week. We'll see how that goes."

"I'm not going to keep bringing you dishes for you to keep shooting down. This is ridiculous. I can make the food on your menu. Just give me the job."

"Logan, I love you. I really do. But no. I need you to cook with heart!"

"I cook with my hands!"

"But not with any heart. Come back when you find it."

I flipped him off.

He laughed again. "And don't forget, you still owe me that hair mask recipe!"

"How are things going so far, being back in town?" Kellan asked me as we sat in the clinic where he was getting his third round of chemotherapy. I hated the place, because it made his cancer seem more real than I was ready for, but I tried my best to hide my fears. He needed me to be his brother who stood by him, not the weak guy who I felt like becoming.

Watching the nurses hook all types of IVs into his arms was hard for me. Seeing how he winced sometimes in pain was almost the death of me. But still, I tried to act normal.

"Things are fine. Jacob's being an asshole, though. He said I had to perfect three dishes before he'd hire me to work in his kitchen."

"That seems fair," Kellan said.

THE FIRE BETWEEN HIGH & LO

I rolled my eyes. "I'm a great cook! You know that!"

"Yeah, but Jacob doesn't. Just test out a few different dishes at the house. No big deal."

He was right, it wasn't a big deal, but it was still annoying seeing how Jacob offered me the job when I first came here but was now putting guidelines on it.

"How has it been seeing Alyssa?" he asked, closing his eyes. "That has to be weird."

"You mean seeing her with or without her clothes on?"

His eyes shot open, shock hitting him. "No! You're sleeping with Alyssa?" he whisper-shouted.

I clenched my teeth together and shrugged. "Define *sleeping*."

"Logan!"

"What?!"

"Why? Why are you sleeping with Alyssa? This is a terrible idea. This is a completely, out of this world, horrible idea. I thought the plan was to avoid her at all costs so you don't fall back into your past. God. You seriously slept with her? How does that even happen?"

"Well, when two people take off their clothes..." I started, smirking.

"Shut up. I was having sex when you were still wearing underwear with superheroes on them. But how did it happen with you two?"

I couldn't tell him that I went to her when I was falling apart, because he'd feel terrible about me not being strong. But I didn't want to lie. So I told the truth. "She always reminds me of home."

He got a cheesy grin. "After all this time, after everything you guys went through, it's still there, huh?"

"It's just sex, Kellan. And we have only done it once. No commitment. No strings. Just a way to let loose."

"No. It's never been just sex between you two. Just to be clear, I always liked you guys together. Erika hated it, but I loved it."

"Speaking of Erika, let's not tell her. She'd freak out."

"Freak out about what?" Erika said, walking back into the room with coffee in her left hand and a textbook in her right. She'd been taking night classes for her master's degree, and when she wasn't taking care of Kellan, her head was in a book. Sometimes even when she was taking care of Kellan, her head was still in a book.

"I broke a saucer at your house by accident," I lied.

She glanced up from her book. "What?!"

"My bad."

She started questioning me about every detail of the incident with the plate that I didn't even really break, and Kellan smirked at me before closing his eyes and waiting to finish his chemotherapy treatment.

Thirty-two hours after Kellan had his chemotherapy, he was determined to play a show at a bar. Erika and I both tried to talk him out of it, but he refused, telling us that he couldn't just give up his dream. A black baseball cap sat on his head every day now as he tried to hide the proof that he was losing his hair, but I knew better.

We never talked about it, though.

Kellan's breaths were heavy as we walked from the house to the car, as if the few steps were almost deadly to him. That worried me so much.

"See, guys?" He took a deep inhale followed by a deeper exhale. Erika helped him into the passenger seat. "I'm fine."

Erika grimaced for a moment before giving him a fake smile.

"You're really doing great. I can't wait to see in a few weeks how the chemo is working, because I know it is. I just have a feeling. And I love that we are keeping our normal lives too. That you're still playing the guitar at places. Routine is important, the doctors say. This is good. This is all good." Erika kept repeating the words, and I placed a comforting hand toward the front passenger seat where Kellan sat.

I saw him give me a weak smile through the rearview mirror.

We only made it a few blocks before we had to pull over. Kellan launched from his seat and started throwing up on the side of the road. Erika and I both rushed to his side, holding him steady so he wouldn't fall over.

This cancer was becoming more real each day.

I hated it.

I hated everything about this disgusting disease. How it took the strongest people in the world and forced them to be weak. How it not only touched your loved ones but sucked them dry.

If there were a magic pill I could have to take away all his pain and transfer it to me, I'd take it every day of my life.

My brother didn't deserve to be going through his current struggles.

No human did.

I wouldn't wish cancer on my worst enemy.

We got him back to the car and drove straight home, knowing there was no way Kellan could've performed in his current state. When we arrived at their house, both Erika and I had to help him walk into his bedroom.

"I'm fine," he said, his voice exhausted. "I just need a little sleep. I should've planned the show further away from the chemo. Just a stupid mistake."

"I'll be in the living room studying if you need anything, okay, hon?" Erika said, helping him lie down and then covering him up. She kissed his nose, and he closed his eyes.

"Okay."

She left the room, and I stayed behind, watching his chest rise and fall. He looked so skinny that it made me ill. *How can I fix you? What can I do to make this right?*

"I'm fine, Logan," he said as if he were reading my mind.

"I know, it's just… I worry, that's all."

"Don't waste your time. Because I'm fine."

I shrugged my left shoulder. *I love you, brother.*

He shrugged his right, as if he could see my action even with his eyes closed.

"I'm gonna go out for a little bit. Have Erika call me if you need anything."

"Going out for some cookies? For a little shake? For some adult activities with a girl named Alyssa?" he teased.

"Kellan, shut up," I laughed.

But yeah.

That was exactly where I was going.

CHAPTER 30
Alyssa

The first time, he stood on my front porch, ran his hands through his hair, and told me not to invite him inside. Then, he came back the next day and the next. And the next. I wanted to know the kinds of thoughts that ran through his mind each day. What his daydreams were like and what his nightmares entailed. But since we weren't talking, I'd have to use his body language to figure it out. When he was angry with his parents, he was rough. When he was heartbroken about Kellan, his body lingered against mine a bit longer.

I stepped to the left of my doorframe. He entered the house.

We didn't make it past the foyer this time. He ripped at my clothes, and I tore at his. He lifted me up against the front closet door and tugged on my hair as my hands became tangled in his. My legs wrapped tightly around his waist, and he didn't warn me before he entered. The shock sent ripples through me, making me moan his name as he began pounding me, each thrust harder than the last. I was seconds away from losing myself against him.

One of his hands gripped my back and the other squeezed my breasts as he rocked in deeper.

Feel.

Taste.

Suck.

Fuck...

We were slowly becoming addicted to the act of him showing up and me inviting him in. Passion was our drug, and we were addicted to the high. I cried out his name as he grunted out mine. We thrust and heaved and clenched and sighed. We caught our breaths as he lowered my feet to the ground. But this time, instead of leaving my house, he started walking toward my living room.

"What are you doing?" I asked as he walked down my hallway, toward my bedroom.

"Put your clothes back on."

"What? Why?"

"So I can take them off again."

CHAPTER 31

Logan

My greatest fucking High…

CHAPTER 32
Alyssa

My most painful Lo…

CHAPTER 33
Logan

"She's not home," a kind voice said.

I'd been standing there for a few minutes, knocking, waiting for her to let me in, but there hadn't been an answer.

"She's working at Red's Piano Bar tonight. She'll be performing there all week long."

"Oh, okay. Thanks."

The voice belonged to a woman who was probably in her seventies and had silvery-gray hair that fell down her back. She was sitting on the porch next door in a rocking chair, reading a novel as she hummed to a tune of her own. As I started down Alyssa's steps, the woman spoke again.

"So what's your motive with Aly, huh?"

"Excuse me?"

"Come here," she ordered, waving me over as she closed her book.

I walked over to her front porch and took a seat beside her.

"My name's Lori, and I've known that girl next door for many years now. Served more pancakes with her than anyone I've ever worked with. She has guys throwing themselves at her daily, yet she never even looks their way. But then this mysterious boy comes to town, and she loses her mind. What's the deal with you?"

"She and I used to be really close. About five years ago."

"Oh," she murmured, nodding. "You're Logan. The boy in the box."

"What?"

"Under her bed, there's a box. You're all that's in it. Memories, keepsakes. The one boy she can't seem to shake." She placed her hand around the locket hanging around her neck. "I know what that's like."

"I'm sure she's over whatever we had years ago. She told me she was."

Lori raised an eyebrow and tilted her head. "Men are stupid."

I laughed.

"There's this guy named Dan. Handsome boy. He came into the diner each week for the past few years to try to get Alyssa to go out on a date with him, and I watched her officially turn him down today. I knew she did it because of her feelings for you."

I wasn't sure what to say to that, so I stayed quiet as Lori kept speaking.

"But just to be clear, she's not a drug. She's not *your* drug, young man." I raised an eyebrow, and a small smirk appeared on her lips. "You think you'd disappear for years, and Alyssa wouldn't mention you every now and then? She told me about your past with drugs and how you got clean. Which is good. But, honey, you can't come back here and use her this way. She's not something you can take in so you can forget about the things around you. She's a girl, a gentle, caring girl who is still crazy about a boy. And what you're doing is selfish. What she's doing is selfish too. See, you're not going to stop using, and she's not going to stop giving. You're both addicted. You're both lighting yourselves on fire as if you don't feel the burn.

"If you care anything about her, you'll stop doing this right now. If you care anything about her heart, you'll stop yourself from breaking it again. Whatever you two are doing might just be fun and games for you, but for her, it's more. It's everything she spent the last few years thinking about. If you end up breaking my friend's heart, you best believe I will break all your fingers and toes, one at a time."

I laughed again, but this time the stern look Lori was giving me made me pause. I swallowed hard. "Okay."

"But for now, you should get home soon," she said, opening her book back up. "A big storm is supposed to be moving in over the next few hours."

I looked up at the sky, the darkened clouds blocking out the moon. Standing, my hands went back to my pockets, and I thanked Lori for the talk.

The next day, Kellan asked me to join him and Erika at his therapist appointment, and there was no way I'd say no. I'd do anything he'd ask of me. The only therapist I'd ever spoken to was during my stay at St. Michael's Health and Rehabilitation Clinic. We'd had individual sessions and group sessions where they made us color and shit. I hated it at first, but after time, it helped. Then, sometimes, I'd start hating it again.

I sat beside my brother and his fiancée in Dr. Yang's office, and I could feel the tension building. Before we left the house, Kellan and Erika had been bickering about small things—a toothpaste tube left on the bathroom countertop, coffee not being finished, Erika's school books all over the dining room table. I'd never seen them fight before, so it was a bit odd.

"Thank you for joining us today, Logan. I know it means a lot to your brother that you're here."

"Yeah, of course." I patted Kellan on the leg. He gave me a forced smile. "Anything for this dude."

Dr. Yang nodded, pleased. "I think it's important to check in every now and then about how things are going. I know Erika mentioned that you moved into the house, which I think could be a good thing for Kellan. Having family around is always helpful. So how about we go around to see how everyone is doing? Kellan, you start."

"I'm fine."

"He's been losing his appetite a bit. And he seems a bit moody lately," Erika chimed in.

"That's perfectly normal with everything that's going on," Dr. Yang assured her.

"I'm not moody," Kellan barked.

Erika frowned. "You snapped at me yesterday, Kellan."

"You were taking my temperature at three in the morning while I was sleeping."

"You looked cold," she whispered.

"And how are you doing, Erika? I know we spoke about how you handle your stress by sometimes breaking things…"

"Yeah. But I'm doing much better."

Kellan laughed.

"I'm sorry?" Erika cocked an eyebrow at my brother. "Is something funny?"

"We have seven new lamps in our closet because one broke. You're losing your mind."

Wow. That was harsh.

I watched the embarrassment turn Erika's cheeks red as she studied her shoes.

Dr. Yang wrote something in his notebook before turning to me.

"What about you, Logan? Do you think Erika is handling Kellan's illness in the best way possible?"

Erika huffed. "Right. Because a drug addict gets to judge me."

That was harsh too.

I sat up in my seat, glancing over at both Kellan and Erika before I replied. They both looked so exhausted. The same way Ma had. Kellan was digging his fingers into the sides of his chair while Erika was fighting off the temptation to cry.

I cleared my throat. "Do I think it's weird that Erika has mini breakdowns where she breaks and buys? Yes. Do I think she judges people for not being or thinking exactly like her? Absolutely." I could feel the daggers Erika was sending my way with her eyes, but I continued speaking. "But she loves him. She cleans up after me. Yelling about it, but she does it. Because she's trying her best to make him comfortable. She might not be handling it to your definition or Kellan's or mine. Maybe not even the best way possible. But she's doing her best. She wakes up every morning and tries to do her best. I don't know if I've ever done my best…" I glanced down at the band on my arm. "But I'm trying. For these two, I'm trying to do my best. Which is all anyone can really do.

"When I was at the rehab clinic in Iowa, they had these quotes in every room by Ram Dass. In the front lobby, there was this quote on the wall that said, 'We're all just walking each other home.' I never really understood the meaning until right now. Because at the end of the day, we're all lost. We're all cracked. We're all scarred. We're all broken. We're all just trying to figure out this thing called life, you know? Sometimes it feels so lonely, but then you remember your core tribe. The people who sometimes hate you but never stop loving you. The people who always show up, no matter how many times you've fucked up and pushed them away. That's your tribe. These people, these struggles, this is my tribe. So yeah, we fall apart, but we'll fall together. We'll stand up—together. Then, at the end of all the bullshit, all the tears, all the hurt, we'll take a few steps at a time. Then we'll take a few deep breaths, and we'll walk each other home.'"

After Kellan's appointment, he and Erika went home to get some rest, and I walked around town all day until night came and I found myself standing in front of Red's Piano Bar. On a chalkboard sitting outside the bar, I saw Alyssa's name as the performer of the night, and a wave of pride washed over me. *She's doing it. She's doing what she loves.*

I stood at the back of Red's Piano Bar, hidden away from Alyssa's line of sight. She sat at the piano, her fingers moving back and forth across the keys, filling the bar with a beautiful melody that too few people in the world would ever experience. I listened closely, song after song, remembering how amazingly talented Alyssa was.

When it came to her final song, she sat up at the microphone sitting beside her and spoke gently. "I finish every show with this song, because it means so much to my heart. It holds a lot of my soul within the lyrics and always reminds me of a time when I once loved a boy… And for a few breaths, a few whispers, and a few moments, I think he loved me too. Here's Sam Smith's 'Life Support.'"

My chest tightened, and I sat up straighter.

Her fingers danced across the keys, and I watched her body move as if she was becoming a part of the piano. It was as if she was nothing more than a willing vessel of art. I couldn't imagine how she could've become any more astonishing. I couldn't grasp how she could've stunned me even more.

But then she parted her lips.

The lyrics flowed from her with such ease. Her eyes shut as she sang; she was losing herself in the words, in the sounds, in herself, in our memories.

It was an honor to witness such a moment. Tears fell from her closed eyes as her shoulders swayed back and forth to the rhythm and sounds she crafted. There was something different about the artists in the world. It almost seemed as if they felt things differently, *deeper* maybe. They saw the world in color, while many only saw the blacks and whites.

My life was black and white before Alyssa showed up in it.

My feet took me closer to the stage, and I stood in front of her, listening to the words that I used to whisper into her ear when we were young. She was so beautiful, so free, when she played her music. When she let go, it had a way of making everyone around her feel as if they were free too. For a few moments as she sang, I was convinced that the chains of life were removed. I was free right alongside her.

I knew Lori was being a great friend, protecting Alyssa the way she did, but what she didn't know was that for me, Alyssa was it. She was the girl in my heart. Even though such a big part of me tried to deny the feelings I held for her, another part of me was still desperate with the want, the need, the love that only she was able to create in my soul.

Alyssa finished her song, thanked her listeners, and then turned toward the audience. I hadn't moved. Her beautiful eyes found my stare. She took a deep breath and shivered a bit when she released it. Her footsteps toward me were tentative. When we stood in front of each other, we kind of smiled yet kind of frowned too.

"Hi," she said.

"Hey," I replied.

We frowned and smiled.

"Can I walk you home?" I asked.

"Okay," she replied.

When we stepped outside, it was still raining. Alyssa shared her polka-dot umbrella with me the whole way to her house.

"You were amazing up there, Alyssa. Better than I've ever heard you perform. Better than I ever heard anyone perform, actually."

She didn't reply, but her lips curved up.

Once we reached her porch, she opened her mouth to invite me in, and I shook my head. "I can't anymore."

The sting of disappointment hit her blue eyes. Then the embarrassment reddened her cheeks. "Oh yeah. No big deal."

I could tell that I hurt her with my simple words.

I was so tired.

It had been such a long day.

A long life.

A long, tiring life.

"I relapsed, Alyssa." I rubbed my fingers against my forehead.

Her eyes shot from embarrassment to worry. "What? What happened? How? With what?"

My voice lowered, and I shrugged. "With you."

"What?"

"I came back, and my world was rocked again. I was back in my past, except this time it was worse because my brother was sick, and I went straight to my greatest high to help me forget for a while. I went to you. You've always been my safe haven, High. You've been my escape route from all the crap that surrounded me. But it's not fair to you or to me. I want to get clean. I want to be able to stand up and not find the need to forget, which means I can't relapse again, and we can't keep doing this. We can't keep sleeping together. But I need *you*."

"Lo…"

"Wait. Let me get this out because it's been spinning in my mind for so long now. I know I'm not the same boy I was back then, but parts of that guy still linger within me. And I know we said the sex wouldn't mean anything, but I think we know that it meant everything, which is why we can't do it anymore. But I need you. I need you to be my friend. Everything in my life has been hard. Everything in life has made me hard. Except for you and Kellan.

"And I know it's selfish of me to ask this of you right now. I know it's selfish, because I need someone to hold me up while I try to hold my brother too, but I need you. I need you to be my friend again, but that's it, because I can't hurt you again. I can't be with you, but I need you. *I need you*. We won't talk about the past. We won't worry about the future. But we'll just be us, be friends. Here and now. If you're okay with that? Because I miss laughing, and I always laughed with you. I miss talking, and I could always talk to you. I miss you. So I was wondering, can we be friends again?"

She leaned against the doorframe, appearing deep in thought before a smile found her lips. "We never stopped being friends, Logan. We were just in a weird time-out."

CHAPTER 34
Alyssa

As tensions between Logan and I finally calmed down and we found our way to a new friendship, the rocky waters between Kellan and Erika began to build. Late one night, after a bad doctor's appointment, the two came into the house fighting as I sat on their couch, setting up Kellan's medicine that Erika asked me to get from the pharmacy. I'd been staying at their place for a few days, just to help out with things. Plus, I was worried about Kellan more than I wanted to admit.

"You're not listening!" Kellan shouted, straining his voice.

"No, I'm listening. What you're saying is that you don't want to marry me."

"Of course I want to marry you, Erika. But it just doesn't make sense now. If I died, you'd be left with all the baggage. All the bills, all the…"

"I don't care!"

"Well, I do!"

"Why are you acting like this?" Erika flipped around to me. "Alyssa, can you tell Kellan how unreasonable he's being?"

My lips parted, but before I could speak, Kellan said, "Don't drag your sister into this!"

I shut my mouth. I would've gone home, but they were standing right in the foyer blocking my path. So I sank into the sofa, trying to become invisible.

She sighed heavily. "Let's not talk about this right now. Let's just calm down. Tomorrow is your chemo appointment, so we should rest before we go to that."

"You're not coming," he said.

"What?"

"I said you're not coming. You flunked your last exam. You haven't been studying as much as you used to, and you can't keep falling behind. I'll have Logan come with me."

"Why are you shutting me out?" Erika whipped around to me again. "Why is he shutting me out?!"

I opened my mouth, and once again, Kellan spoke before I could. "Stop bringing her into this! You aren't coming to my chemotherapy appointment, all right?"

"Why not?"

"Because you're smothering me!" he shouted, louder than I'd ever heard him yell. "You are smothering me with questions and pamphlets and pills and your goddamn wedding planning and your goddamn lamps! I can't breathe, Erika!" He swung his arms in irritation, knocking a lamp off the side table. As it crashed, the room went silent. Kellan's eyes grew heavy with guilt as tears began to fall down Erika's face. Kellan lowered his voice, stepping closer to my sister. "I'm sorry, I just—"

She shrugged. "I know."

Suddenly Logan came crashing out of the bathroom with a towel around his waist, dripping wet with water. His hair was drenched with some weird-looking concoction that was slimy and green, and his eyes were wide in panic.

"What's happening?!" he said, flustered, almost slipping on the water trail he created himself. He looked so serious yet so ridiculous that the three of us couldn't help but start laughing hysterically.

"What the heck is on your head?" I exclaimed.

He narrowed his eyes, confused by our laughter. "It's the third Monday of the month. It's an egg and avocado mask for deep conditioning."

We laughed harder, and the room that had previously been filled with anger and confusion was replaced with family and laughter.

"You know what we need?" Kellan said, lightly kissing Erika's cheek.

"What's that?"

"A music dance break."

"What's a music dance break?" Logan and I said in unison.

They both ignored us. "Kellan, no. It's been a long day," Erika disagreed. "And like you said, I need to study…"

"No. It's happening. Music dance break."

"But…" she groaned.

"I have cancer," he said.

Her mouth dropped open and she smacked him in the arm. "Did you just play the cancer card on me?"

His smile grew. "I did."

I waited to see Erika yell at him, to tell him how his words hurt her, but instead she smiled. They exchanged glances and looks that only they understood, and she nodded once. "Fine. One song. One, Kellan."

I'd never seen him smile so big. "One song!"

"Our song," she ordered.

He hurried out of the room, leaving a slimy Logan and confused me standing there. Then Kellan came out with two conga drums and two rain sticks, handing one to me and the other to Logan.

"What's going on?" Logan asked. "What the hell am I supposed to do with this?"

Erika stared at Logan as if he was a complete buffoon. She took the stick from his grasp and turned it upside down, making the rain sound. She handed it back to him.

"Duh, Lo," I mocked.

He flipped me off.

Butterflies formed.

That was nothing new.

Kellan sat in front of the conga drums and started playing them. It took me a second to pick up on the beat of the song, but when it clicked in my head, my heart melted for the type of love my sister and Kellan had. He was playing Ingrid Michaelson's song "The Way I Am."

Their song.

Kellan sang the first verse to Erika as she smiled, swaying back and forth. Logan and I added in the rain sticks and began to dance with Erika as Kellan pounded against the congas.

Erika sang the second verse, and the love between her and Kellan filled the house with light as the words of the song fell from her tongue. Words about loving each other no matter the pain, words about being there for each other even when walking through the flames of life.

It was beautiful.

When we reached the long musical moment with no lyrics, Logan took both Erika's and my hands and spun us around, still wearing his towel, still with green goop dripping off his hair. Then, the room grew quiet when Erika began to sing the final verse—the verse that made tears fill everyone's eyes. She sang the words about loving him when he lost all his hair as she ran her fingers through Kellan's locks, leaning her forehead against his lips. He kissed her gently, and they finished singing the lyrics together as one.

The last noise heard was Logan's rain stick dying down.

"Wow," he said, wrapping his hand over his mouth, staring at his brother and Erika. "You two are fucking perfect."

Erika laughed lightly before looking at Kellan. "I don't want to marry you."

He sighed. "Yes, you do."

"No. Well, yeah, I do. But not until you're better. Not until you're healthy. We'll wait. We'll kick cancer's ass. Then you'll marry my ass."

He pulled her close to him, kissing her hard. "I'm going to marry the hell out of you."

"Heck yeah, you are."

"Oh my God. Get a room," Logan moaned, rolling his eyes. "I'm going to go wash this crap out of my hair."

"Speaking of…" Kellan cleared his throat and narrowed his eyes. "Do you guys think you could do something for me?"

Logan shook his head back and forth with disgust. "This is a terrible idea."

"For the first time ever, Logan and I agree on something," Erika said, tossing her hands up in shock.

"I say just go for it." The four of us were scrunched in the bathroom, a pair of hair clippers in my hand.

"Thank you, Alyssa! Finally, someone on my side. Besides, babe." Kellan turned to Erika with a big grin. "A ton of people are shaving their heads now."

"Well, he's not wrong there," Logan agreed. "It's kind of what people do in Hollywood. Shaved heads is the new trend."

"Then you shave yours," Erika challenged, taking the clippers from my grasp, then holding them out to Logan.

His eyes widened with horror, and he held a finger up to her. "You watch your language."

"But Logan's right. A ton of celebrities have shaved their heads for roles," Kellan tried explaining to his panicked fiancée.

"Name some."

"Bryan Cranston!" I said. "For *Breaking Bad*."

"Joseph Gordon-Levitt did in *50/50*!" Logan tossed in.

"I'm sorry, can we not name actors who were playing terminally ill patients when they shaved their heads?" Erika requested. Fair enough.

"The Rock!"

"Hugh Jackman!"

"Matt Damon!"

"Jake Gyllenhaal—twice," Logan exclaimed.

"Really?" Kellan asked. "Twice?"

"*Jarhead* and *End of Watch*."

"Badass," Kellan said and nodded, holding out his fist, which Logan bumped.

"Total badass."

What losers.

"You guys." I stood up straight and turned on the clippers. "It is time."

Erika held her breath and covered her eyes. "Okay. Do it!"

"Do it!" Kellan exclaimed.

"Do it! Do it!" Logan chanted.

So I did it.

CHAPTER 35
Logan

"What are you doing here?" Alyssa asked, opening her front door, finding me standing there with a brand new door and a tool kit.

"I couldn't help but notice the few times that I've come to your house that there was some work that needed to be done."

"What are you talking about?" She smiled. "This house is the definition of perfection."

I cocked an eyebrow, walked over to her porch railing, and pulled it straight up, seeing how nothing was securing it to the steps of the porch.

She giggled. "Okay, so it's not perfect. It's also not your job to fix." She bit her bottom lip. "Are you wearing a tool belt?"

"I'm definitely wearing a tool belt, which makes it my job to fix. So if you could please step aside and let me put a door on your bathroom, that'd be great."

I spent the next six hours fixing things around her place, and she helped me hammer a few things into place. The last thing I did was climb on top of her roof and try to patch up a few spots.

"Do you know what you're doing?" Alyssa shouted up to me. She refused to climb up to the roof, because unlike the billboard, there was no railing for protection.

"Of course I know what I'm doing," I shouted back.

"But how?"

I turned to her and gave her a sly smile. "I saw a documentary once on roofing."

Her eyes bugged out and her hands waved back and forth. "Nope. Nope. Get down, Logan Francis Silverstone. Now! Watching a documentary does not make you a professional."

"No, but the tool belt does!"

"Logan."

"Alyssa."

"Lo."

"High."

"Get down now. Come get some water. Just… I'll hire a person to check out the roof, okay? Then you won't feel like you have to fix it."

I chuckled and started climbing down the ladder. "Good. Because I had no clue what the heck I was doing."

Once my feet hit the ground, she shoved me hard and narrowed her eyes. "Don't be an idiot like that ever again. Okay?"

"Okay."

"Pinky?" she asked.

I wrapped my pinky with hers, pulling her closer to me. My heart started racing from the small touch, and I studied her trembling lips as she stared at my mouth. "Pinky."

We stood close to each other, somehow growing closer and closer as each moment passed. I felt her lips slightly touch mine, but we weren't kissing. We were simply somehow turning two people into one, taking in each other's breaths.

"Lo?" she whispered, her air brushing against my skin.

"Yes?"

"We should stop standing so close now."

"Okay."

She nodded once and stepped back. "Okay." She ran her fingers through her hair and gave me a tight grin. "You should go get some water or something. You've been working like crazy. I'm just going to my bedroom to take a breath or five for a minute."

I agreed and headed to the kitchen for a glass of water. I wondered if she felt everything for me that I felt for her whenever she stood near me. I wondered if she had to fight off the feeling of longing as much as I had to.

As I opened her refrigerator, I paused, seeing all the fresh foods she had. "Did you just go grocery shopping?" I hollered toward her bedroom.

"Yeah, I went yesterday."

My mind started racing, looking at the vegetables and uncooked sausage. I opened her cabinets, searching. "Do you mind if I make something really quick?"

"No. Go for it. Anything is up for grabs."

Awesome.

I started moving things around, grabbing pots and pans. Within minutes, chicken broth was heating on her stove, and I began chopping up mushrooms and fresh garlic.

"I gotta say, when you said you wanted to make something really quick, I thought you meant like a Hot Pocket." Alyssa smiled.

"Sorry," I breathed out, standing at her stove, browning the sausage in a pan. "Jacob offered me a job at his restaurant. But he's forcing me to perfect three dishes before he gives me the job. And he's being a total dick about it, turning down each thing I bring him. So I was going to test some of the food on you if that's okay."

Her eyes widened with pleasure. "Oh my God, I haven't had a Logan meal in forever. I will gladly be your guinea pig. What are we making?"

"Risotto," I replied.

"Doesn't that take a while?"

"Yup."

She didn't know that I was watching her from the corner of my eye, but she smiled. I smiled knowing she was smiling.

We spoke about random things as I stood by the stove, stirring the rice in the broth. "So you're thinking about opening a piano bar?"

"Yeah, well, seriously thinking about it. Remember when we were kids and talked about it?"

"LoAly?"

"*AlyLo*," she corrected with a smirk. "Yeah. I mean, I wouldn't name it that seeing how that was kind of our thing, but I don't know. It's just a dream. That's all."

"A good dream, which you should make a reality."

She shrugged, folding her arms on the table and resting her head on top of them. "Maybe. We'll see. My friend Dan has shown me a few different properties that might work. I know it's too soon to be looking at buildings and stuff, but it's just fun. Seeing the places makes the dream seem a little closer."

After the risotto was done, I put it on the plate and set it in front of Alyssa.

She grinned from ear to ear, clapping her hands like crazy. "Oh my God, it's happening! I know I missed you, Logan. But I think I missed your food even more."

"Fair enough. Now here." I handed her a spoon. "Eat up."

She dug in quickly, and when it met her lips and she began chewing, she frowned.

"What? What is it??" I asked, my voice heightened.

"Nothing. It's just not…amazing?"

"What? There's nothing wrong with this dish."

Her lips parted, and she nodded. "Yes, there is."

"No, there isn't. Look. The sausage is cooked flawlessly, the mushrooms are roasted perfectly, and the blend of seasonings is remarkable. This is a freaking perfect dish."

She frowned and shrugged her shoulders. "I mean, it's okay. For what it is."

I huffed. *For what it is?* Alyssa had a lot of nerve. "There's nothing wrong with this dish."

"There is."

"No, there isn't."

"It's"—she bit her bottom lip, made a wavering back-and-forth gesture with her hands, and shrugged once more—"bland."

"*Bland*?!"

"Bland."

"You just…" I took a deep inhale and exhaled hard. "Did you just call my food bland?"

"I did. Because it is."

I placed my hands on the edge of the table and leaned into her, extremely annoyed. "I've been cooking since I was a kid. I've been cooking this dish for three years straight through culinary school. I could make this food in my goddamn sleep, and it would taste like something I'd feed to the president. My food isn't bland. My food is flavorful and delicious. And you are just nuts!" I hollered.

"Why are you yelling?" she whispered.

"I don't know!"

She laughed, making me want to kiss her. "Logan…try the food."

I grabbed the spoon from her hand. Diving into the dish, I tossed the warm risotto into my mouth. The moment it hit my lips, I spit it back out onto her plate. "Oh my gosh, that tastes like ass." Since I could make this dish in my sleep, I hadn't tasted it before I put it in front of Alyssa.

She nodded apologetically. "When I said it was bland, I was being polite."

My shoulders slumped, and I fell against the ground. "How did I start sucking at cooking? That was the one thing I was good at."

"You don't suck at cooking. You just lost your passion probably. Don't worry. We can find it. If you come back tomorrow, I'll help you try to cook something else. We'll keep trying until you perfect three dishes that Jacob could never turn down."

"You'd do that for me?"

"Of course."

We stayed up that night, eating disgusting risotto and remembering what it felt like to be happy with each other. For the following two weeks, I showed up at her house, and we cooked and cooked until we found three dishes that tasted like heaven. It felt good to be around her. It felt free. We talked, laughed, and made messes. It felt like all those years ago, when all we did was laugh with each other. Alyssa coached me through perfecting every single one of my dishes, and I was so thankful that she had.

I set the final chocolate cake in front of her, and she moaned before it even hit her lips. "Moaning over my cake before you've even tasted it?" I asked.

"Definitely moaning over your cake before I've even tasted it." She opened her mouth, and I grabbed a fork, scooped up some cake, and placed it in her mouth. As she began chewing, she moaned louder. "Oh my God, Logan."

I beamed with pride. "If I had a dollar for every time I've heard that."

"You'd have no dollars and no cents," she mocked. "No. Seriously, you have to try this," she said, but instead of getting a fork for me, she drove her hand into the cake and shoved it into my face. "Isn't that good?" She giggled like a five-year-old as I wiped chocolate from my eyes, nose, and mouth.

"Oh yeah. It's so good. I bet you want more," I said. Right as she went to dash, I wrapped my arm around her waist and pulled her close to me. With my free hand, I scooped up cake and shoved it into her mouth. She squeaked.

"Logan! I can't believe you," she said and laughed, smearing her chin against my chin, rubbing it deeper into my slight five-o'clock shadow. "It's in my hair!"

"It's in my nostrils!" I replied, shaking it from my face the best I could, laughing at the sound of her laugh.

We kept snickering for a while until the moment passed. My hand was still wrapped around her, and when our sounds ceased, our heartbeats increased.

I'm falling in love with you.

My mind was so flooded from missing Alyssa for all those years that I almost forgot why I had to miss her. *Because loving me is dangerous. Change the subject.*

I took a step backward, releasing my grip on her. "Alyssa."

"Yeah?"

"You have a guitar in your bedroom. Do you play?"

She waved her hands back and forth. "Kind of. It helps keep me creative. I'm okay at it, nowhere near as good as I am with the piano."

"Kellan's been unable to play. His hands are shaky, and he sometimes forgets his own lyrics. I can tell it's eating him up."

She frowned. "I can only imagine what that's like. Being unable to do what you love."

"Yeah. I was wondering. I know you said you're not great at playing, but can you teach me? Can you teach me whatever you can so I can maybe play for him?"

"There it is again." She breathed out a small sigh.

"There what is?"

"The small glimpse of the boy I used to love."

CHAPTER 36
Logan

The next week, I brought Alyssa with me as I sat in Jacob's restaurant for my final examination of food. Seeing as how she was my inspiration behind the dish, it felt right that she'd be the one sitting beside me as Jacob told me to piss off and find a new line of work. Crisp-tender roast duck with a raspberry-rosemary sauce, roasted fingerling potatoes dressed with olive oil and seasonings, and garlic brussels sprouts.

My heart was pounding in my chest as I watched Jacob make the same mundane facial expression as he chewed. Alyssa's foot tapped nervously beside me, and she chewed on her shirt collar, which made me smile. I didn't know who was more worried about the duck not meeting Jacob's standards—Alyssa or me.

"You have to dip the duck into the sauce!" Alyssa chimed in before going back to chewing on her shirt. "Oh! And the brussels sprouts. Dip the brussels sprouts in the raspberry sauce too!"

He did as she said, and I cringed watching. He put his fork down and sat back in the booth, and a small smile graced his lips. "Well, fuck me sideways, that's good."

A bit of confidence found me. "Yeah?"

"No. Like—it's good. Like out-of-this-world, best-thing-I've-ever-eaten good." He went back to spooning more into his mouth. "Holy shit. Whatever you did to this dish, I want you to do to my menu each and every day you come into work."

"So…I got the job?"

"Keep cooking like that and you can have the whole restaurant," he said and laughed. Then he grew serious, pointing a finger at me. "That was a joke. The restaurant isn't for sale."

I laughed. "Well, the job is good enough for now."

Pride filled me up inside, and I almost burst.

Alyssa was beaming from left to right as she reached out, tossing her hands around me. "I knew it!" she whispered against my ear. "I knew you could do it."

I breathed in her peach shampoo.

"All right, children, break it up. Go out and celebrate tonight. Logan, you start on Monday."

We all stood up and Jacob went for a handshake, but I scooped him up into a bear hug and spun him around in circles before kissing his forehead. "Thanks, Jacob."

"Anytime, friend."

As Alyssa and I went to leave, I paused. "Oh yeah, Jacob, wait." I reached into my back pocket and pulled out a piece of paper with the recipe for my hair mask.

He snickered. "Were you holding out on giving me the recipe until I gave you the job?"

"There might have been a small possibility that I was holding off until you gave me the job."

He nodded, proud. "I would have done the same thing."

Alyssa and I stayed out on the town for the remainder of the night, celebrating me getting my first official chef job. We ended up in a cheap diner with hamburgers and French fries stacked in front of us, taking on the battle of who could eat the most without getting sick.

I felt like for the first time, I was happy again.

But I should've known it wouldn't last long. Because after the highs always, *always* came the lows.

"You eat here too, son?" was heard from behind me, and my jaw clenched. I turned to see my father smiling my way like the asshole he was. He had his arm around a girl, and when I locked eyes with her, I saw the fear resting in her stare. My mind flashed back to the night I first saw those eyes.

"Do you know how beautiful your eyes are?" I asked, changing the subject. I began kissing her neck, listening to her moan.

"They're just green."

She was wrong. They were a unique shade of celadon, holding a bit of gray and a touch of green to them. "A few years back, I was watching a documentary on Chinese and Korean pottery. Your eyes are the color of the glaze they used to make pottery."

"Hey." I swallowed hard, tearing my stare away from Sadie. "What's up?"

"What's up?" he echoed. "You say *what's up* as if the last time you saw me, you didn't try to start a fight."

Alyssa was holding her purse close to her, and I could see the panic in her stare. She was terrified, the same way Sadie looked. The same way most women appeared when they were near my dad.

"Look, I don't want any trouble," I said, my voice low.

"Oh, so now I'm trouble?" he snickered, talking loud because he wanted everyone to notice our interaction. That was the kind of person he was, the show-off. He stepped in closer to me as I sat, hovering a few inches above me. "Don't forget the person who took you and your mom in all those years ago, Logan," he growled, somewhat as a threat. He stared at me with hate in his eyes for a few seconds before he smirked big and patted me on the back. "I'm just fucking with you, buddy. Can we sit? Can we join you?" He didn't wait for a reply before sliding into the booth beside Alyssa.

Alyssa tensed up and appeared seconds away from crying. I took her hand in mine, lightly squeezed her fingers, and pulled her closer to me.

I wanted to ditch the place and take Alyssa home. I hated how my father made women's skin crawl out of fear.

"This is my girl Sadie," he said, wrapping his hand tightly around her waist, pulling her into him.

I cringed, feeling my temper building, but tried not to let it get to me. I held my hand out to Sadie for a handshake. "Nice to meet you," I offered. She didn't extend her hand, and she broke her eye contact.

Ricky spoke for her. "Oh no, no, no. No touching." His voice was drenched in the same threatening manner that it always was when he spoke to Ma. He thought it meant something that he was a big powerful dick, so he belittled women as a way of feeling strong.

It just made him look weak to me.

"Sadie doesn't really like to be touched by other men, do you, Sadie?" Dad said.

She didn't reply, because he wouldn't let her. If I hadn't spoken to her that one night, I would've assumed she was mute, seeing how she hadn't spoken one word since I saw her in the diner.

"Do you need something, Ricky?" I asked him, growing more and more upset.

He tossed his hands up in defense. "Whoa there, stranger. I just wanted to say hi." His cell phone went off, and he glanced at Sadie. "Gotta take this. Don't move." He stood up and headed outside to take the call.

My stare shot to Sadie. "What the hell are you doing with him? Is that the boyfriend you were talking about?"

"I—I didn't know..." Her voice was shaky. "I saw you at the train station after I tried to leave him, and I wanted to tell you. But I knew it'd only make more trouble. I want to leave him, but every time I try, he sends people to find me. I can't..."

"Does he hurt you?" I asked.

Her stare fell to the ground.

I dug into my back pocket and pulled out my wallet, scrambling to get money. "Here. Take this. Go get on the closest bus, and get away from him."

Alyssa's eyes studied mine, but she didn't ask what was going on. Her hand landed on my leg for comfort the whole time.

"I can't leave. I can't," Sadie said, her eyes tearing up.

"Why not?"

"I'm pregnant," she whispered. "I'm pregnant, and I have nowhere and no one to run to. He pulled me away from my family. He destroyed all my relationships. And now he's all that I have."

"Sadie, listen to me. For your kid, the best thing you can ever do is get on a bus and never look back. You don't want to have a child with that man. I've been that child. Trust me, it doesn't turn out well."

She looked down, shaking slightly. "Okay," she whispered.

Alyssa appeared confused but scribbled her number onto a

napkin. "If you need anything, you can call me or Logan. I put both of our numbers down."

Sadie wiped the tears from her eyes. "Why are you being so nice? You both hardly even know me."

"What? Of course I know you. You taught me Spanish," I joked, trying to break up the tension.

She gave me a small smile and collected the money.

"Go out the back door in the kitchen. I can take you if you want." I stood up, took her hand, and started walking her to the back. We almost made it until I felt her being yanked away from me.

"What the hell does *don't move* mean to you, woman?" Dad hissed at her. His arm wrapped around her waist, and he squeezed her so tight that I saw the pained expression hit her eyes. "Time to go."

Sadie looked at me with pleading eyes, and I stepped forward. "I don't think she wants to go."

"Excuse me?" he asked. He ran his fingers in Sadie's hair and pulled her even closer, tighter. "You don't want to go with me?"

She didn't say anything.

Dad continued. "I do so much for you, Sadie, and this is how you repay me? I love you. Don't you know that?" He bent down and kissed her, the same way he used to kiss Mom when he fed her his lies of control. She kissed him back too, just like Mom used to kiss him.

I knew right then that Sadie wasn't going to leave. She was too far tangled into his web.

"We'll catch up later, Logan," he said to me. It sounded more like a threat than a promise for a happy get together.

I wasn't shocked, though. My father knew nothing about happiness, but he was a professional at disasters.

When they left, I felt disgusted. I remained silent, snapping the band on my wrist.

Alyssa walked over to me. "Are you okay?"

I shook my head.

"We can go outside for air if you want."

"Yeah, okay." I needed more than air, though. I needed my father to disappear, allowing everyone who ever crossed his path to finally be freed from his chains.

CHAPTER 37
Alyssa

As Logan and I walked outside, he clenched his fists, reddening from the annoyance of his father. I didn't know the history that Logan and Sadie had, but I knew he was afraid for her well-being, as he should've been. Being around Logan's father was terrifying. I couldn't imagine being Sadie, unable to escape his chains.

"Are you okay?" I asked.

"Just need a moment." He placed his hands behind his neck and started pacing around the parking lot. There were cars parked on the large plot, and people were outside in the nice weather, socializing and laughing, while Logan was doing the complete opposite. He was dealing with those demons that liked to haunt him. *He deserved a break.*

I leaned against the side of the building, waiting for him to calm down. He kicked the tall strands of grass with his shoes, back and forth.

"Are you thinking about using?" I asked.

"Yup," he muttered, shutting his eyes and walking in circles.

Poor guy.

"You know what would make this moment better?" I asked, placing my hands on my hips as my left foot rested against the side of the building.

"What's that?"

"You know what we should do to really make you feel better?"

"Uh, no. But I'm guessing you have an idea?"

"Oh, do I ever!" I locked eyes with him. "Are you listening?"

"Yes."

"No, I mean, are you really, *really* listening?"

He laughed. *Good.* I was so happy he was laughing. I laughed too, because he was so handsome. I laughed because he was my friend again. I laughed because my heart knew that would've never been good enough for me.

"Yes, I'm listening."

I stood up tall, pushed out my chest, and said, "Karaoke."

"Oh God, no."

"What? Come on! Don't you remember when we went out for karaoke when we were younger?! And you did Michael Jackson's 'Billie Jean' with all the pelvis humping?" I reenacted his hip movements from the past.

He snickered. "Yeah. I also remember being coked up when I did the pelvis humping."

My face dropped in shock. "What? You were high when you did that?"

"Yeah. Otherwise, I would've never agreed to doing karaoke, trust me."

"Oh. I just thought you were excited about their Michael Jackson and Justin Bieber collection. Anyway. Today, we are going to do karaoke at O'Reilly's Bar."

"No way."

I nodded, taking his hands into mine. "Yes way."

"Alyssa. I appreciate that you're trying to make me feel better and stuff, but seriously, you don't have to. I'm better now. You made me better. Plus, there's no way in hell I'd ever do karaoke again."

CHAPTER 38
Logan

I was doing karaoke again.

Somehow Alyssa managed to pull me onstage in O'Reilly's Bar and put a microphone in my hand. She promised we'd do a duet so I wouldn't be performing on my own, but I could still feel the nerves in the pit of my stomach. She picked the song "Love the Way You Lie" by Rihanna and Eminem.

"You know the words?" she asked me. "I sing it all the time when I'm driving in my car, so I know the lyrics by heart."

"I can follow along on the screen."

She smiled wide. I smiled wider.

My greatest High.

When the music started playing and the first lyrics started coming on the screen, no sound came from either Alyssa or me. The people in the bar started shouting at us to sing, but neither one of us were.

The DJ turned off the track and gestured toward us. "Um, you do know that you have to open your mouth to sing, right?"

I looked at Alyssa with confusion. "Why weren't you singing? It said it was Rihanna's part."

"Oh. I don't sing her part. I like Eminem's rapping parts."

"What?" I hissed, stepping closer to her. "I'm not singing Rihanna's part."

"Why not?"

"Because I'm not a chick."

"But you have that beautiful high-pitched voice, Lo. I think you'll make a beautiful Rihanna," she mocked.

"I'm hitting replay one time, folks. It's now or never," the DJ said.

"I'm not doing this, High," I said as we stood nose to nose with our chests out.

"Oh, you're doing it."

"No."

"Yes."

I shook my head. "No."

She nodded. "Yes."

"Alyssa."

"Logan."

"High."

"Lo."

The intro music started, and I kept shaking my head left and right, telling her there was no way I was going to do it, but when Rihanna's part came on, the microphone rose to my lips and I began singing the female part of the song, high-pitched, sounding like fucking hell.

Alyssa covered her mouth to keep her uncontrollable chuckles to herself. I gave her a look to kill before turning around to face the audience and fully embracing my feminine side. I thought I did pretty good. I thought I was the one to make our performance magic.

But then something happened.

Eminem's verse came up, and Alyssa transformed into something I've never seen before. She stole the DJ's baseball cap, tossed it on her head backward, and started marching back and forth on the stage, getting the audience involved in the performance, making them wave their hands as she rapped.

Alyssa Marie Walters was rapping to Eminem. And she was fucking incredible. She put her all into it—hand gestures, facial expressions—giving it everything she had. She was so wild and beautiful in that moment. Free.

When the chorus came up, she looked at me, and I started singing again, high-pitched and terrible.

Then she rapped again, nailing every word.

When it came to the last verse, the hardest verse she had to rap, she took a deep breath. She locked eyes with me, and before she started, her shirt collar rested between her lips. She nodded once. I nodded once. She dropped the collar and started rapping the final verse directly to me.

And it was fucking sexy.

Her body swayed back and forth. She became the words. Once she finished, she dropped the microphone, the crowd went wild, and I sang the final Rihanna chorus to her.

When we finished, we couldn't stop laughing. We wrapped each other in a tight hug as the people in the audience cheered us on, begging for an encore.

We performed five more songs before we retired to a booth in the back of the bar for a few celebratory drinks.

We stayed most of the night, chatting about anything and everything. We laughed more than we had in a long time. For a while, it felt like it used to.

Her laughs became my inhales. Her smiles were my heartbeats.

I watched her mouth move as she told a long story. Truth was I stopped listening. I stopped listening a long time ago, because my mind was somewhere else.

I wanted to tell her how I felt about her, all over again. I wanted to tell her how I was falling for her once more. I wanted to tell her how I still loved her wild hair and still loved her mouth, which was always chattering about something or another.

I wanted to…

"Logan," she whispered, frozen in the booth. My hands had somehow landed against her lower back, and I guided her closer to me. My lips hovered inches away from her mouth. Her heavy exhales were mixing with my deep inhales as both of our bodies shook in each other's hold. "What are you doing?"

What was I doing? Why were our lips so close? Why were our bodies pressed against each other? Why couldn't I break my stare? Why was I falling in love with my best friend all over again?

"Truth or lie?" I asked.

"Lie."

"I'm not addicted to your smile. Your eyes don't make my heart race. Your laughter doesn't give me chills. Your peach shampoo doesn't drive me crazy, and when you chew on your shirt collar, I don't fall deeper in love with you. Because I'm not. I'm not in love with you."

Her inhales grew deeper and her exhales were heavy. "And the truth?"

"The truth is I want you. I want you back in my life, in all ways and more. I can't stop thinking about you, High. Not to escape reality but to embrace it. You're my heart. You're my soul. I want you. All of you. And more than anything right now, I want to kiss you."

"Lo…" Her voice was shaky. "You're still the first person I think of when I wake up. You're still the one who I miss when you're not beside me. You're still the only thing that ever felt right to me. And if I were honest, I'd say that I want you to kiss me. I've wanted you to kiss me all my life."

I locked my fingers with hers.

"Nervous?" I asked.

"Nervous," she replied.

I shrugged.

She shrugged.

I laughed.

She laughed.

I parted my lips.

She parted her lips.

I leaned in.

She leaned in.

And I was reminded of the yesterdays that set my world on fire. We kissed for a long time in that booth, making up for all the mistakes of our past and forgiving each other for all the mistakes of our future.

It was beautiful. It was right. It was ours.

But of course with all the highs always came the lows.

Alyssa's phone rang, and we pulled away from each other. When she answered, I could tell something was wrong. "What's up, Erika?"

Pause.

"Is he okay?"

My gut tightened as I sat up straight.

"We'll be there soon. Okay. Bye."

"What is it?" I asked as she hung up.

"It's Kellan. He's in the hospital. We have to go. *Now*."

CHAPTER 39
Logan

"What happened?" I asked, rushing into Kellan's hospital room. Kellan was lying in his bed, IVs hooked up to his arms. "Kel, are you okay?"

"I'm fine. I don't know why she called you guys. There's nothing wrong."

"He was walking to the bathroom and he passed out in the hallway," Erika said, sitting in a chair, rocking back and forth slightly with her hands tucked under her thighs.

"I came to right away," he argued. "I'm fine."

"Kellan, you couldn't walk, and you forgot my name."

Kellan opened his mouth to speak, but a sigh left him instead. He closed his eyes. He was tired, breaking down more and more each day, and I couldn't help but wonder when the chemotherapy would start fixing him. It seemed as if it was only wearing him down.

Erika stood up, taking Alyssa and me to the side of the room to talk while Kellan fell asleep. She wrapped her arms around her body and leaned against the closest wall. "The doctors are running a few more tests. He's just so tired and weak. The nurse said they can send us home with a wheelchair and it might help him get around, but he said he didn't want it. He's being so prideful. But he needs…" She wiped her hands over her eyes before resting them on top of her head. "We just need to help him. He's not the type to ever say he needs help. He's always been the one who helped others. But he needs our help. Even if he tries to push us away."

"Anything you need, I'm there," I said. "Anything he needs."

Erika gave me a tight smile. Her eyes were heavy too. Sleep deprived. I was almost certain whenever Kellan closed his eyes at night, hers stayed wide awake.

"You need help too, Erika. You don't have to do everything. That's why I'm here."

"It's just…" Her voice trembled as she glanced back to Kellan. "It's just time to start realizing that things are going to get a whole lot worse before they get better. That scares me. I'm terrified. Logan, if anything happens…if anything happens to him…" She began to cry, and I pulled her out of the hospital room, into the hallway, and wrapped her in a tight hug. "I can't lose him. I can't."

I'd never seen Erika fall apart. She was always the one who had everything together. To see her so destroyed spoke volumes on how serious the current situation was becoming.

When she pulled herself together, she took a step back and wiped away her tears. "I'm fine. I'm okay. I'm good," she said, reassuring herself as much as us. "They are going to keep him overnight. I'll stay here with him."

"I can stay," I offered. "I know you have your finals coming up."

"No, it's fine. I'm okay. I'm good."

"Sis," Alyssa whispered, wiping away the tears from her sister's eyes.

"I'm okay. Really. You two get home. I'll text you if anything changes."

I glanced toward the hospital room. "Can I just sit with him for a second?"

She nodded. "Yeah. Definitely. Alyssa, want to come with me to find coffee?"

The two wandered off, and I went into the room and pulled a chair up beside Kellan's bed. The machines around him kept beeping and humming as I watched his chest rise and fall. Even breathing looked hard for him lately.

"Are you sleeping?" I whispered.

"No," he replied. "Just sleepy."

I pushed my thumbs against my eyes to hold back the emotion. "What the hell are you doing in here, Kel? It was my job to end up in places like this, remember? Not yours."

He gave me a weak smile. "I know, right?"

"You okay?"

One deep inhale. One coughing exhale. "Yeah. I'm okay." He tilted his head in my direction, and his always kind eyes gave me a slight grin. "I'm killing her," he whispered, speaking of Erika.

"What? No."

He turned away, trying to hide the tears falling against his cheeks. "I am. Watching me die is killing her."

"You're not dying, Kellan."

He didn't reply.

"Hey! Did you hear me? I said, 'You're not dying.' Say it."

He looked to the ceiling, then closed his eyes. The tears were still falling down his cheeks. "I'm not dying."

"Again."

"I'm not dying."

"One more time, big brother."

"I'm not dying!"

"Good. And don't you fucking forget it. Everyone's okay. We're all going to get through this together." I took his hand in mine and squeezed it lightly, trying to give him some comfort.

"Everything's okay. You're right. Sorry, I'm just—"

"Tired?"

"Tired."

I stayed with him longer than I thought I would. Erika came back to the room, but I asked if I could be the one to stay with Kellan that night. She agreed, and Alyssa decided to stay with her, making sure she wasn't alone.

I didn't sleep that night. I stayed up, watching the machines and my brother's breathing.

When morning came and he opened his eyes, he gave me a half-way grin.

"Go home," he said.

"No."

"Go. Go live your life, Logan. Don't you have someone to be falling in love with?" he asked.

"What do you think I'm doing right now?" I replied as I laid my head on the bed.

He smiled my way and shrugged his right shoulder.

I smiled his way and shrugged my left.

I wish I could say things with Kellan were getting better, but it appeared that they were only growing tougher. If he wasn't in the hospital, he spent most of his time in bed. The once-smiling brother of mine was slowly turning into someone who showed hardly any emotion. The gentle Kellan snapped more and more at Erika for anything she did, which made her even more nervous.

It was heartbreaking, because she truly was doing the best she could do.

He never yelled at me, which I wished he would. Erika seemed on the verge of having a breakdown. The fall school year was coming back around, and she seemed overwhelmed with the planning of her classes, along with the fact that she failed her summer class for her master's degree. Her stress level was high.

"Take her out," Kellan sighed as I sat him up on the living room sofa. He was getting sick of staring at the walls in the bedroom, growing a bit claustrophobic.

"Take who out?"

He gave me a you-know-who-I'm-talking-about look. "Alyssa. On the coffee table are two tickets to the opera tonight in Chicago. There's an overnight hotel stay too. I think she would like that. Erika and I were going to go for our honeymoon but…" His voice faded as he closed his eyes. "Take her out."

"I'm not driving all the way down to Chicago and staying overnight when you aren't doing that well."

"Yes, you are."

"No, I'm not. You had chemotherapy yesterday. You always get sick a few days later."

"I'm fine. Besides, Erika will help me."

"Kellan."

"Logan." Kellan pushed himself up to a sitting position on the couch. "You deserve to be happy."

"I am happy."

"No. You're existing. Going through the motions of life. Which makes sense. Everything you've been through, everything you've seen, it had to become somewhat of a sick routine that was impossible for you to break away from. But the only time I've seen you happy—and I mean really happy—was when you were with Alyssa."

"Kellan, stop."

"Remember when you came begging me for money to buy a suit that fit just so you could take her out to a piano recital in Chicago? You beamed with hope. I'd never seen hope from you."

"With good reason. Hope is a waste of time. Remember how she and I never actually made it to Chicago, because Ricky pissed me off and I fell off the deep end?"

He rolled his eyes. "That's not who you are anymore. Take her out."

"No."

"Yes."

"No."

"Yes."

"No!"

"I have cancer."

I rolled my eyes. "Dude. Low blow. How long are you going to play the cancer card?"

He smiled at me, reached his hand out in my direction, and patted me on the shoulder. "Take her out, okay?"

I nodded once. "Okay."

CHAPTER 40

Alyssa

Hi," I said, my voice breathy as Logan stood on my porch in a suit and bow tie. His hair was slicked back, and he was beaming.

"You look beautiful," he said, taking in my long black dress. "So beautiful."

I blushed. "You do too. I mean handsome. You look handsome."

He reached out for my hand, and I took his in mine. As he walked me to the car, he opened the passenger door and helped me inside. My heart was pounding against my rib cage as the butterflies in my stomach somehow transformed into dragons, setting me on fire. I was so nervous.

When he asked me if I'd go to Chicago with him to see an opera, I had to make sure I wasn't dreaming. We were never able to go on any fancy dates all those years ago. We were never able to fall in love the way we truly deserved to love each other. So the fact that today, Logan was in a suit that wasn't too big for him and I was in a dress that was too fancy for me was amazing.

I still love you.

"Are you excited?" he asked as we drove down the freeway.

"Yes."

I still love you.

"I've never done anything like this, ya know? Seen an opera. I mean, I've been to your piano recitals, which were breathtaking, but I've never seen something like this."

"You'll love it," I said. "When I was in college, we had to go to shows for one of my music classes. The opera is quite the experience."

He smiled. "Thanks for coming with me, High."

Whenever he called me High, I felt like I was eighteen all over again.

I still love you.

The show was amazing, and as we sat in a corner box watching it, I noticed Logan tearing up from the action. His eyes never left the characters onstage, and mine hardly ever left him. It was crazy how it happened. How one boy could still, after all these years, influence l every beat of my heart.

After the show, we walked outside in the cool autumn Chicago weather. We stood so close to each other that every now and then, our arms would brush up against each other. The hotel we were staying at was right down the street from the opera house, which was wonderful.

"Erika and Kellan are stressed," Logan said, breaking me from my thoughts.

"Yeah. Extremely stressed. Erika called me the other night as she sat in her car crying her eyes out. She feels as if she's at the end of her rope and like Kellan is pushing her away."

"Do you think he's pushing her away?"

"I don't know. I think he's just scared."

"Yeah. Me too. I've been thinking…we should do something for them. I don't know what, but I want to do something to make them feel better."

"That's a great idea," I agreed, opening the door to the front lobby of the hotel. "And I think—"

"I'm still in love with you."

What? Did I just speak the words that have been dancing through my mind all night long? The words that I've felt for the past five years?

No. They didn't come from my lips.

With a slow turn, I stared at Logan, standing on the sidewalk, with his hands stuffed in his slacks. He swayed back and forth.

"What?" I said, my heart pounding.

"I'm still in love with you," he repeated, walking closer to me. "I've tried to stop it. I tried to ignore it. I tried to wish it away, but it won't leave. Whenever you're near me, I want you closer. Whenever you laugh, I want the sound to never fade. Whenever you're sad, I want to kiss your tears away. I know all the reasons that I shouldn't want to be with you. I know that I can never be forgiven for what happened all those years ago, but I also know that I still love you. You're still the fire that keeps me warm when life becomes cold. You're still the voice that keeps the darkness at bay. You're still the reason my heart beats. You're still the air in my lungs. You're still my greatest high. And I am still truly, madly, painfully in love with you. And I don't think I'll ever know how to stop."

"Logan…"

He kept walking toward me, making my heart speed up until I felt faint.

"Alyssa…"

"Lo." My fingers slowly laced together with his.

"High."

Him.

Me.

Us.

We drew closer. Our bodies wrapped together, and I felt him trembling as my fingertips rested against his chest.

"Nervous?" I asked.

"Nervous," he replied.

My lips hovered millimeters away from his. His breaths became mine, and mine were solely his. He was my life support, making my heart rise and fall, over and over again.

I shrugged.

He shrugged.

I laughed.

He laughed.

I parted my lips.

He parted his lips.

I leaned in.

He leaned in.

And we were both still so very much in love.

For a few brief moments, he let me into his heart, and I allowed him into mine. His skin met my skin. His lips met my lips. That night, we held on to each other. We stopped our minds from wandering off. We didn't speak of yesterday, and we refused to speak of tomorrow.

But we did remember, and we did dream.

We remembered everything we were and dreamed of everything we could someday become. Every time he moved into me, I whispered his name. Every time he pulled out, he whispered mine.

"I love you," I said softly against his ear.

"I love you," he replied gently, kissing my neck.

We loved each other that night. We loved each other with no restraints, no restrictions, no fear. We loved each other with every kiss, every touch, every climax.

We loved the pain, we loved the scars, we loved our wild fire that could never be extinguished.

We loved that night.

Yes...

We loved so slowly.

When I awakened, I still felt as if I were dreaming, because I woke up in his arms. His eyes were open, and he placed a gentle kiss on my forehead.

"Hey," I yawned, rubbing my eyes.

"Hey," he replied.

"Is it time to get up?"

"No." He shook his head. "It's only three in the morning."

I sat up slightly, concern building inside me. "What's wrong?"

"Nothing."

"Logan. Tell me."

"I'm just worried, that's all. Kellan had his chemotherapy a day ago, and since I've been back, I've never not been there. He sometimes gets sick in the middle of the night, and I'm worried, that's all."

I climbed out of bed and started collecting his things, then I tossed on my clothes.

"What are you doing?" he asked.

A pair of pants slapped him in the face. "Get dressed. We're going home."

The drive home was quiet, but he held my hand the whole way. I knew it seemed silly, but on that car ride, I fell even more in love with him. He pulled up to my house to drop me off and leaned forward to kiss me.

Oh, how I loved his kisses.

"Call me if you need anything," I said. The sky was still dark, the sun still sleeping. He agreed to keep me updated. "Oh, and I have something for you." I reached into my oversize purse and pulled out a stack of DVDs. "I collected these over the past years, thinking they might be documentaries you'd be interested in. I watched a few and loved them. The one on the phoenix was my favorite and reminded me of you."

His lips parted, and his voice cracked. "Why didn't you ever give up on me?"

I shrugged. "Because some things—the best things—are always worth fighting for." I kissed his lips and started to climb out of the car.

"Oh, and, High?" He reached into the glove compartment of the car and pulled out a DVD. "This is for you."

"What is it?"

"I made a documentary while I was in Iowa."

"What?" I asked. "What is it about?"

"Us," he replied a bit shyly. "It's called *Highs and Lows*. Every message you left me has a response on that. One thousand and ninety replies. Plus a few in-between moments."

"Lo…"

"It's not all good, but it's real. It's raw. But I thought you should know that I did respond. To every single message. And I want you to know that you're the one who helped me get through every second of getting clean. Your voice saved me."

The moment I got into my house, I tossed the DVD into my laptop, and I held my breath for an hour straight. Some of his replies he spoke to me; others he simply spoke to the camera, as if it were a diary of sorts. Each reply told me what I'd wished I could've heard all those years ago. Each reply matched how my heart bled for five years straight.

Reply #1

_____

I'm sorry. I'm sorry. I'm sorry. I'm so fucking *sorry, High.*

Reply #56

———

It's my fifty-sixth day at rehab, and I'm lonely. I still don't know what this all means. Being alive, being dead. Inhaling, exhaling. The simple idea of existence was always confusing to me. But then you walked into my life one day, and everything started to make a little more sense.

Maybe the point of life is to teach us that we aren't always going to be our past mistakes. Maybe the point of life is to open ourselves up to the things that we fear most—like love.

Maybe the whole point of my life was to simply find you, even if it wasn't meant to be forever.

And that thought alone is enough to get me through each night of loneliness.

Reply #270

The baby would've been born this month. You left me a message telling me this, but I already knew. I can't sleep. I can't eat. I can't stop thinking about lying beside you, holding you close to me. But I'm not better yet. I'm still lost. I'm not strong enough to love you the way you deserve to be loved. So here I wait. Until I'm something you can be proud of.

Reply #435

So this is my apartment. I don't know if I've shown you before, but here it is. We have all the basics. Kellan helped me. Over here, you'll find Jordy the mouse. He comes out to play every now and then. And that's pretty much it. It's small, but it's mine, I guess.

I know you're mad at me.

But I miss you so much it hurts to breathe some nights.

You asked me what I do when it rains?

I lie in bed and think of you.

Reply #1090

You said you were done calling me. I'm happy to hear that but at the same time broken. I want you to be happy. I want you to find someone worthy to love you. I want you to fall in love with a heart that beats like mine beats for you. I want you to laugh so loudly, and I want someone to fall in love with the sound of your laughter, the way I love those sounds.

I want you to have your happy ending.

I want you to move on.

I tell myself each day that I'm not in love with you anymore, that I've moved on.

But somehow that's not true. Each day it happens, right before I close my eyes to sleep. I see your face, your smile, your soul, and in the quiet whispers of the night, I fall in love with you all over again.

I hope that never changes.

And selfishly, I hope a small part of you always loves me too.

CHAPTER 41
Logan

Walking into Kellan's place, I paused a moment when I heard the sound of upchucking. I rushed to the bathroom where the sounds were traveling from and found Kellan on the floor, his head in the toilet as he threw up everything he had inside him.

"Jesus, Kel," I muttered, reaching for a towel to wet. I bent down beside him as he gagged, unable to throw anything up because he hadn't much left inside.

"I'm okay," he muttered before the dry heaving began.

My hand landed on his back. There wasn't much I could do other than be there with him through the pain.

"What's happening?!" an alarmed Erika said, poking her head in the bathroom. Her eyes widened as she deliberated over which direction she should go—stay in the bathroom with Kellan, or go toward the living room. "Why didn't you wake me?" she asked me.

"I just got home."

Her hands raked through her hair. "Okay. He needs the nausea pills." She hurried away, her feet hammering against the wooden floors. She came back with a glass of water and a little pink pill. "Here you go, Kellan."

"No," he whispered. "I don't want that."

"It will help with the nausea."

"I don't want that."

Erika's chin quivered, and she pushed the glass and pill toward him. "Kel, come on. It will—"

"Just leave me alone!" he hollered, pushing the glass from her and making it fly to the ground and shatter.

Erika leaned back, grimacing. Her lips trembled as her breaths sawed in and out. She placed the pill on the bathroom sink. "It's right there if you need it."

After I helped Kellan back to his bedroom, he took the pill from me. I took a few tentative steps toward the kitchen, where I found Erika going through her cabinets. In front of her was a box of new glassware, which she was unloading.

"Erika, he's just tired."

She nodded repeatedly, pawing her hands through her hair. "Yeah, I know. I know. It's fine. I just wanted to get these glasses switched in before morning. I'm so glad I bought these. I knew they'd come in handy, and they are actually better than the ones before. Stronger. I don't know why I didn't switch before."

She closed the box after all the glasses were switched and headed for the living room, where she stood with her hands on her hips, staring blankly ahead.

"What are you doing?" I asked.

"I think if I move the sofa to face the east wall, more people could see the television. Yeah, I think that's a good idea."

"Erika."

"Or maybe I should buy a new television. I saw a sale in the paper and—"

"Erika, come on. Go to bed."

"No. No. It's fine. I have to clean up the glass in the bathroom. It was seriously so lucky I had the replacements."

"Erika."

She burst into sobs, covering her face. *Jesus*. "Why isn't he like that with you, huh?! Why doesn't he yell…? Why doesn't he…?"

"I left before and had no plans on coming back. He probably thinks I'll leave again. Or worse, that I'll start using."

"I'm broken. I'm so broken. I'm not prepared for school to start. I failed my summer night class. Failed. I never failed anything in my life. And now Kellan's mean. Mean. Kellan has never been mean. I don't know how much more I can take." She continued to sob, and I wrapped my arms around her.

I wasn't sure what to say or what kind of comfort to deliver to her. She wasn't wrong. It seemed each passing day, Kellan grew darker and darker toward her, pushing her away. "Do you want to smoke some weed?"

She pulled away from me and cocked her head, shaking it. "No, Logan. I do not want to smoke some weed."

"Okay."

Silence.

"Do you want to get drunk?" I asked.

She narrowed her eyes at me, pinched her bottom lip, and swayed, debating.

Erika drank, I didn't. We'd been sitting on her patio for the past forty-five minutes, and for the first time ever, I witnessed a drunken Erika.

Her laughter echoed through their backyard, and every now and then, she'd snort before taking a swig from her bottle of whiskey. I smoked a joint, which mellowed me out.

"You're the best," she said, slapping my leg.

"You hate my guts."

"I do. I hate your guts." She reached for the joint between my lips, and I pinched my lips around it, refusing to let it go.

"I think you should just stick to your whiskey."

"'I think you should just stick to your whiskey,'" she mocked me before laughing again. "You know what I hate most about you?"

"What's that?"

"Everyone loves you, no matter what you do."

"Bullshit."

"No." She nodded. "Really. Especially Kellan and my sister. They think you are some kind of god. Logan Silverstone can do no wrong! They both love you more than they could ever love me."

I frowned. "That's not true."

"No, it is. I mean, let's face the facts. You crashed Kellan's car. You almost burned down my first apartment. You broke my sister's heart when you drove into a building. You ran away, ignored her for years, and still—she'd freaking marry you tomorrow if you asked. Kellan didn't go a day without mentioning your name. Your mom cried every day after you left. She even managed to get clean for a while because she wanted to make you proud, before your crazy father dragged her back into that crap and landed her in the hospital. Screw whatever kind of crap you used that sent you to rehab. The truth is the biggest drug in this small circle of people is you. They are addicted to you, and they won't stop using."

My throat went dry, and it became hard to swallow. "What did you just say?"

"Uh, I just said a lot. You want me to repeat it all?"

"No." My head shook. "The part about my mom. My dad put her in the hospital?"

Erika looked up fast, locking eyes with me. "Oh my gosh." Her eyes bulged and she shook her head. "Don't tell them that I mentioned that. Please. They didn't want you to know, because they didn't want you to feel guilty for not being there. Please don't say anything."

I put out the joint, stood up, and then headed back inside. "Go to bed, Erika."

CHAPTER 42
Alyssa

The next day, Logan asked me to go with him to visit his mom. We stopped by Bro's Bistro first to pick up some food for her, and as he ran into the restaurant, I waited outside in the car for him. My eyes traveled across the street when I heard yelling from the alley a few steps away from the car.

Opening my door, I started walking in the direction of the sound and my heart leapt out of my skin as I saw Logan's father standing over Sadie, screaming at her. She was shaking against the concrete wall of the shop next door.

"I'm sorry!" she cried as he raised his hand and slapped her hard across the face. I listened to her whimpering as her body slid down the wall into the fetal position.

"Hey!" I screamed, running down the dark alley toward the two. "Back off," I hollered at him.

He boxed Sadie in with his arms and glanced my way. His eyes were bloodshot and cold, vicious. "Fuck off," he ordered.

Sadie's eyes met mine with nothing but fear. The bruises slowly forming on her face made my stomach twist. I didn't know what else to do as I watched him bend down and whisper something in her ear that made her cringe with fright.

"Leave her alone, jerk!" I screamed.

His hands wrapped around Sadie's wrists, and he started pulling her in the opposite direction of me. "You stupid bitch," he muttered to her, dragging her beside him.

Without thought, I rushed down the alley and shoved him from behind. "Let her go!" I screamed, slamming my fist into his back.

He dropped her hand and, without any hesitation, swung around and hit me right in the eye and sent me slamming against the wall, making my body slide down to the ground from the sudden loss of balance.

Before I could stand, all I saw was Logan come charging down the alleyway, and I watched as he slammed his fist against his father's jaw, knocking him to the ground.

Sadie rushed over to me to help me stand. "Are you okay?" she asked, panicked, but I was fine, if not just shaken from the whole situation.

"I'm good, I'm good," I said.

My eyes fell to Logan, who was standing over Ricky, slamming his fists into his face over and over again. His eyes were hard, his stare cold, and he kept swinging.

"Logan, no!" I shouted. I yanked on his arm. His eyes were wild, the fire inside him burning him to ashes.

Logan.

Lo.

My most painful low.

"Logan, that's enough. He's passed out. It's okay." I kept my voice gentle, trying not to show how scared I was. He went back to swing at his father, but I held on to his arm. "Look at me, Lo. Please," I begged. "Logan, you are not him," I promised, making him pause. "You are not him. You are not your father."

He stopped.

"You're okay, Logan Francis Silverstone," I swore, tears falling down my cheek. "You're okay. Give me your hand," I ordered.

He did.

I watched his breathing slow as he climbed off Ricky, and he stared at his bloody knuckles. I reached for his hands, but he yanked them away. His eyes fell to Sadie's face, which was almost as bad as his father's. "*Shit,*" he exhaled. "Come on," he said, walking off.

Sadie and I followed behind him as he led us to TJ's doctor's office.

After banging on the door, TJ came down in his pajamas and unlocked the door. "What the heck, Logan? It's Sunday. Sunday is *rest* day."

Logan didn't say anything, but he stepped to his side, revealing Sadie and me.

"Shit," TJ muttered. "Come in."

We stayed there until we were all fixed up, and TJ checked on Sadie's baby, who was thankfully okay. When we left, I told Sadie she could stay with me, but before she could reply, she received a text from Ricky.

Ricky: Tell your hero that he's going to pay for this.
Starting with his mom.

"Oh no," I murmured as Logan's eyes widened with fear. "Call the cops."

CHAPTER 43
Logan

Rushing to Ma's apartment, I pushed the door open, my chest heaving. "Ma! Where is he?" I shouted. My heart almost stopped beating when I saw Ma on the ground, being kicked in the stomach repeatedly by the devil himself. I leapt at him and tossed him across the room with all my strength. I hurried to Ma's side, trying to wake her up.

A snicker was heard behind me as he stood up. "Well, isn't this a grand family reunion? Don't mind your mama there. She's just taking a nap."

I stood up and charged at him, wanting to tackle him to the ground, but I paused, hearing Alyssa in my head. *You're not your father.*

"Just leave us alone, Ricky." He looked a mess, as if he'd been using a lot of his own drugs.

"Not until I get Sadie back. You had your fun. Now give her back," he hollered, walking toward me.

"Ricky…you need help, man."

"Fuck off, asshole. Give me Sadie."

"She's not your property. She's not going with you."

He ran his hands through his hair, pulling on it out of anger. "I was there for you, boy! When you had nobody, I took you under my wing."

"Getting me hooked on drugs? Yeah, how thoughtful of you."

He rushed toward me and wrapped his hand around my neck, pressing our foreheads together. "You don't talk to me any damn way you want, son."

Even though I wasn't the tiny kid I used to be, Ricky was still much bigger than I was. He was even scarier when doped up too. There was no telling what he'd do, but all I knew was I'd rather him do it to me than those two girls sitting in the car downstairs.

"Go home, Ricky. It's over."

"It's over?" He pushed me away and then swung his fist into my eye. The pain that followed was hard-core. I stumbled backward and tried not to fall, gripping the sagging sofa.

"I'm not going to fight you, Ricky," I muttered, my fingers falling to my eye.

"Yes, you are," he muttered, moving in and slamming his fist into my gut.

I felt the vomit rising up from my stomach, and I did my best to push it down. "No, I'm not."

"Why not?" he asked, pushing me to the ground and slamming his foot into my stomach. "Why not? Because you're weak? Because you can't be a real man?" he screamed, kicking me repeatedly.

"No," I muttered, spitting out the blood that was in my mouth. "Because if I did, I would be just like you."

"I'm so tired of you," he muttered, running his hands against his mouth before reaching into his back pocket and pulling out a gun. "I'm tired of you interfering with my life. I'm tired of you stepping in between my situations. I'm tired of your face. So we're just going to end this now."

He pointed his gun toward me, and I shut my eyes, but when I heard the sound of the bullet, I felt nothing.

My eyes opened, and I saw the cops standing behind me and Ricky lying on the floor, shot in the shoulder.

The cops and paramedics rushed into the scene. It was all a blur as I watched them race to Ma and then to Ricky. Alyssa spoke to the officers with Sadie, explaining what happened. I tried to open my mouth, but my jaw was so swollen that it hurt to speak. A paramedic came over to me to check out my face, but I shrugged them away.

"I'm fine," I choked out, my throat burning. They ignored me and started cleaning my cuts, speaking of stitches to my nose and chin.

"We'll have more questions at the hospital," the officer told Alyssa. "We'll follow behind you as you drive over."

She nodded, then headed over to me. She grimaced as her fingers lightly touched my face. "Oh, Lo…" she whispered.

I huffed out a chuckle. "Y-y-you…" I paused, cringing at the pain in my jaw. "You think I'm bad, you should see the other dude."

She didn't laugh.

I guess because it wasn't funny.

"Come on," she said. "Let's go get you fixed up."

I wanted to say something sarcastic. I wanted to make her feel better because I could tell she was distraught. But no words would leave me. My mind was whirling, thinking about Ma, if she'd be okay. I couldn't stop wondering how long she had been hit before I arrived. I couldn't stop thinking about how I should've been there to protect her. I couldn't stop thinking about how many times I swore I hated her, but the truth was I loved her.

I loved her so much. And I let her down. I let her down when I went away.

LOGAN, THIRTEEN YEARS OLD

Grandpa sent me a documentary on hamburgers for my birthday. I'd already watched it three times, but I placed it back into the DVD player. It was pretty interesting, and I was pretty bored before I got the documentary because I had watched most of the ones at the library already.

"What are you doing?" Ma asked, standing in my doorway.

"Nothin'," I replied.

"Can I do nothing with you?"

I looked up and gasped. Ma looked beautiful. Her hair was combed into a high ponytail, and she had tied a red ribbon around it. She was wearing makeup, something she never did, and she wore a pretty black sundress that normally sat hanging in the back of her closet.

"You look amazing," I breathed out.

Her muscles were twitching, but that was kind of the norm with Ma. She was always fidgeting and twitching with tremors, but after a while, it didn't bother me. It was just a part of her. "Yeah? I don't know. I'm going to this meeting later today." She smiled and curtsied. "It's a meeting about helping people get clean, ya know? I want to stop using, Logan. I want to be a better mama for you."

My eyes widened. I felt like I was floating as my stomach fluttered. "Really?" Ma never talked about getting help. She always said no one could help her.

"Yeah." She sat down on my mattress. "You'd have to go stay with

Kellan and his dad for a while, though. I want to go to rehab. I really want to make something better for us."

"You're leaving me?" I said, my hands clammy.

"Only for a little while. Then I'll be back better than ever."

"You'll come back for me?"

"I'll come back for you."

I sighed in relief.

"You think you can take a break from watching your DVD and come make a lasagna? We can celebrate before I leave."

My eyes beamed and I nodded my head. "Yeah!"

We cooked together. I made the sauce, and Ma layered the noodles and cheese. After it was done, she had me move the small television from my room into the living room. We sat on the sofa, watching the documentary on hamburgers, and ate our hot lasagna out of the pan.

"Ma?"

"Yeah, Logan?"

"Why are you crying?" I asked.

She gave me a tight grin and shrugged. "Just happy, that's all, sweetie. I'm just happy."

I smiled too and went back to eating. The lasagna burned the roof my mouth, but I didn't mind at all, because Ma was going to rehab. Then she'd come back to me, and we'd start our real lives together. We were getting better. Soon our normal life would be eating dinner together and watching documentaries. She'd come to my parent-teacher conferences and graduations. She'd slow dance with me at my wedding. She'd read my future kids bedtime stories.

We'd have a future together, and it would be perfect.

I kept smiling and smiling and smiling.

Because I'd never been so happy.

CHAPTER 44
Alyssa

Logan walked away with a fractured nose, two black eyes, and a broken wrist. He was lucky, seeing how the damage to his face looked fifty times worse than it actually turned out to be. We sat in the lobby, waiting to hear about his mother's condition. I closed my eyes, praying that she was going to be fine. I knew Julie had always brought so much pain into Logan's life, but there was no doubt that she meant the world to him.

The cops came over to speak with us.

"Sorry to interrupt, you guys, but we just wanted to update you. After everything we spoke about, we are currently obtaining a search warrant for your father's house. The gun he had was illegally in his possession, and we found drugs on him at the scene. He has quite a history of coming in contact with the police, so I think we'll be able to really nail him this time. For now, we'll keep him in custody for the attack on your mother. That should give us enough time to get the court's warrant. We're going to get this guy."

Logan nodded. I thanked the officers, and they wished us the best, saying they'd be in contact.

"What a relief," I sighed.

Logan's head rested in his palms as he kept nodding. "Yeah."

I rubbed his back as the doctor approached us.

"Hey, so just an update."

"A lot of updates today," Logan murmured.

The doctor gave a tight grin. "Yeah. So your mother's condition is improving, but the level of narcotics in her system is pretty worrisome for us. We're going to keep her here for the next few days to help flush her system. She has two broken ribs from where she was kicked, but we can't give her too much medicine for the pain due to the narcotics. We're kind of playing it by ear at this point. If you have any questions, please don't hesitate to ask."

I thanked the doctor, and Logan's head remained in his palms.

"See, Logan? Everything's okay. Everything's going to be fine. Do you want me to call Kellan and let him know?" His brother hadn't been informed of anything. Logan didn't want to worry him until he knew all the details.

He groaned, looking up. "No. I should be there to tell him in person. Just in case he reacts badly. I don't want to tell him over the phone."

"That makes sense. That's a good idea."

"High?"

"Yeah?"

"I just want you to know you have the right to opt out now. Out of all this."

"What are you talking about?"

"My life," he said, strain evident in his voice, hinting at the pain in his jaw. He cringed and started rubbing it. "My life is a mess. It always has been, and I'm giving you a get-out-of-hell-free card. I'm in love with you, and that's why I'm giving you an out. You deserve more than this messed-up life."

"Hey," I whispered, moving closer to him. My lips fell against his ear, and I combed his hair back. My heart broke seeing the blood on his face and in his hair. It was all so heartbreaking—the life he'd lived. "I'm not going anywhere."

He nodded constantly, clasping his hands together, his eyes glassy. "I'm a mess, High. I'm a mess. I've always been a mess. I'll always be a mess."

"Logan, stop. You're not who you were back then. Okay? You're not the product of your yesterdays."

"But you deserve the world. You can do better. You deserve more."

"I could have a decent life with someone else," I said. "I could have the white picket fence, the normal job, the normal kids, the normal husband. I could have a comfortable life with someone who I'd be content with but never fully love. But that's not what I want, Logan. I want you. I want the scars. I want the burns. I want your mess. Your scars, your burns, your mess—that's my heart. You are everything I ever wanted and everything I'll ever need. Your hurt is my hurt. Your strength is my strength. Your heartbeats flow through mine. So no, I'm not going to opt out. I don't want to run away because things are hard sometimes. I want you. All of you—the good, the bad, the pain, the anger. If you're walking through hell, I'm holding your hand the whole way through. If the fires in our lives keep rising, we'll burn as one. You're it for me, Logan. Yesterday, today, tomorrow—I'm yours. You're my eternal flame."

He turned to me and kissed me. I kissed him back, a bit too hard, and he whimpered at the touch.

"Sorry," I said and laughed gently, kissing his forehead. "Come on.

Let's go to my place, get you cleaned up, and then I'll drop you off at Kellan's so you guys can talk."

When we got to my house, I turned on my shower, undressed Logan, and helped him inside. The warm water fell against his body as he closed his eyes, taking in deep breaths.

"I'll be right outside. I have a few of your old clothes from way back when that I can grab for you," I said.

"No. Shut off the light and come here," he said, his eyes still closed.

I did as he said. I removed all my clothes, and I climbed into the shower with him. He pulled me close, wrapping his arms around me, his skin on my skin, his forehead against mine. All that could be heard was the water falling against us and our breathing.

We stayed there for a long time, until the water ran cold, and then we stayed longer.

"For always, High?"

"For always, Lo."

CHAPTER 45
Logan

When Alyssa dropped me off at Kellan's place, she left me with a level of peace. My father was in custody. Ma was unable to leave the hospital, which meant she wouldn't be able to come in contact with any drugs for a small bit of time. Maybe things were slowly turning around. *Maybe.*

I stepped into a darkened house. Kellan sat on the sofa.

"What's going on?" I asked, flicking on the light switch.

He cringed at the abrupt flood of light, but he didn't say anything. He had tears rolling down his face as his hands shook, and he tried to open a bottle of his pain pills. When he was unsuccessful, he threw the pill bottle across the room.

"Argh!" he shouted, pounding his hands against his head.

"What's going on, Kel? Where's Erika?"

"She went to her mom's house." He stood up slowly, his legs shaking, and stumbled over to the pill bottle. He picked it up, tried to open it once again, and failed. His breaths were heavy as he leaned against the wall and kept trying.

"Here, let me," I offered. I reached for the pills, and he shoved me away.

"Leave me alone."

"No."

"Yes."

I started wrestling him for the pill bottle, and I snatched it from his grip. I opened it and placed a pill into the palm of his hand. He slid down against the wall to the floor and sat.

"I don't need you and Erika to babysit me and open damn pill bottles."

"Yes, you do."

"No, I don't."

"Kel, yes, you do!"

"No, I don't!" he hollered, his voice cracking as he broke down crying. He wrapped his arms around himself and turned away from me, trying to keep the tears to himself. "I'm dying, Logan. I'm dying."

I slid down to the floor and sat beside him with my back against the wall. "Don't say that."

"It's the truth."

"'Be here now,'" I said, quoting Ram Dass. "That was the quote at the rehab clinic that was right over each bedroom. They told us to stop blaming ourselves for our yesterdays and to stop worrying about when we left the clinic. We were meant to just be there, in the moment. Be here now, Kellan. Right now, you're here. You're just as alive as Erika, Alyssa, and I am."

"Yeah. But I'm going to be dead a lot sooner than all of you."

"That's debatable. I'm a pretty big screwup."

Kellan laughed and shoved me lightly. *Good. Laughing is good.* We leaned back against the wall.

"'Be here now,'" he murmured to himself.

"So when is Erika coming back?" I asked.

"She's not. I told her to go for a while."

"What?"

"I couldn't keep putting her through this, Logan. Every time I coughed, she thought I was dying. She deserves a normal life."

"Is that what you told her?"

He grimaced. "Not exactly."

"What did you say?"

"I told her that I never wanted to marry her. I told her that we were over and I was sick of her nagging. I told her to leave and not come back."

"You pushed her away by being mean."

He nodded, sniffling. "It was the only way she'd go. I couldn't keep breaking her heart."

"Trust me, big brother, her heart is broken." He frowned, knowing I was right. "Let's just say that the roles were reversed. Let's say Erika had the cancer, and you were the one taking care of her. How would you feel if she said those words to you?"

His hands rolled over his face nonstop. "I know. I know. I miss her already. But I don't know how to fix it. I don't know how to make it easier for her."

"She didn't sign up for easy, Kellan. She signed up for you. Through all of it, she signed up for you. Don't worry, though. We'll fix this."

"When did you become so wise?"

I smirked. "When Alyssa gave me the same exact speech about how she signed up for me, which included all the baggage that came along with me."

He laughed. "I should've known you weren't that wise."

"Yeah, well, I'm working on it."

We sat silent for a few minutes. "Uh, Logan?"

"Yeah?"

"What the hell happened to your face?"

I chuckled and began to tell him about Mom and my father.

He reacted much better than I'd hoped yet had the same thought as I did. "Well, at least she can't get to any drugs while she's in the hospital."

Ah, my brother. My best friend.

Alyssa: You're okay, Logan Francis Silverstone.

Me: I'm okay, Alyssa Marie Walters.

She texted me those words every few hours. When Kellan was ready, he and I went to the hospital to see Ma. She was in quite a bit of pain, because the doctors couldn't give her much medicine due to her addictions. It was hard seeing her that way, but it wasn't the worst I've ever seen her.

Kellan sat in a wheelchair, and I pushed it toward her bed. He took her hand into his and gave her a small smile as I stood back watching.

"I'm so sorry, baby," she cried.

He placed their hands against her face, and he shook his head.

"I'm so sorry for messing up so much," she said. "I've screwed up everything."

"Be here now, Ma," he replied. "It's okay."

She bit her lip and looked down at her hospital gown and all the cords and bandages attached to her body. "I want to go to rehab," she said softly.

Kellan and I nodded in agreement.

"Me too," another voice said.

I turned to see Sadie. She had glassy eyes and was fidgeting a little, but she gave me a smile.

"Okay," I said.

She nodded. "Okay. I don't know how I'm going to do it. Have this baby on my own. I don't have anyone."

I nudged her. "It's fine. That kid, he's going to be my brother. And where I come from, you do anything for your brother. I'll help you. You have family now, Sadie. You don't have to figure it all out on your own anymore. Promise."

CHAPTER 46
Alyssa

Two weeks had passed since the incident with Logan's parents. Julie entered rehab and had been there for days, struggling but fighting for her life. Sadie was getting clean too, finding her footing.

Everything was getting back to normal. Except for the fact that Erika was still staying with our mom, which was far from normal. It was actually a bit terrifying.

On Saturday afternoon, I headed over to Mom's house with a box in my hands and pounded on the front door.

When it opened, Erika cocked an eyebrow. "Hey, Aly. What's up?"

"Um, what's up is the fact that you're staying with Mom. You know what? Never mind. Go get your things. It's time to go."

"What are you talking about?"

"Remember your life? Your fiancé? Yeah. It's time for you to go home. Kellan—"

"Doesn't want me. He doesn't want me there, Alyssa."

"He needs you."

Mom appeared in the doorway, her eyes narrowed. "What are

you talking about? Erika has finally come to her senses. She's getting her life back before she makes a huge mistake. I'm so proud of her for realizing this."

"Mom, can you do something for me?" I asked.

"What?"

"Just mind your own damn business. Just for once in your life, mind your business."

She huffed, but before she could reply, I yanked Erika out of the house and closed the door behind her.

Erika frowned. "Listen, Alyssa. I tried with Kellan. I really tried. But he made it loud and clear that he didn't want me there, so I'm not."

"Come home, Erika. Right now."

"No."

"Fine." I opened my box and arched an eyebrow. "But I tried to warn you."

Her eyes widened when she saw her plate collection in the box. "What are you doing, Alyssa?" I started tipping the box over, and she jumped as they all crashed to the ground. "Oh my gosh!"

"Logan! Come here." I called him over, and he hopped out of the car with a box in his hands. "Tell Erika to come home."

Erika was shaking, biting her bottom lip. Logan walked over to her, stared her in the eyes, and smiled. "You're my sister."

"Stop. I'm not."

"You scream at me. You hate my guts. You treat me like shit. You call me stupid. You're my sister, Erika. And screw Kellan right now. Right now, *I* need you to come home. I can't help him without you."

"I can't," she said. "I can't do this."

Logan nodded, opening the box with Erika's favorite glassware. "Come home."

"I am home."

"Okay." He started tipping the box over, and she cringed.

"No, Logan! I just bought—"

Crash! Glass pieces went scattering across the ground.

"Oh my God! What is wrong with you two?!"

"We want you to come home. That's all," I explained.

"I can't keep doing this. I can't do dysfunctional anymore."

I gestured toward the windows of the house where Mom watched our every move, pounding on the glass, yelling for Erika to come back inside. "And you think *that's* normal?"

"Go away, you two. Please. Kellan doesn't need me."

"Yes, I do." We all turned to see Kellan walking toward us with a box of his own. He stood at the edge of the driveway and locked eyes with Erika. "I miss you. I want you. I need you, Erika." He dumped all the items in his box to the ground and released the box. "Come home."

Erika laughed, and then we all started laughing with her. Mom opened the front door, came rushing out, and ordered Erika to come back inside, but she refused to listen.

We all walked back to the cars, leaving our pain in the broken pieces of glass on the ground and starting over again—together. Kellan rode home with Erika in her car, and Logan drove mine.

"Hey, I was thinking… Want to have some crazy, wild sexual escapades before the event at Jacob's restaurant tonight?"

I shrugged, unamused. "I guess. Or we can watch the new documentary on Michael Jackson that I bought yesterday and eat leftover pizza and raspberry Oreos."

His eyes widened. "Oh my God. I love it when you talk filthy to me."

He kissed me, and I knew that our forever was beginning that very minute.

"Okay, so here's the plan. I go to Jacob's restaurant and help set up all the final details. You go to Kellan and Erika's place, pick them up, and talk them into coming out for drinks, which Kellan will agree to. Erika will refuse going out and then somehow still end up coming because she loves Kellan and will do anything to make him happy," Logan explained, standing up to leave after we watched the documentary.

"Right."

"God. I'm nervous, and the party isn't even for me," he said and grinned.

I gave him a kiss as he hurried out of the house. "Are you sure you don't want a ride to Jacob's?"

"No, I'm fine. It's nice out. I'll see you soon!"

After he left, I headed straight over to my sister's place, where she did exactly as Logan thought she would and refused to come.

"I just don't think it's a good idea to go out for drinks, Alyssa. We're both pretty tired." Erika frowned. "Maybe next week."

"Ah, come on! It will be fun! Plus, Logan's working tonight at Jacob's, so we can annoy him by ordering food and sending it back nonstop. It will be so epic!"

Kellan smiled. "That does sound kind of fun. And I miss fun."

Erika narrowed her eyes. "You want to go?"

He nodded rapidly.

"Seriously? You're not tired?"

He shook his head rapidly.

She sat in deep thought for a moment as Kellan and I gave her the biggest puppy-dog eyes she'd ever seen. When she finally gave in, we both cheered with excitement.

"One appetizer and one drink! Water for this dude," she said, nodding toward Kellan.

"Just so you know, I'm going to sip my water really, really slow."

When we arrived at Jacob's restaurant, Erika frowned. "Why is there a closed sign on the door? It's six in the evening."

"I don't know. That's weird." I grabbed the handle and turned, opening the door. "It's unlocked. Come on. Let's see if Jacob is here."

The moment we stepped inside, Erika gasped as she saw all the wedding decorations. The place was packed solid with all their friends, shouting, "Surprise!"

"What's going on?" Erika asked, her eyes shooting back and forth.

Jacob came over, wrapping his arm around Kellan. "I'll take care of this guy, and, Alyssa, you help your sister out. The ladies' room is free for you both."

"For what?" Erika asked, still flustered, but I grabbed her arm and pulled her along with me. When we stepped into the bathroom, her hands covered her mouth. "Why is my wedding dress here, Aly?"

I smiled, almost feeling her overwhelmed energy. "I thought you knew? You're getting married today."

"What?"

"I said, you're getting married today." Her eyes started to water, and I shook my head. "Oh no. No crying. The makeup artist is going to be here in a few minutes. And we have to get you ready."

"You mean… That wedding out there… Those decorations, those people. That's my wedding?"

I nodded.

She huffed, placing her hands on her hips in disbelief. "You did this for me?"

"It was Logan's idea."

She bit her bottom lip and started shivering.

"Aw, honey. Don't cry."

"I'm not," she sobbed, covering her face with her hands. "That was just a really, really nice thing for him to do."

We hurried to get her ready, getting her into her beautiful white wedding gown, pinning her hair up in a delicate bun, and we laughed and laughed while drinking champagne.

"Are you ready, sis?" I asked, standing behind her in my maid of honor dress.

"Yes. I just wish Mom was…"

I frowned. "I know."

"But it doesn't matter. Tonight is about Kellan and me. Tonight is ours."

When we walked out to the restaurant, Jacob was standing onstage with a microphone in his hand, ready to officiate the ceremony. To his left was Kellan in a suit and tie, and beside Kellan was Logan. My eyes danced across his face, taking in all of him. His smile was wide and spread to his eyes. His beautiful locks of hair were missing, though. All his hair was gone, freshly shaved to match his brother. Not only did Erika tear up, but water fell from my eyes.

I loved him.

For always. For always. For always.

"You stay here," I said to my sister. "Don't move until you hear me playing, then go meet your soon-to-be husband."

Erika was still in a beautiful shock, but she nodded.

I headed over to the piano and began to play as I watched my sister walk down the aisle toward the love of her life. Tears fell down her cheeks, and tears fell down mine.

They deserved this moment. They deserved it more than anyone in the world. Jacob read his script, and the two lovers exchanged their vows, promising each other the hard days and the calm days. The painful heartbreaks and the beautiful heartbeats. The forever and always. When they kissed, everyone in the room felt the love they shared.

Then, they were rushed out of the room, laughing and crying and loving. Logan grabbed the microphone from Jacob and waited a few more minutes before I gave him the sign that Erika and Kellan were ready for their grand entry. His lips parted, and he smiled as he spoke. "Ladies and gents, it is my pleasure to introduce to you for the first time ever, Mr. and Mrs. Kellan Evans!"

He gestured over to Erika on the left side of the room and then gestured toward Kellan on the right, and they walked out, meeting each other in the middle of the dance floor.

"Before we dive into a night of fun, I figured I'd give my best man speech now. So wherever you are, grab a drink, and listen up." He gave a tight smile, and I saw the tears form in his eyes that he tried his best to blink away. "My brother, Kellan, is a superhero. He might not save cities, he might not wear a cape, but he changes lives. He's always lived each day as if it was filled with magic. He smiles even when it hurts. He believes in love and life and happy endings. He believes in family. I mean, he believed in me when I probably didn't deserve it. He and I grew up different. When he believed in happiness, I was stuck in tragedies, but he still loved me. He loved me through my struggles, through my internal fires, through my pain. He loved me unconditionally, with no limits to that love. And because of that love, I knew I'd never be alone.

"He and Erika love in the same way. Erika loves my brother to her core. She'd go through hell and back to keep him smiling, even when it hurts. She's caring, she's smart, she's gentle. She welcomed me into her home, even though I left messes in every room, because she loved him. She loved him for all that he was and all the heavy baggage that came with him—including me. She loved him before cancer, she loved him during cancer, and I swear to God, she'll love him after cancer. Because her love is unconditional.

"These two individuals are superheroes of love. They showcase how when things get hard, there are always smiles to be found. They sacrifice for each other because they know that their love is real. Even when it's dark, their love somehow shines. These two individuals taught me to embrace love. To believe in happily ever afters. To give my all, unconditionally. So to that, I raise my glass." He lifted a glass into the air and stared at his brother and Erika. "To the good days, to the bad days, to the unconditional love that these two taught me to believe in. May we all search for that kind of love. May we all discover that kind of love." His eyes moved over to me, and a single tear fell down his cheek as one rolled down mine. "And when we find it, may we hold on to it for always and always and always."

I blew him a kiss, and he caught it in his heart before turning back to the couple.

"To Kellan and Erika and their forever kind of love."

Everyone cheered, everyone drank, and everyone loved.

Logan wiped at his eyes and laughed. "Now, please, everyone clear the dance floor as the beautiful married couple share their first dance."

I joined Logan onstage and took the microphone from his hand. "Your hair is gone," I whispered, running my hands over his bald head.

He shrugged. "It's just a haircut."

"No." I kissed his forehead. "It's so much more than that."

"I love you," he whispered.

"I love you," I replied.

He moved over to the guitar and picked it up, sitting on top of the stool as I moved to the piano, placed the microphone near me, and waited for him to begin strumming. When I heard the sounds that he only recently learned to play, I smiled, joining him as I played the keys and began singing the intro to Ingrid Michaelson's song "The Way I Am."

Their song.

Kellan and Erika swayed back and forth on the dance floor, falling deeper in love, minute by minute. During the guitar solo, Logan spoke into his microphone as the front door opened to the restaurant. "Please welcome the mothers of the bride and groom to the party."

Everyone's eyes widened and cheered as Julie and my mom entered the room together. My heart started pounding against my rib cage as I turned to Logan, shocked. "How?"

He shrugged. "I made a few stops before coming over here."

You're my world. My whole, wide world.

The wedding was going amazingly well, with more laughter and happy tears than I'd seen in a long time. When everything wound down, we all walked out to the parking lot of the restaurant, Kellan and Logan still in their suits and Erika and I still in our dresses.

"Thanks again, Logan and Alyssa. For everything. Tonight was everything I ever dreamed of," Erika said. The way she looked at Kellan and the way he stared at her showed me what true love really looked like.

"No problem. Kellan, I know you have your doctor's appointment tomorrow, and I'll be there. But I think tonight I'll stay at Alyssa's so the newlyweds can have the night to themselves," Logan said.

Kellan smiled and agreed, but Erika yipped. "No!"

"What?" I asked.

"We have to make one stop before anyone goes their separate ways," she explained.

"Okay. Where's that?" Logan asked my sister.

A wicked grin fell against Erika's lips, and that smile told me exactly where we were about to go.

The four of us stood in aisle five of Pottery Barn, staring at the different plate sets. Erika's eyes were narrowed, deep in thought, as the rest of us swayed back and forth.

"Did you really have to break all my things?" she questioned, tilting her head to the left, looking at something that cost more than my bridesmaid dress.

"It was Logan's idea," Kellan said, throwing his brother under the bus.

"Alyssa went along with it," Logan replied.

"Kellan told me you wouldn't mind," I chimed in.

"Whatever. I blame you all equally."

"You can't blame me!" Kellan said defensively. "I have—"

"Cancer, we know!" Logan, Erika, and I moaned in unison.

He laughed.

"Okay. On the count of three, everyone point at which set I should get before we move on to the glasses. One, two, three!"

"That one!" we all shouted, pointing at different items, then we all began to argue, shouting over one another, laughing, and smiling.

Once the plates were chosen, there was a sense of peace that washed over the once hectic aisle five. I looked around at the people who knew all of one another: the good, the bad, and the destroyed. I saw it. It was still there. Through all the pain, tears, and destruction, somehow our love for one another survived. Somehow we were all still connected.

My people.

My family.

My tribe.

Somehow, we were unbreakable.

CHAPTER 47
Logan

TJ's office was cold. Colder than it needed to be. But I was used to it by now. I hadn't missed one appointment with Kellan since I returned to True Falls.

On the left corner of his desk was a jar of jelly beans along with red licorice sitting on the right side. *At least he got rid of the black licorice.*

I crossed my arms, pressing them against my body for heat. *Shit.* I was freezing. My eyes moved to the chair right next to me where Kellan sat.

When I looked up to TJ, I saw his lips moving pretty quickly. He kept explaining the situation over and over again. I couldn't be certain, though, because I wasn't listening anymore.

I didn't know the exact moment when I stopped hearing the words flying from his mouth, but for the past five or ten minutes, I was simply watching his mouth move.

My hands gripped the sides of my chair, and I held on tight.

Erika sat on the other side of Kellan's chair, tears falling against her cheeks. "It's working?" she said, breaking me from my daze.

"It's working." TJ's voice was filled with hope. He even had a smile on his face. "The chemotherapy is working. We're not out of the woods yet, but we are moving in the right direction."

The overwhelming feeling of hope took my breaths. The panicked heartbeats that rolled through my system were terrifying.

"I—" my voice started, but then it paused. I felt like I should say something, because Kellan wasn't talking at all. Yet I didn't know what the right words were. Were there any right words in a situation like this one?

My fingers gripped the chair deeper. My right hand brushed against my cheek, and I cleared my throat. "It's working?" I asked.

TJ started speaking, but I stopped listening again. I took Kellan's left hand and squeezed while Erika squeezed his right.

My brother, my hero, my best friend was fighting cancer.

He was *beating* cancer.

And I could finally breathe.

That night, Alyssa and I climbed up to the billboard and stared at the stars tossed across the sky. We shared raspberry Oreos and kissed until we needed a breath, remembering everything we'd been through and dreaming of everything that was coming our way.

"I liked the DVD you gave me about the Greek mythology of the phoenix," I said as our legs dangled off the ledge of the billboard. "I love the idea of the bird dying but then somehow rising from the ashes, reborn, receiving a new chance at life."

She smiled. "Yeah, you're the phoenix, Logan. You've come so far, seen so many things, and you've been reborn."

I shook my head. "I looked deeper into different mythologies and different beliefs on the phoenix and what it stood for. Although I appreciated the story of the Greeks, it was the Chinese beliefs that got me the most."

"What did they believe?"

"The phoenix was commonly seen as a pair, a male and a female. The two phoenixes together stood for yin and yang. They were two parts of a whole. The female phoenix was the passive, gentle, intuitive one, while the male was the assertive one, the one who took action. Together they stood for unforgettable partnership. In parts of the world, the two phoenixes symbol is given as a wedding gift—a sign of forever and happily ever afters."

"That's beautiful," she said.

"I thought so."

We took a moment to stare back up at the sky.

"High?"

"Yes?"

My palms were sweaty as I reached into my pocket and pulled out a small box.

She took in a small breath when her eyes fell to the box, then her eyes locked with mine. "What are you doing, Lo?"

"Truth or lie?"

"Lie."

"I'm doing absolutely nothing."

Her bottom lip trembled. "And the truth?"

"I'm beginning to rise from the ashes. I'm only in the early stages of rebirth, but I know as I ascend, I want you to be locked with me forever." The small box opened, and I pulled out the engagement ring, which showcased two phoenixes coming together, intertwined with a diamond in the middle of their wings. "You're my healer. You're my strength. You're my ever after, and if it's all right with you, if you're okay with it, I'd love for you to be my wife."

"Really?" she asked softly.

"Really," I replied.

Her voice was shaky as she moved in closer to me, resting her lips against mine. "For always, Lo?"

I took her hand into my hand and slid the ring onto her ring finger, kissing her gently. "For always, High."

EPILOGUE
Logan

SEVEN YEARS, ONE WEDDING, ONE FULL RECOVERY, TWO BABIES, AND A STRONGER LOVE LATER

I was happy.

I didn't have much to my name, and I didn't have many stories of success to pass on to my children. I wasn't some millionaire genius. I didn't have three bachelor's degrees. I'd probably be working most of my life to make ends meet, but I'd always make them meet because I had love. I had three people counting on me to keep going when times were hard. I had three people believing in me and my faraway dreams.

Alyssa and I were able to start one of our dreams together: High & Lo Restaurant and Piano Bar. We'd been running it for two years now, and after our children, it was one of my greatest accomplishments. Still, I strived for more.

One day, I'd give my children and my beautiful wife the world. My children would never know what it meant to be unloved. They had been cherished before they'd even entered the world.

Alyssa, my beautiful love, had saved my life. She had given me a reason to live, and it was an honor to be loved by her. I promised her heart I'd never forget the way she gave me all of her when I had nothing left to give in return. She promised me I wasn't the product of my yesterdays and knew I was destined for amazing tomorrows.

She was the fire in my soul that kept me warm at night.

"That's too high," my five-year-old son, Kellan, cried as we walked over to the billboard ladder. He was named after his uncle, who still was chasing his dream of becoming a successful musician and was getting closer each day.

His younger sister, Julie, sat on my shoulders, looking up. "Yeah, Daddy! Too high!" she agreed. She was named after her grandma, the woman who knew more dark days than light but now was able to walk in the sun and for the past seven years kept her demons at bay. Not every day was easy, but each day was a blessing.

I smiled at Alyssa, who had warned me that the kids would think it was too scary, but I wanted them to see the stars that night from the same place I'd first fallen in love.

"We have blankets," Alyssa said. "We can always lay them out down here and look up."

"Can we do that, Dad? Can we just look up instead of climbing?" Kellan asked.

"Of course. That's even better."

That night, we were quiet, staring out into the starlit sky that was fading into darkness. My arms were wrapped around Alyssa's waist, and she leaned back against me, allowing me to be the one who held her up. Each night, we watched the sun set no matter where we were, and we'd wake early to witness it rising again. That was the thing about life: even when the days faded to black, you were always given another chance, a second moment to try again to rise from the ashes.

The kids ran around, playing, as Alyssa and I stared at the lives we'd created. They were our happily ever after, the gifts that brought us so much joy.

My gosh, I was happy.

I was so damn happy, secure, and loved.

As the sky became black and the cool winds brushed against us, I whispered against Alyssa's ear, pulling her closer to me. "For always, High?"

"For always, Lo."

I shrugged.

She shrugged.

I laughed.

She laughed.

I parted my lips.

She parted her lips.

I leaned in.

She leaned in.

Our lips locked, and even though my feet were planted firmly on the ground, I'd never in my life felt so high.

Enjoy this brand-new annotated chapter as Brittainy Cherry takes you on a tour of the world of The Fire Between High & Lo.

get ready for tears...

CHAPTER 1

Logan

**TWO YEARS, SEVEN GIRLFRIENDS, TWO BOYFRIENDS,
NINE BREAKUPS, AND A STRONGER FRIENDSHIP LATER**

I'd watched a documentary on pie. *I love keylime pie ♥²*

Two hours of my life were spent sitting in front of a tiny television, watching a library DVD on the history of pie. It turned out pie had been around since the ancient Egyptians. The first documented pie was created by the Romans; they made a rye-crusted goat cheese and honey pie. It sounded completely disgusting, but somehow, at the end of the documentary, all I wanted was that freaking pie.

I wasn't much of a pie eater, more into cake, but at that moment, all that flew through my mind was the thought of a flaky crust.

I had all the things needed to go upstairs to our apartment to make the pie too. All that stood in my way was Shay, my now ex-girlfriend, who I'd spent the past few hours sending mixed signals to.

I was crappy at breaking up with girls. Most of the time, I'd text them a simple "Not working, sorry" or have a five-second phone call to cut it off, but I couldn't with this one, because Alyssa told me breaking up with someone over the phone was the worst thing a person could ever do. *Alyssa is right!* [3]

So I'd met up with Shay in person. Terrible idea.

Shay, Shay, Shay. I wished I hadn't found the need to have sex with her that night—which we had. Three times. *After* I broke up with her. But now it was past one in the morning, and...

~~She. Wouldn't. Leave.~~ → *Go home, Shay!* [4]

She wouldn't stop talking either.

The cold rain whistled as we stood in front of my apartment building. All I wanted to do was go to my bedroom and relax for a bit. Was that too much to ask? Smoke a bit of pot, start a new documentary, and make a pie or five.

I wanted to be alone. No one liked being alone more than I did.

My cell phone dinged, and I saw Alyssa's name appear on the screen with a text message.

Alyssa: Is the good deed done?

I smirked to myself, knowing she meant me breaking up with Shay.

Me: Yeah. *Break ups suck always* [5]

I watched the three dots appear on my phone, waiting to see Alyssa's reply.

Alyssa: You didn't sleep with her though, did you?

More dots.

Alyssa: Oh God, you slept with her, didn't you?

Even more dots.

Alyssa: MIXED SIGNALS! *very mixed!* 16

I couldn't help but chuckle, because she knew me better than anyone else. Alyssa and I had been best friends for the past two years, and we were the complete opposite of each other. Her older sister was dating my brother, Kellan, and at first, Alyssa and I were convinced we had nothing in common. She happily sat in church while I smoked pot around the corner. She believed in God while I danced with demons. She had a future while I somehow seemed trapped in the past.

But we had certain things in common that somehow made us make sense. Her mom barely tolerated her; my mom hated me. Her dad was a jerk; my dad was Satan.

When we realized the small things we did have in common, we spent more time together, growing closer each day.

She was my best friend, the highlight to my shitty days.

Me: I slept with her once.
Alyssa: Twice.
Me: Yeah, twice.

She knows him TOO WELL!

Alyssa: THREE TIMES, LOGAN?! OH MY GOSH!

"Who are you talking to?" Shay whined, breaking my stare from my phone. "Who could possibly be more important than having this conversation right now?"

"Alyssa," I said flatly.

"Oh my gosh. Seriously? She just can't get enough of you, can she?" Shay complained. It wasn't new though; every girl I'd dated in the past two years had a way of being extremely jealous of Alyssa's and my relationship. "I bet you're screwing her."

"Yeah, I am," I said. That was the first lie. Alyssa wasn't easy, and if she was, she wouldn't be easy with me. She had standards—standards I didn't meet. Also, I had standards for Alyssa's relationships—standards no guy could ever meet. She deserved the world, and most people in True Falls, Wisconsin, only had crumbs to offer. *He loves her !7*

Aw 18 "I bet she's the reason you're breaking up with me."

"Yeah, she is." That was the second lie. I made my own choices, but Alyssa always backed me, no matter what. She always gave me her input, though, and let me know when I was in the wrong in all my relationships. She was painfully blunt sometimes.

"She wouldn't ever really get with you, though. She's a good girl, and you—you're a piece of shit!" Shay cried. *Self aware, King! 19*

"You're right." That was the first truth.

Alyssa was a good girl, and I was the boy who never had a chance of calling her mine. Even though sometimes I'd look at her crazy blond curly hair and my mind would think about what it'd be like to maybe hold her close and slowly taste her lips. Maybe in a different world, I would've been enough for her. Maybe I wouldn't have been screwed up since I was a kid and would've had my life together. I would've gotten into college and had a career, something to show for myself. Then I could've asked her out and taken her to some fancy restaurant and told her to order anything on the menu because money wasn't an issue.

I could've told her how her blue eyes always smiled, even when she frowned, and that I loved how she chewed on the collar of all her T-shirts when she was bored or anxious.

I could've been someone worthy of loving, and she would've allowed me to love her too.

In a different world, maybe. But I only had the here and now, where Alyssa was my best friend.

I was lucky enough to have her in that form.

"You said you loved me!" Shay wept, allowing the tears to fall down her cheeks.

How long had she been crying? She was a professional crier, that one.

I studied her face as I slid my hands into my jean pockets. Goddamn. She looked a mess. She was still high from earlier, and her makeup was smeared all over her face.

"I didn't say that, Shay."

"Yes, you did! You said it more than once!" She swore.

"You're making shit up." I would've traced my memory to see if those three words slipped out of my mouth at some point, but I knew they didn't. I didn't love. I barely liked. My fingers brushed against my temple. Shay really needed to get in her car and drive far, far away.

"I'm not stupid, Logan! I know what you said!" Her words were confident in the belief that I loved her. Which, as a whole, was pretty sad. "You said it earlier tonight! Remember? You said you fucking loved me?"

Earlier tonight?

Oh crap.

"Shay, I said I love *fucking* you. Not that I fucking *love* you."

"Same thing."

"Trust me, it's not."

She swung her purse in my direction, and I allowed it to hit me. Truth was I deserved it. She swung again, and I allowed it once more.

She swung a third time, and I grabbed the bag, yanked it—and her—toward me. My hand landed on her lower back, which she arched at my touch. I pressed her body close to mine. Her breaths were heavy and tears were still rolling down her cheeks.

"Don't cry," I whispered, turning on my charm to try to get her to leave. "You're too beautiful to cry."

"You're such an asshole, Logan."

"Which is exactly why you shouldn't be with me."

"We've been broken up for three hours, and you've become a completely different person."

"That's funny," I muttered. "Because last I checked, it was you who became different, when you hooked up with Nick."

"Oh, get over it. That was a mistake. We didn't even have sex. You're the only boy I've slept with in the past six months."

"Uh, we've been dating for eight months." *I hate cheating!*

"What are you, a math guru? That doesn't matter."

Shay was my longest relationship in the past two years. Most of the time, it was a month tops, but with Shay, we made it a total of eight months and two days. I didn't know why exactly, other than her life was almost a carbon copy of mine. Her mom was far from stable, and her father was in prison. She didn't have anyone to look up to, and her sister was kicked out of their house by their mom because she got knocked up by some jerk.

Maybe the darkness in me saw and honored the darkness in her for a little while. We made sense. But as time went by, I realized that it was because of the similarities that we truly didn't belong together. We were both too messed up. Being with Shay was like looking at a mirror and seeing all your scars staring back at you.

"Shay, let's not do this. I'm tired."

"Okay. I forgot. You are Mr. Perfect. People make bad calls in life," Shay explained.

"You made out with my friend, Shay."

"It's just that: making out! And I only did it because you cheated on me."

"I'm not even sure how to reply to that, seeing as how I never cheated on you."

"Maybe not with sex, but emotionally, Logan. You were never fully there and committed. This is all Alyssa's fault. She's the reason you never really committed to me. She's such a stupid bit—" *too far!*[13]

I held my hand up to her mouth, halting her words. "Before you say what you're about to say, don't." I lowered my hand, and she remained quiet. "I told you from day one who I was. It's your own fault for thinking you could change me."

"You're never going to be happy with anyone, are you? Because you are so hung up on a girl that you'll never have. You're going to end up sad, alone, and bitter. Then you'll figure out what you had when you were with me!"

"Can you just leave?" I sighed, brushing my hand against my face. I blamed Alyssa for this.

"Break up with her in person, Lo. That's the only way a real man would do it. You can't break up with someone over the phone."

She had some awful ideas sometimes.

Shay kept crying.

God, those tears.

I couldn't handle the tears.

After a few snotty sniffles, she glanced at the ground before holding her head high, a spark of confidence finding her. "I think we should break up." *hahaha!*[14]

I appeared shocked. "Break up?" *We already did!*

"I just feel like we're two people going in two opposite directions."

"Okay," I said.

Her fingers flew over my lips and she shushed me, even though I wasn't talking. "Don't be so emotional about it. I'm so sorry, Logan. But it's just not going to work out." *She is wild* 15

I snickered internally at her, making it seem like the breakup was her idea. I stepped back and placed my hands on my neck. "You're right. You're too good for me."

Why are you still here?

She moved over to me. "You'll find someone good. I know it. I mean, granted, she might look like an ape, but still." She jogged toward her car, opened the door, and climbed inside.

As the car pulled off, my gut tightened, and regret overtook me. I started sprinting toward her car in the pouring rain, shouting her name. "Shay! Shay!" I waved my hands into the darkness, running for at least five blocks before she came up to a red light. I banged on her driver's window and she screamed, out of fright.

"Logan! What the heck are you doing?!" she cried, rolling down her window. Her confusion turned into a proud smirk and she narrowed her eyes. "You want to get back together, don't you? I knew it."

"I…" I huffed. I wasn't an athlete at all; that was more of my brother's field of expertise. I tried to catch my breath, holding my hands against the edge of her window. "I—I…n-need…"

"You need what? What, baby? What do you need?" she asked, running her hand gently against my cheek.

"Pie."

She sat back, confused. "What?"

"Pie. My pie supplies that we bought earlier. They're in the back of your car."

"Are you freaking kidding me?!" she screeched. "You chased me down for blocks and blocks for pie ingredients?!"

I arched an eyebrow. "Um, yeah?"

She reached into the back of her car, snatched the bag up, and slammed it against my chest. "You are so unbelievable! Here's your stupid crap!"

I smirked. "Thanks."

Her car pulled off, and I couldn't help but laugh when I heard her shout, "You owe me twenty bucks for that goat cheese!"

The second I stepped foot into my apartment, I pulled out my cell phone and sent a text. *Always texting* [16]

Me: Next time I break up with a girl, I'm doing it via text
message.
Alyssa: That bad?
Me: Dreadful.
Alyssa: I feel bad for her. She really liked you.
Me: She cheated on me!
Alyssa: And yet you still found a way to sleep with her
three times.
Me: Whose side are you on?

Dots.

Alyssa: She's such a monster! *Loyalty* [17]
I'm so happy she's out of your life.
No one deserves to date such a psychotic person.

She's disgusting.

I hope she accidentally steps on Lego pieces for the
remainder of her life.

There was the response I needed.

Alyssa: Love you, best friend.

I read her words and tried to ignore the pull in my chest. *Love you.*
I never said those kinds of things to people, not even to Ma or Kellan.
But sometimes, when Alyssa Marie Walters said she loved me, I kind
of wished I could say it back.

But I didn't love.

I hardly liked.

At least that was the lie I told myself daily to keep from getting
hurt. Most people thought love was a reward, but I knew better than
that. I'd seen my mom love my father for years now, and nothing good
ever came from it. Love wasn't a blessing, it was a curse, and once you
invited it into your heart, it only left scorch marks.

Pain! 18

Annotated Chapter Guide

Images and words on page 343: Drawing of hearts rising from the opening paragraph. Drawing of a cloud surrounding the chapter number. Drawing of a cake with three lit candles in page margin.

1. *Get ready for tears...*
2. *I love key lime pie.* ♥
   Underlined text next to drawing of cake: "a pie eater, more into cake."

Images and words on page 344: Drawing of hearts along the upper-right side of the page. Drawing of stars above a text message.

3. *Alyssa is right!*
4. Underlined text: <u>"She. Wouldn't. Leave."</u> *Go home, Shay!*
5. *Breakups suck always.*

Images and words on page 345: Drawing of flowers along the top and bottom of the page. Drawing of a long, squiggle line down the left-hand side of the page. Drawing of stars around the author's comment: "She knows him TOO WELL."

6.　*Very mixed!*

Images and words on page 346: Drawing of a long, squiggle line down the right-hand side of the page.

7.　"Alyssa wasn't easy, and if she was, she wouldn't be easy with me. She had standards—standards I didn't meet. Also, I had standards for Alyssa's relationships—standards no guy could ever meet. She deserved the world, and most people in True Falls, Wisconsin, only had crumbs to offer." *He loves her!*

8.　*Aw!*

9.　Circled text: "You're a piece of shit!"
"'You're right.' That was the first truth.'" *Self-aware king!*

Images and words on page 347: First three paragraphs circled. Drawing of hearts midway down the page.

10.　*I love friends to lovers.*

11.　Underlined text: "it's not." *Heavy on it's not.*

Images and words on page 348: Drawing of clouds and a sun in the upper part of the page. Drawing of a squiggly line on its side. Drawing of flowers at the bottom of the page.

12.　*I hate cheating.*

Images and words on page 349: Drawing of a long squiggle line down the left-hand side of the page. Drawing of a cluster of broken hearts.

13.   Underlined text: <u>"She's such a stupid bit—."</u> *Too far!*

14.   *Ha ha ha!*

Images and words on page 350: Drawing of clouds and a sun in the upper part of the page. Drawing of half a pie.

15.   *She is wild.*

Images and words on page 351: Drawing of a long squiggle line down the left-hand side of the page.

16.   *Always texting.*

17.   *Loyalty.*

Images and words on page 352: Drawing of hearts and flowers at the bottom of the page. Final paragraph bracketed.

Underlined text: "Love you."

18.   "At least that was the lie I told myself daily to keep from getting hurt. Most people thought love was a reward, but I knew better than that. I'd seen my mom love my father for years now, and nothing good ever came from it. Love wasn't a blessing, it was a curse, and once you invited it into your heart, it only left scorch marks." *Pain!*

Acknowledgments

So many people helped bring this novel together, and I don't know where to start thanking people, so I'll start with my best friend. To my mom: You helped me get through writing this book. I don't know where I'd be if it weren't for you. You make life better for so many souls, and I'm so happy to call you my best friend.

To Alison, Allison, Christy, and Beverly: Thank you for taking the time to help beta read Alyssa and Logan's story. You've helped me figure out so many issues with the storyline and gave me the best feedback. You are all so close to my heart, and I can never thank you enough.

To my agents who believe in me when I can't even believe in myself: You've made all my dreams come true. Thank you.

To the readers: Thanks for taking a chance on me and my novels. You changed my life more than you'll ever know.

Lastly, a big thank-you to my family. I'd always choose you. XOXO!

About the Author

Brittainy Cherry is an Amazon bestselling author who has always been in love with words. She graduated from Carroll University with a bachelor's degree in theater arts and a minor in creative writing. Brittainy lives in Milwaukee, Wisconsin, with her family. When she's not running a million errands and crafting stories, she's probably playing with her adorable pets.

Website: bcherrybooks.com
Facebook: BrittainyCherryAuthor
Instagram: @bcherryauthor